BLOOD & STEEL

BLOOD & STEEL

A Love Story

JT Buckley

Blood & Steel
Copyright © 2013 by J. T. Buckley.

 www.carnoriapublishing.com

Library of Congress Control Number: 2013917575

ISBN: Hardcover 978-0-9906545-0-6
        Softcover 978-0-9906545-1-3
        Ebook 978-0-9906545-2-0

Cover Art and Design by Aidana WillowRaven
Copy editor: Lynda Dietz

Rev. Date: 10/12/2014

To my wonderful wife, Sherry, whose help and support
made this book turn from a dream to a reality.

PROLOGUE

Romania, 1920

S aria walked over to her window and smelled the flowers
as she had so many times before. She loved her visits to
the Colony. Her home, the growing city of Los Angeles,
seemed so dirty in comparison. She heard a knock at her door. Outside stood Nickolea, her adoptive father's Romanian servant, holding a bouquet of flowers in his hand. She allowed him in, and he
placed them in the vase she kept on her dresser for them, prompt-
ing a smile from her as he turned around.

"I brought your favorites, Lady Saria," he said.

"They are beautiful, Nickolea. Thank you," she replied.

"They are not as beautiful as you," he replied, shyly looking
away. "I have to go back to work. I saw them and had to pick
them for you."

Saria watched him as he walked out. From the first time they
met, she had been instantly attracted to his muscular physique.
She found his olive complexion a bit exotic and his golden-brown
eyes mesmerizing. She had asked her father about him, and all he
had told her was Nickolea had served the family faithfully as his
family had for centuries. Nickolea made her days a little brighter with the flowers he brought every morning. His attentions
pleased her. She walked back to the window, half-covered her face
with the curtain and watched Nickolea as he brushed down the
horses— always so gentle with them.

He looked back, saw her at the window, gave her a little
smile and waved. His smile made her feel faint. She walked over
to the dresser, pressed her face into the flowers, and inhaled their
fragrance. Her face showed a matching smile as she opened her

door and walked downstairs.

Her adoptive father, Stefan, was sitting next to the fireplace, reading. Her adoptive mother, Ecaterina, was knitting next to him. Saria walked over to them and sat at their feet. She loved the carefree life at the Colony. She loved the vacations when she was not attending another enclave. She finally built up enough courage to look up at her parents and ask.

"So what makes a good mate?"

"You'll know when you find him." Stefan had given her the same response for centuries.

"Stefan, you could give the girl a little more," Ecaterina lovingly chastised her husband. She turned to Saria. "First of all, looks are not everything. This may sound a bit corny but you will just know. He will just be . . . different from other men."

"Like making my day brighter with his presence?" Saria asked.

"Yeah, something like that. By the way, how are things going in Los Angeles?" Ecaterina asked, changing the subject.

"It's okay. The vampire population is small, and our coven is even smaller yet. Most of the vampires are Thins, which I find very odd. I haven't seen many Gluts. I don't understand why there aren't more there. But even the Thin population is small."

"Watch that gutter speak. Contractions are laziness of the tongue," her mother chastised. She then changed back to their previous subject. "It takes time. America is a very young country. You cannot expect a large population in just 150 years. Plus, there have been five wars in that time. It puts a strain on the population, both human and vampire."

"Sorry, Mother," she said with her eyes down. "I understand, but as an Elder, everyone looks to me for answers and I do not have any. They are concerned about the lack of growth. I have trouble making them understand."

"Just keep reminding them growth will come. It just takes time. Patience is the vampire's best friend. Time is the thing we have the most of."

"Thanks for the reassurance, Mother, but you still haven't

fully answered my first question. What do you think about Nickolea as a mate?"

"If you have to ask us, then he is wrong for you," Stefan replied from behind his book. "Like your mother said, you will know."

"Saria, he is a nice boy. But he is a servant. Part of his job is to make you feel special. You have to learn that difference."

"And he has bad teeth," Stefan interjected.

"What has that got to do with anything, Father?"

"Bad teeth make bad vampires," he replied.

"What?"

"It is not that he doesn't take care of them. They are poorly formed, which means he will have bad fangs. Bad fangs make bad wounds. Bad wounds leave scars and proof of a bite. Ergo, bad teeth make bad vampires. You will find a man with good teeth who will make you feel more than special. I also have a bad feeling about him. I cannot quite place it but I sense something very wrong in him."

Saria stood up and grimaced as she left the room. As she walked down the hallway, Nickolea stepped out of the shadows. He put his finger to his lips, gently held her hand, and led her to the stables. He led her to one of the horses he had been grooming earlier.

"She has nice flanks, don't you think?"

"Yes, quite nice. You did a beautiful job grooming her."

"Thank you. I must tell you your beauty outshines everything I have ever seen."

"Really?" she said, moving a little closer.

"Saria, I love you. I have always loved you. But I am a servant. You are the master's daughter."

Nickolea continued to flatter and arouse her with his charm and charisma. Saria felt the butterflies in her belly begin to flutter. *This must be love. He must be the one. It feels so different from the last time. Father said I would know. However, he is a servant, a human.* How could she love him? Nickolea looked deep in her eyes. "Saria, I love you with all my heart and want to be with you forever. I know I am merely a mortal servant, but you have my undying devotion forever."

Saria began to feel faint. Nickolea put out his arms and caught her. He leaned down and kissed her passionately. She returned his kiss. They lay down in the hay and continued to kiss, their bodies moving together in a dance of passion.

***

Exhausted, Saria lay next to Nickolea. After a few minutes, he turned over, kissed her and said, "The only way we can be together forever is if you change me. We can't go to your father for his blessing, with me being a lowly servant. Only as an equal will he even consider accepting me."

Saria looked in his eyes. She saw desire and hopefulness. Finally she spoke. "The process is not hard, but it is very painful."

"I will tolerate any agony for you, my love."

Saria pulled a ring out of her purse. A sharp razor covered one side. She bit her lip as she used it to rip open her pale, delicate skin.

"You must drink my blood," she said to him. "Drink it now."

Nickolea greedily licked up the blood as she'd commanded. He then sucked the wound to get as much as he could from it. He smiled at her with her blood covering his face. Within seconds, the change began to take hold. He screamed in agony as every cell in his body began to mutate as the virus forged his DNA, making him into something different.

Saria heard a storm brewing outside. She could hear thunder rumble outside the stables. Lightning crackled. The rain started to batter the stable roof. The wind whistled so loud, she could barely hear herself think. She started to become afraid as the storm intensified. She could see the dark clouds and lightning through the windows in the upper level of the stables. She held Nickolea close and tried to comfort him as the transformation continued. He shoved her away as he continued to scream and writhe. The horses began to buck and lurch in their stalls. They threw their bodies against the stall doors, trying to escape them. Saria was becoming terrified. The horses' whinnying added to the cacophony. She could hear the dogs snarling and barking at the doors of the stables.

Soon, the transformation was complete. He lay on the hay, still and silent, covered in sweat. The storm became just a heavy rain. She continued to caress his toned frame and tried to comfort him. His pale skin looked gaunt. Soon he awakened. He smiled and opened his mouth to reveal his misshapen fangs. She looked in his eyes and saw desire and pure joy. She smiled.

"There are some things you need to know about being a vampire. You should never provide proof of our existence. You should drink from several people to quench your thirst, never all from one."

"Okay," he said absentmindedly. He could feel the power in his new body. He could feel the strength.

"We are shepherds of the humans, not wolves . . ."

He only half heard what Saria was telling him as he felt the power he had craved for so long.

"Let's go talk to your father."

They walked out of the stables and headed for the house. Nickolea kept himself a step or two ahead of Saria. Once at the house, he opened the door and went in, letting the door close behind him. Saria opened the door and followed him. She reached the sitting room after him, but he had already started speaking.

"Since I am now a vampire, and we love each other, I demand you give us your blessing."

Saria looked at him strangely as she stepped into the room. *This is not the man I was with in the stables*, she thought.

"First of all, whelp, you do not barge into my house and demand anything. You ask politely. Second, what makes you think that being a vampire has anything at all to do with receiving my blessing? I am just as likely to give my blessing to a human as a vampire." Stefan turned to Saria. "You turned him? You turned him against our wishes?"

She lowered her head. "Yes, Father. I love him."

Stefan shook his head. "I cannot give my blessing, Saria. You should kill this thing you have created. It is less than worthless. It will destroy us all."

"No, Father, I love him." She began to cry at her father's displeasure.

Nickolea looked at Stefan and smiled a vicious smile. He then turned to Saria.

"Let's go back to America where we can marry if we want. We do not need his blessing."

Nickolea turned and walked out. Saria looked at her father and saw the disapproving look on his face. She then followed Nickolea with her head down. She glanced back at Stefan and could see a tear in his eye. She mouthed "good-bye" and followed Nickolea. He stood outside and waited for her impatiently. They walked to the closest main street and hailed a hansom cab. Saria watched out the window through the rain as the horse's hooves clopped on the cobblestones. She watched as the lights of the manor disappeared. They arrived at the port and she bought the last first-class tickets on the only ship in port headed to New York.

They boarded and went to their stateroom. Saria sat on the bed and signaled for Nickolea to sit next to her. He waved her away and walked out to the deck. She lay back on the bed waiting for him to return and finally fell asleep. During the remaining trip, they spent time together walking on the deck and feeding sporadically. Saria continued with her attempt to teach him the laws governing vampires. He feigned interest when she spoke but did not listen. The trip to New York was long for her and luckily, uneventful. Once in New York, they wandered around, looking at all the activity and the new buildings going up. She bought train tickets with stops across the country, wanting to show him her world along the way. Their first stop was in Chicago where they spent several weeks. She introduced him to all the local covens and their leaders. Next, they traveled to New Orleans, the home of the largest coven in America, and mingled with the locals. During their stay, she introduced him to the coven leaders. He was beginning to act like the man she had met in Romania, not the man she'd left with.

After several weeks, they traveled to Denver to spend some time in the mountains. Several times during the trip, Nickolea came back with a bloody face, an obvious sign he had been hunting alone. She would chastise him for his disregard of vampire law as she cleaned him up. She tried to go hunting with him several times, but he refused her and continued to go alone. This bothered her and she told him of the dangers but he ignored her warnings.

Finally, they arrived in Los Angeles and traveled to her home. It was a beautiful second-story apartment in a nice part of town. They put their luggage on the bed and began to unpack. Soon she had everything put away. Saria reached to kiss Nickolea. He returned the kiss.

"So, Saria, how did you become the dame of your line again?"

"I killed my sire. He was going to kill my human mother and father, and I couldn't allow that. He had already killed my older brother. He wanted to become king. I thought he loved me but he was just using me."

"So if a vampire kills his sire, they become the sire—or dame, as the case may be?"

"Yes, they inherit the entire line as I did," she replied, a bit confused.

"Good," he said flatly. "I have something to admit to you."

"What is that, darling?"

"I only used you too. See you in hell, harlot."

Nickolea pulled a large pistol from behind his back and shot Saria straight in the chest. Her chest exploded, splattering blood around the room. She flew back onto the bed and lay very still. He rolled her over and stabbed her through the back with a large knife, making sure it pierced her heart and her lung. He looked at her, satisfied, and then gathered his clothes. As he opened the door, he looked back one last time and smiled a vicious smile, then spat on the floor.

After a few hours, Saria began to rouse. The room was spinning around her. She tried to stand but could not. She was too weak. She could feel the hunger clawing at the back of her mind. She flailed her arms, reaching for the knife in her back. The wound in her chest had already begun to heal but her rapidly beating heart was visible through the rent flesh. She pulled herself up and sat on the side of the bed. She bit her lip to keep from screaming as she slid down the edge of the bed onto the floor. She could feel the knife ripping through her flesh as it pulled out. It clanked to the floor as she landed against the hard wood.

Once the knife was out, she sat for a few minutes as she regained enough strength to stand. She changed her clothes and stumbled over to the window. It was twilight. She walked out on the balcony and looked below her. A bum was sitting among the trashcans. She leaped down and fell, scattering the cans. She pulled herself up and staggered toward the bum, grabbing him and biting deeply into his neck. He screamed. She drank and drank the man's blood until she forced herself to stop. She licked and sealed the wound. She dropped his unconscious body on the ground.

She felt a little stronger. She hunted all night to sate her thirst. Victim after victim she drank like an animal. Blood covered her face and clothes. Slowly she regained her strength. She returned to her apartment. She undressed, threw away the bloody clothes, and looked in the mirror as she washed up. The bullet wound that had split her chest in two was gone; her flawless skin was completely healed. She stared for a moment then asked her reflection, "How could I have been so stupid to fall for that again?"

Chapter I

A hooded figure squatted on the fire escape. He looked out into the twilight of early morning, waiting for his prey to pass by. Soon three men walked into the alley. They approached a bum under him. One of the men grabbed the bum and threw him to another of the men. He extended his fangs and bit the old man.

The figure leaped down and landed on the first vampire. He drove him to the ground and firmly planted his foot on the back of his neck. The vampire holding the bum threw him down the alley and dove toward the hooded man. All the vampire saw was a flash of silver as the figure drew his katana and removed his head in one stroke. Bright red blood splashed across the man's face. The other vampire turned and started to run. The man threw a weighted rope toward him, caught him around the neck, and jerked him off his feet and through the air toward him. Another flash of the sword and his head rolled across the alley, too. The hooded figure looked down at the vampire under his boot.

"If I tell you, you will kill me. If I don't, you will kill me. A Shadow never leaves a *rogue* alive, do they?"

"You are correct. However, by telling me, you may receive mercy in whatever afterlife you believe in. What do you have to lose?"

"I lose my head either way."

"How about this option: if you tell me, I will make it swift and painless like your friends there. If you don't, I will slowly drain your blood until the hunger takes you," he said, rubbing the flat of his sword against the vampire's neck. "The excruciating pain will loosen your tongue and you will beg me to take your head."

The vampire swallowed and then smiled. "How about we take another option?"

About that time, the hooded man ducked as a blade passed over his head. He quickly turned around to see another vampire with a shocked look on his face. The man's sword flashed and took the new vampire's head. Having to step off the one vampire to dodge the blow allowed the formerly trapped vampire to jump up, pull a knife, and try to stab him in the back. The hooded man spun around and beheaded him. Disgusted, the man piled the dead vampires in a heap and threw a match on the pile. They burst into a bright flame, burned for a minute, and were consumed completely. Rick Smythe jerked off his blood-saturated hood, walked over to his car, threw it in the passenger seat and drove home.

He walked into his home and headed for the shower. He removed the bloody uniform and handed it to waiting hands. His housekeeper took the uniform and asked.

"Any luck, my lord?"

"No, Amaya, he still eludes me. The hood is in the car; please get it and wash everything. These rogues bleed a lot. I don't like what that implies. I guess I will be going out again tonight."

"My lord, you need to sleep. You are a human. Let me call for another to hunt the beast."

"Okay, Amaya, go ahead and call in Taiga. He can handle the shift tonight."

"Very good, my lord. I have your clothes for the day laid out on the bed. Have a good day today."

"Thank you, Amaya—oh, and I will grab something to eat on the way to work."

Amaya nodded as she walked out carrying the blood-soaked uniform. Rick stepped into the shower. He stood, letting the warm water soothe the bruises from the last few nights of searching. He still hadn't found the rogues' leader. He also knew Amaya was right; he could not keep going without sleep. He was only human. The only human in the Shadow. He stepped out and started getting ready for work. He turned on the local news for the LA Area and saw that the "vampire killer," as the media had named the rogues, had struck again. Rick found it amusing the media had called it right for once. The victim's neck was broken, with multiple bite wounds on his neck and no blood in his body. All the signs of this particular coven. Rick sighed. While he was hunting them, they were still out killing. *Maybe I should call in the Clan*, he thought. *No, it is still too soon.*

As a psychologist, Rick had seen many patients with a vampire fixation. Most of them were teens who had a hard time fitting in, so they thought being a vampire made them cool. Society's fixation with romanticizing vampires in movies and books made things worse. As a hunter, he had also seen and killed many rogue vampires. However, it still concerned him that these were real vampire attacks. It was the work of an entire rogue coven. Each rogue coven had a particular pattern of behavior. What bothered him worst of all was this particular pattern was occurring across the country, not just in Los Angeles. He knew LA had always been a hotbed of vampire activity but it had never been this bad or this blatant. That was the reason he was here.

He had hoped working for the Los Angeles County Department of Health and Human Services with the homeless might give him a hint. It was a good strategy in New York and provided many clues, but here it provided nothing. None of them had seen or heard anything they were willing to discuss. With them, he had only encountered the run-of-the-mill psychoses such as paranoia and schizophrenia. He really loved his new cover, though. He could actually help people, and that was why he'd gotten into the psychology field in the first place.

He grabbed his briefcase, checked his pockets for his phone, wallet, and keys, and then had an uneventful drive down the 110 Freeway. He parked in the employee lot of his workplace and looked at the aging building. It was a big change from the high-society clinic he'd had in New York. The county did not have the money for fancy buildings, but if he'd wanted that, he could have started a Beverly Hills practice. However, none of this had brought him any closer to the rogue leader.

He sighed and walked in. He had considered dropping the cover completely, but he shared the office with Saria de la Rosa, a beautiful social worker employed by the county. When he opened the office door, she was already there and hard at work. He liked working with her because she was as passionate about helping people as he was. She also volunteered at a halfway house for at-risk teens. He had thought about joining her, but he was already very busy with his project for getting assistance for the mentally ill homeless so they could return as productive members of society, and making sure there were not any rogues left loose. They made a great team. He set his briefcase down, and Saria looked up.

"Good morning, Dr. Smythe," she said with a smile.

"Good morning, Ms. de la Rosa. Why the formality this morning?"

"Oh, no reason, just felt like it," she said. Her smile grew larger.

"You just think you are so cute, don't cha," he replied, smiling himself.

"Of course I do. Do you have anything good on the calendar today, Rick?" she said with a self-satisfied smirk.

He opened his calendar on his computer. "Just the usual—a couple of paranoids, a couple of schizophrenics, and a banker who 'just couldn't take it anymore.' Like I said, the usual."

"What, no megalomaniacs? You should have one of those here—did I ever mention my ex was a megalomaniac? Anyway, you should be done by lunch. There is a new place on Sunset we should try."

"We should talk about that ex of yours sometime. He sounds like a real piece of work." Rick turned his chair to face her. "Not another new burger place, is it? You know how tired I am of burgers."

"Nope, Czech. I just love food that's out of the ordinary. Besides, Sally recommended it."

"Sally, huh. Have you already forgotten the last time she recommended a place? It was in Compton, and I almost got shot."

"Hey, the food was good, and that is all she had said. Besides, this is on the strip. I don't think you will have the same problem."

"I have to admit that the food was good and so was the atmosphere. But we have been having lunch together for months now. Why do you always get to pick?"

"All right then, you pick."

"Czech is fine. I just wanted to feel like I had a say in our little relationship."

"Oh, so it's a relationship now, is it?"

"Yeah, friendships are defined as a relationship. Purely platonic, but a relationship nonetheless. You don't have to be jumping in bed to have a relationship," he countered.

"Oh, so Mr. Afraid of Commitment is in a relationship. And what is wrong with jumping in bed? As long as you watch the ceiling fan."

"Come on, Saria, you know how I feel about coworker relationships. That is not what I meant."

Saria put on her sternest face for the few seconds before she burst out laughing. Rick looked at her. He knew she had gotten him again with one of her "jokes." He smiled at her.

"When am I going to learn? You get me every time. I don't know why I let you, but you do get me every time. This time we take your car."

"You got it, Rick. Yours is much too conspicuous anyway. We'll meet here at the office about noon." She was still giggling a bit.

"I'll be here with bells on, Saria."

Saria stood and left the office. Rick shook his head and looked at the files on his desk. He grabbed the first one, stood, and walked to the door. He opened the door and called the name of his first client. An older gentleman stood up and walked over to the door. Rick closed the door behind them and directed him to a chair in front of his desk.

"So, Mr. Andrews, are you still hearing the voices. . .?"

***

Rick finally finished with his last client. He looked at his watch. It was eleven forty-five. He still had a few minutes before Saria returned. He stood and walked into the restroom. He removed his shirt and bared his tight chest and his chiseled abs. The bruises had already started to change colors, though they were still tender. He walked over to the sink and washed his face. He straightened his sandy blond hair. That made him feel a little more refreshed. He turned as he was buttoning his shirt. Walking through the door was Saria.

"Dang, again I walk in seconds too late." She crinkled her nose. "One of these times, I am going to catch you with your shirt off," she said, looking deep into his ice-blue eyes.

He smiled and replied, "You'll just have to be a bit faster next time."

She smiled back. "Are you ready to go?"

"I am."

They walked out and locked the door. They walked down the hall to an old elevator. As it opened, he gave a flourish, allowing her in first. She gave a mock look of surprise and walked in. He pushed the button for the ground floor, and the elevator creaked and moaned as it descended. Once the doors opened, they went to the back door leading to the employee parking lot, got into Saria's car and headed for the restaurant.

After they had driven for a few minutes in silence, Saria asked, "So what is your take on the 'Vampire Killer'? Who do you think it is? Maybe a cult?"

"No, it is probably a single individual with a vampire delusion. Cults usually drink other members' blood, not strangers'."

"What about the wounds? There are always multiple marks. You don't think it could be a real vampire, do you?"

"Since I don't believe in vampires or werewolves, I sincerely doubt it. As for the multiple wounds, it's probably a violent manifestation of a repressed trauma. Maybe they're projecting their anger or even hate from abuse or something like that. It has been seen in many cases of violent delusional thinking. It has to be someone who's delusional, because we have become so domesticated as a species that violence this brutal is not even conceivable by a sane person."

"Do you believe in the supernatural at all?"

"I guess I do believe in ghosts. I feel they are psychic recordings of traumatic events—what is popularly called a repeating phantasm. However, I haven't seen enough evidence to convince me of intelligent hauntings. Vampires and werewolves are just manifestations of our fear of the animalistic urges in all of us. The jury is still out on aliens, too."

"Silly doctor, aliens aren't supernatural. I find it interesting that you clumped vampires and werewolves together."

He raised an eyebrow at her. "I guess I am buying into the societal belief that they exist together and are mortal enemies unable to ever reconcile."

"They might be able to if the werewolves weren't so hardheaded and stubborn," she stated offhandedly.

Rick looked at her. She was looking forward with a little smirk on her face. Her eyes were what struck him the most. They were a beautiful gray-green, a very unique variant of hazel, occurring in only a small portion of the population. He had noticed the perfect form of her jaw. The smooth curve leading from her ear to her chin was perfectly formed. Her pale skin was very attractive, especially contrasted by her raven-black hair. Her skin color was something he had found odd, being in Southern California and given her Hispanic ancestry. She had told him her family had come from Spain to California while it was still a Spanish colony. But her skin tone was a bit out of the ordinary even in those circumstances. He could see her neck muscles curving to her shoulder. The curve of her shoulder was leading to her . . . He snapped himself out of the trance he had placed himself in, and hoped she had not noticed.

He turned and looked out the window just to avoid staring at her. He knew from personal experience that workplace romances did not work out. That experience was part of the reason he'd left the East Coast. The more he thought about it, he'd had more reasons to leave the East Coast than to stay. He watched as they turned onto the famous Sunset Boulevard. It amazed him how it seemed that at every corner they turned in the city, they passed some iconic landmark. That was the only similarity between his home and New York. He looked back at her beautiful neck. His attempt to divert his attention from the stunning woman in the car with him was an abysmal failure.

"So do you believe in vampires and werewolves, Saria?" he asked

"Like you said, the jury is still out. We have had a great many strange things happen here in the last few years. Did you hear about the wolf attacks in the city a couple years ago? They had a forensic vet working on the case. He was the one who identified the bites as wolves, very large wolves."

"That is odd, and now we are having 'vampire' attacks. It does make one question their beliefs. But you have to remember we are in LA. It's the land of fruits and nuts. Look at most of the actors around here."

Saria put on her best fake-hurt look at his comment about her town. They both laughed. Soon they were pulling into the restaurant. They parked in an out-of-the-way spot and went into the building. The room was dim. They walked over to a table off to the side and sat down, and a server walked over and took their order. They watched the crowd; it seemed large for lunchtime. Rick turned to his companion.

"The food must be good here. Look at this lunch crowd," he said.

"Yeah, they sure are packed in. Hmmm," she said as she looked into the crowd.

"What is it?"

"Never mind. Thought I saw someone I knew. I must have been mistaken. So . . . we have been working together several months now, and I know very little about you except that you left a successful practice in New York. What are some of your interests?"

"I sold my practice in New York because I was tired of all the rich kids and their ridiculous problems. I really wanted to help people. I moved to LA because no one really knew me here. Now the other psychologists do because of some of the papers I have written. But as to my interests, I like sailing, running, and am an avid collector of oriental weapons and swords."

"Cool. I am an avid martial artist and have what some people call a macabre interest in the supernatural, especially vampire history. I want to know what the interest in vampires in the human psyche is all about. I discovered that most cultures have vampire legends. You know, kind of like the stories of dragons and were-wolves."

"Really? Now that's interesting. I didn't know that. So I bet this current problem has really piqued your interest. It certainly has mine. You know, I have always wondered why our culture romanticized such an evil creature concept. How can you have a romantic relationship with a creature that wants to drink everyone's blood, and the fact that its skin is cold like a corpse? It borders on a secret desire to commit necrophilia."

Saria flinched a bit. "Wow, you have a pretty strong opinion."

"Oh, I'm sorry. I had to deal with a lot of kids in New York who wanted to be vampires. They took Goth to a whole new level. That is why I began to study these developing new vampire cults. It is frightening what is happening to our youth. This is above and beyond the gang problem. I helped the NYPD with a few of those gang cases. The combination of gang mentality and vampirism could make someone be brutal."

"You know, in several cultures, vampires are not undead creatures. They are living, breathing people. They just require blood to survive. You know, I would really like to see your collections, and I could bring some of my vampire research. Maybe it can help you with yours. We can both get something we want."

Saria bit the nail of her right pointer finger and smiled a quaint little smile. Before Rick could say anything, the food arrived. The fragrance of it filled his nostrils and drowned out all other scents, especially the scent of Saria's perfume. He had always found that intoxicating. He could not place the fragrance. It was on the tip of his tongue, but there was something different about it that he had never smelled before.

"Saria, what is that perfume you are wearing? I have been trying to place it since we met. I just can't figure it out."

She smiled. "It is actually a fragrance of my own creation, made from the essential oils of several common flowers in Romania. I spent time there doing an international internship. My apartment was above a beautiful garden, and I loved the smell so much, I collected the essential oils of all of them and mixed them until I got the same aroma. It reminds me of a wonderful time in my life."

"Now that is a beautiful story. I was offered an international internship to London. Yeah, I passed on it. If I'd had one to Eastern Europe, I would have taken it in a heartbeat. You are very lucky."

"Yeah," she said wistfully, "I was. It kind of helped me find myself. I was lost and felt so very different until that period in my life. It was after I was first betrayed by someone I thought I loved and who loved me."

"Wow, it was good that you had an opportunity like that after such an emotional upheaval. I'm still trying to figure out who I am. You said 'first betrayed'?"

"Maybe I can help you with that," she said, smelling the food. "Yeah, it happened more than once. We can start discovering who you are tonight, when I come to see your collections."

"I haven't said yes yet," he said, laughing.

"Oh, but you will. Besides, how can you refuse an evening with a beautiful woman willing to bring takeout?" she asked with a quaint smile.

"Takeout? No way. If you're going to be my guest, I will cook. What do you like?"

"Oriental, any kind, or anything European. I just like food," she said, snickering.

"How does six o'clock sound?"

"Delightful. Do I need to bring wine or anything?"

"No, I also collect wines and have a very well-stocked cellar. Now let's enjoy this wonderful food."

"Definitely."

They both reached for their napkins and their hands brushed, each jumping as a tingle of electricity sparked between them. They quickly pulled their hands back, began to eat, and spent the next hour eating and chatting. Rick saw a glint in her eyes. It was something he felt he had seen before but could not quite place it. Her voice was intoxicating, and he loved to hear it and the way it flowed. He watched the movements of her mouth and her neck. With her head tilted away from him, he could see light glisten off her skin and the veins of her neck slightly protrude as she spoke. He felt strangely attracted to her. He desired her. It was more than mere sexual attraction; he kept that in check. It was something else. What was it about her that brought out these animalistic desires from him and what was that shock he'd felt when their hands touched? He prided himself on his self-control. However, this woman was making it very hard and he did not think she was doing it on purpose.

She brought out feelings he had buried deep. All he wanted to do was to grab her and kiss her. He focused on the food before him. It seemed to have lost all taste in comparison with her beauty. He took bite after bite, almost mechanically answering her questions and making small talk the entire time, admiring her.

Saria saw the change in the color of his face and the change in his breathing. She knew his heart was racing. She reached out and took his wrist and could feel his pulse quicken at her gentle touch. She could almost feel the desire in him. She could smell the blood running through his veins. She did notice one thing: her thirst for blood was almost nonexistent. That was something she was never without but now she was. She continued to ask small, easily answered questions. She smiled a little smile. She wanted to kiss him, but was afraid she would scare him away. That was an urge she felt stronger than she did any thirst for blood. She could tell he was keeping something back. She could not quite figure out what, though.

She felt so comfortable with him. She felt she could tell him anything about herself. Well, almost anything. There were things about her past he was not ready to hear. She looked over the crowd for the face she'd seen before. She was very glad that she did not see it again.

"Enough is enough; who are you looking for? I have watched you scan the crowd several times," he said between bites.

"I thought I saw someone I did not want to earlier. Now I am afraid he will show up."

"Let me guess, the megalomaniac ex?"

"Yeah."

"Don't worry about him. I will have him psychoanalyzed so fast, he'll be crying for Mommy."

"I wish it were that easy. For some reason, all he wants is to see me hurt."

"Hmmm, he sounds like a real piece of work. Did he break up with you, or did you break up with him?"

"Embarrassingly enough, he broke up with me. I thought I loved him and could change him. I know, I know—you cannot change someone who doesn't want to change. This happened before I learned that part. I brought him here, so I feel responsible for him."

"People are responsible for their own actions, so don't be so hard on yourself. Besides, I'll watch out for you if he comes around. I can be pretty handy."

"I wouldn't be so sure. Thanks for that. But he is pretty dangerous."

"I can be too. You know, this has been nice; we usually go out to lunch and talk about work. This has been a nice change. We should do this more often."

After they finished their meal, they paid and left. The drive back to the office was very different. The feelings of desire had subsided, and it was back to two friends riding back from lunch. It was an amazing change in him. He could not figure out what had happened in the car ride over and then again in the restaurant. He did not feel a tinge of the strong desire he had felt before. Everything was back to normal except for the usual feeling of sincere interest in her. A little stronger than he had felt before, but it was the same feeling. However, he was starting to be concerned about what she had told him about her ex. He sounded like a problem. Maybe he was involved in this whole thing somehow. *Well, that was a stretch*, he thought to himself.

They arrived back at their office. Rick checked his appointments and saw someone had cancelled all his afternoon appointments. He had a note that the LAPD chief had called and wanted him to come to the station. He showed the note to Saria.

"Wonder what they want?"

"Maybe your past is coming back to haunt you. You are the resident expert on vampire psychoses and delusions around here. You have published at least two papers on the subject. I read them both as part of my research. I guess the chief read them too. Have fun playing with the LAPD. I will see you at six. I can get your address and home phone number from the file. I'll text you a vCard with my info. Don't keep the chief waiting."

Saria smiled innocently and batted her lashes as he rolled his eyes. He reached into a file cabinet and pulled out several files. He placed them in a briefcase, sighed, and headed out the door to the police station downtown. Saria watched him walk out the door and smiled. Once she was alone, she said aloud with a green fire in her eyes, "You will be mine, Dr. Smythe. I haven't felt like this about anyone in a very long time, if ever, and I won't let you go."

Chapter II

Rick walked up to the front door of the downtown office of the Los Angeles Police Department. He looked at the iconic building. It was just as majestic as any picture or other facsimile, such as the metal engraving on the officers' badges. He walked into the building and a police officer met him at the door.

"Sir, how may I help you?" the officer said, stopping him.

"I am Dr. Richard Smythe. The police chief is expecting me."

The officer's entire demeanor changed. "Yes, sir, he is. I am Sergeant Lewis. Please follow me."

Rick followed Sergeant Lewis down the cavernous hallway to the elevators. The sergeant pushed the button and called in his radio for a replacement to come to the front while they waited for the elevator to arrive.

"I am sorry, sir. These elevators are as old as the building and are quite slow. The city has promised a refurbishing of them, but it will take a while. Good news is that they work. Otherwise, five flights of stairs would get old." Sergeant Lewis smiled.

"No problem. My office is in the Department of Human Services building. Now those elevators are old."

"Yes, sir, that's for sure. I think those elevators are older than I am. I have waited on them and decided to climb the six flights of stairs instead."

Both of them laughed. When the elevator finally opened, they entered. Sergeant Lewis pushed the floor button, and the doors closed. The elevator ride was shorter than the wait would have insinuated. Sergeant Lewis led Rick through the squad room. It was a flurry of activity. They walked to a small office in the back.

Sergeant Lewis knocked and a gruff "Come in" came from inside the room. He opened the door, and a husky, balding man sat behind an old oak desk.

"Chief, this is Dr. Smythe," Sergeant Lewis stated, introducing Rick.

The chief looked up. "So you're the vampire expert, are you? We have a hell of a mess, and I'm hoping you can help us. The damn media is having a heyday with this crap."

"I wouldn't exactly call myself a vampire expert. But I have done quite a bit of research into the delusions surrounding that phenomenon."

"So you're a vampire expert. Follow me."

The chief stood up and led Rick over to a corkboard with pictures and ribbons covering a map in the main squad room. "This is a map of all the attacks with pictures of the victims and the crime scenes. As you can tell, there is no obvious pattern. The murders are spread all over the city. The MO is all the same. The victim has multiple sets of dual punctures in the neck in the region of the carotids, and the neck is broken. No witnesses have come forward. All the victims are different. They are from different socioeconomic backgrounds. There are both males and females. The only thing they have in common is that they are all now dead and exsanguinated. That is another thing: with the viciousness of the attacks, there is no blood at the scene except for a few drops. So what's happening here?"

"Because of the cause and method of death, I would say it's a person with a vampire delusion and a single killer. However, a single killer would keep to a single area or maybe two. With the dispersion of the attacks, it could be two or even more killers. Since there is no specific victim type, that also precludes any lashing out because of repressed trauma. Hmm, this is a complex case. Are there any other wounds other than the neck?" Rick grasped his chin in contemplation.

"There have been a few defensive wounds and bruising of being handled roughly. They are indicative of a violent assault. There have not been any signs of rape or any other sexual assault. In addition, their wallets or purses have not been touched. It was as if they were attacked specifically for their blood."

"If this is not a single individual and turns out to be a group, then that would be frightening because it means we have a group of people preying on other people. The next big question is: Do we have a group of feral people or a cult of murderers? Neither option is a very good one. I have something to show you."

Rick put his briefcase down and took out the files he had placed in there. He took out pictures and statements he had collected from around the country. He spread them out across the table. Most of them had the same or similar MO.

"This is information I have collected from other cases across the country. Most of these were isolated incidences, or the attacks were in a localized area. I have not seen any in such a broad area and spread out as far as these are. I was thinking these were separate cases. But they seem like something more."

"This is an interesting development. Lewis, put this on the wire. See how many cases we're actually looking at."

"Sure thing, Chief." Sergeant Lewis looked at Rick with an ever-so-slight glare as he headed to a computer across the room. "We should have everything in a day or two."

"I'll tell Detective Stevens, since he's the lead investigator. I will call you when we have more info, Dr. Smythe."

"Please, call me Rick."

"All right, Rick. We will see you in a couple days. Can I keep this information?"

"Of course, anything to help. I have copies anyway."

"Thanks."

Rick left the squad room and went back down the elevator. He got in his car and left for home, going over a mental shopping list for the dinner he was going to prepare. He could not stop thinking about Saria. He sat in his car and remembered the fragrance of her perfume. He could see her bare neck in his mind's eye. He could not wait to be close to her, to touch her, even to caress her. He stopped by the store on the way home. He collected everything he needed. He moved quickly and efficiently. He rushed through the checkout and was quickly on his way home.

***

Nickolea sat in his chair, looking down on the vampires around him. Finally, he stood and addressed them.

"Who is killing our brothers and how is he doing it? He is taking out not one, not two, but groups of at least three. I want answers."

"But lord, he is but a shadow. No one escapes his blade. He seems to be hunting someone or something."

"Who or what is he hunting?"

"Probably me." A man entered the room dressed in black ninja robes.

"What do you mean, Shinto?"

"Your minions are correct. He is a Shadow. The Shadow is a clan of vampire hunters from Japan. They killed the rest of my clan. They are all vampires themselves, save one. The clan is led by a human. No one outside the Shadow knows who he is, not even me."

"You need to kill him. But kill him after you provide this service to me: I need to know who Saria's new boyfriend is. I need to know everything about him. I saw them together in a restaurant and she looked happy. I can't have that. She has to be miserable. She has to want to die when I kill her. I want her to ask me to kill her. Only then will I let her miserable existence end. She teased me for years, flaunting her power. I had to pretend to love her to get her to give it to me. It disgusted me even to touch her."

"I will find out who this man is. However, you will owe me. I think he and I have crossed paths before. If we have, he owes me a blood debt. I will have him pay it in his blood, gallons of it. He and that Clan he works for will pay. Maybe he will reveal to me who the human leader is."

***

Rick arrived home and quickly began preparing dinner. He told Amaya she could go home and be back on Monday. She nodded and left. He pulled out recipes for minced meat rolls and cabbage with noodles. Since they were both common dishes in Eastern Europe, he hoped Saria liked them. He started the preparations, pulled down a Cabernet Sauvignon, and set it out so it was room temperature. He went back to the prep area and continued making dinner. Once he had it almost complete, he ran upstairs, took a shower, and dressed in a polo shirt with slacks. He looked at the clock. It showed 5:35 p.m. He put on his cologne and went back to the kitchen. He finished dinner and sat, waiting for Saria to arrive. He did not have to wait long. Soon, she buzzed the box at the gate.

"Pull around and into the garage," he said. "The neighbors have a thing about cars parked in front of the house."

She pulled around and into the garage. He met her at the door. She was dressed in a tight, lacy black dress that showed her every curve. She had a perfectly formed and toned body. She was beautiful. He stood for a second absorbing her completely, then he slowly spoke.

"Why, Saria, you look absolutely beautiful tonight. Won't you come in?"

He moved aside, allowing her into the house. She walked into the foyer and looked around at the marble-and-alabaster architectural components and the Greek and Italian statues. She walked to a room to the side, where she could see a glimpse of a Japanese spear. She walked into the room and was amazed at what she saw. On one wall was an example of swords from every era. She was in awe. She had never seen such a collection.

In the center of the room was an empty black walnut sword stand with gold-inlaid dragons for legs. It was sitting on a table covered with a gold-trimmed white linen tablecloth. It had embroidered gold dragons running parallel to the stand. Saria looked at it queerly. It was a very elegant display to sit empty.

"That is the display for my pride and joy. It is on its way from my residence in Japan," he stated in response to her unspoken question. "I just had the display made and it was delivered yesterday. I thought I would see how it fit in the room."

"It is such a beautiful display to sit empty. The sword that it is made for must be beautiful and precious."

"There are only a few out there. It is very . . . rare," he said with reverence.

"This is a very impressive collection, Mr. Smythe. A very impressive collection indeed. May I?" she asked, pointing at a naginata.

"Yes, all these are originals that were used in combat. So they are touchable."

Saria picked up the naginata, a wide-bladed Japanese spear, and spun it around. It was obvious to Rick she knew how to use it. She started doing kata with it. He watched with interest. Each movement flowed into the next unless it was a sharp blow. Those stopped with exact precision. As she moved, he could see an almost unearthly grace to her movement. Her movements were hypnotic. Rick could not turn away as he watched her. Finally, she stopped and put the spear away.

Rick looked to the side and pulled down a nondescript katana. It was in a plain bamboo scabbard and the hilt had dragons carved into it and was wrapped in eel skin. He pulled it out of the sheath. Saria looked at the blade. Obviously made by a master of the art, it had all the appropriate markings of a sword made in the ancient ways. She took the proffered hilt and was amazed at the balance of the weapon. She swung it easily and could stop the blade just as effortlessly. She handed the weapon back to Rick. As he was sheathing it, he stopped and almost instinctively bumped his hand against the blade drawing a mere drop of blood. Saria frowned a little.

"Oh, the blade cannot be drawn and sheathed again without tasting blood. It is an old tradition. I keep it up. I promised my master I would when he passed it to me. Legend has it that Amakuni Yasutsuna and his son, Amakura, made this particular sword. They are the legendary creators of this style of katana. I know it has been passed down for the last thousand years from master to student. It is old enough to have been created by them."

"It has never been sheathed without tasting blood in all that time?"

"As far as I know, no it hasn't. Interesting, isn't it?"

"Yes, it is. So is it time to eat?"

"Of course; follow me."

Rick led her to the dining room and pulled out her chair. She sat, and he brought the food to the table and opened the warming dishes. He served her, and then made a plate for himself. He walked over to his wine bucket and brought the bottle over, cautiously opened it, and handed her the cork. She sniffed it then handed it back. He took the cork, and then poured a bit in a glass. She sniffed it and rolled it around in the glass. She then tasted it and gave him a smile. He poured them both a glass.

"So, Saria, do you like the choice of dishes? Both are common Romanian dishes."

She took a sampling bite of both, looked back at him, and smiled. "They are wonderful. You are very thoughtful. Where did you find them?"

"The Internet."

She laughed. "You are wise and you are also a wonderful cook. Your wine choice is perfect. You are a man of many talents."

"Why, thank you. The Internet can make you a connoisseur of many things." He smiled.

They finished eating, and he cleared the dishes away. He put on some soft music as background sound. They walked over to the couch and sat down. They looked into each other's eyes, but soon Rick broke the eye contact, frowning in concern. He could still see the glint and thought he knew what it was. However, he could not see it well enough to know for sure.

"I have a question for you. When I was at the police station, they showed me pictures of the victims and the crime scenes. They were very similar to the pictures I had collected in my research. These other incidents were scattered and isolated in different parts of the country. However, we have had as many incidences in the last couple of weeks as I had discovered before in several years. It seems they are escalating. The thing that bothers me is that they are identical. There are multiple pairs of bite marks, and the victim is exsanguinated with minimal loss in the area of the attack. Many times, their wallets or purses are untouched. Just the blood was taken. Does any of your research show anything like that?"

"Not really. So you think these attacks are linked in some way all over the country?" Saria frowned at him. He could see she was contemplating something.

"Yes I do," he replied. "It is all too coincidental to be otherwise."

Saria pulled out the information she had brought for them to look at. She spread the information out on the coffee table. She smiled at him as he dug through it. He looked like a kid in a candy store.

"This is a lot of information. This has information about sightings for hundreds of years, in just about every country in the world. Some of these countries don't even exist anymore. This is wonderful. Look at these drawings."

He picked up a set of drawings on old vellum. They depicted a victim with multiple pairs of puncture marks. It went on to show a group of creatures with great cloaks. They appeared to be descending on the victim.

"This is our eyewitness. This is a description of how the attacks occurred. So if this was to occur, someone had to see it—a bum, a passerby, someone. However, if I was to see a group of vampires descend on someone, I don't think I would believe what I was seeing. Maybe that is why there are no witnesses—traumatic amnesia."

"They see something their brains can't process as real, so they forget it?"

"Not exactly forget. Lock away."

"That is a very interesting theory. So how do you find these amnesiac witnesses?"

"I have no idea. We have to do something to trigger their brain to unlock the memory."

"You are way past my experience. How do we unlock their memories?"

"Unfortunately it takes years to break through the barriers the brain puts up to protect the psyche. So, that is probably a dead-end trail. If we, I mean the police, could find the leader, maybe we could stop this."

"Leader? What happened to your single attacker theory?"

"All the clues seem to be pointing toward a group—a coven, if you will. Those groups usually have a charismatic leader who holds them together. Catch the leader and they usually go away. 'Cutting off the head of the snake,' they used to say in the NYPD gang unit," he said.

"Oh yeah, I had forgotten that you helped them out some. Did you see many of these . . . covens . . . in New York?"

"Not really. Mostly just punk gangs and organized crime. There was a case or two periodically but not very often. They classified them as independent homicides so I was not usually involved with those cases."

"Interesting. Hey, why don't we go out? I have been hearing about this new club, Pandemonium. I hear the music is good and they have a large dance floor. I haven't been dancing in a while."

"Sounds great. Let's take my car. I have to make a call first, though," Rick stated.

"Where is the bathroom so I can freshen up?"

"Down the hall, second door on the left."

Rick watched her walk down the hall and turn toward the bathroom. He picked up the receiver of the phone and walked over by the window. Taiga was standing just outside. He looked Taiga in the eyes.

"Hello, yes, I am going to the Pandemonium. I will be back late. Please send a car by to check on the property. Thanks. I appreciate it."

Rick hung up the phone and turned around to see Saria right behind him.

"Everything okay?"

"Yeah, I just called my security company to send a patrol by since I wasn't going to be home. Just a service they provide in this area. If you're ready, let's go."

"I'm right behind you."

Rick glanced out the window to see a shadow move out of sight. They walked to the garage and Rick opened the door for Saria. After she sat, he closed it tightly got in on his side, and they headed for the club.

"I have been meaning to ask you. Where do you keep the car you drive to work? When I parked earlier, I noticed that you did not drive this 1965 Jaguar XKE to the office."

"It's actually a *1963* Jaguar XKE," he corrected smiling. "I have a storage down the road that I park in on weekends and pull out my baby here." He patted the dash gingerly.

"How about we do the whole thing and drive down Sunset with the top down."

"You got it."

Rick pulled off to the side of the road and put down the top. He secured it, pulled back on the road, and headed down the road along the ocean. Saria looked across the water. She could smell the sea air and it took her back to the crossing of the Atlantic to Mexico. Her parents had sent her with a single attendant, an older man who was to watch over her until they reached California and the safety of her uncle's house. He had a tendency to drink too much and pass out. During one of those episodes, two sailors decided they were going to take advantage of the young girl aboard their ship. Her vampire hearing detected the men before they even made it to the door.

She had been developing a thirst and the rats on the ship was not sating it. She slowly and silently moved to the door. She stood next to it and jerked the two men off their feet as they crept into the room. She quickly bit deep into the first one's neck and drank deeply. He thrashed around, making a lot of noise until she snapped his neck to keep him silent. Once she had finished with him, she turned to the other one. He had crawled into a corner and was holding up a cross and praying for deliverance from this evil creature.

"Your god will not help you. You came with plans of an impure nature and now you will die the same way," she snarled at the man as she wiped his shipmate's blood from her face.

The thirst was demanding more. She stepped closer to the man. He struck out at her but she caught his hand and crushed it. She grabbed his shirt and lifted him from the floor, bit deeply into his neck, and felt the warm blood gush into her mouth. His fear tasted good. She drank all she could and then dropped his limp body to the floor. Her thirst sated, she looked at what she had done. She fell to the floor and prayed for God to forgive her and to free her from this curse. She stripped the clothes from the corpses and used the cloth to clean the blood from the floor. She cleaned herself up and changed her clothes. She threw the corpses and all the bloody clothes off the back of the ship.

"Saria?" Rick asked, breaking her reverie.

"Yes?"

"You were staring into space and crying. Are you sure everything is okay?"

"Yeah, this song reminded me of a bad memory. It was my mother's favorite. I just miss her and my father so much sometimes. You know they died when I was young. My adoptive parents are the most wonderful people but I still miss my birth parents sometimes."

"I understand that. My parents were killed when I was very young and my uncle raised me. He was a good man and did his best, and I wasn't the greatest kid. You sure you still want to go?"

"Of course, a little melancholy isn't going to stop us from having a good time, is it?"

"I guess not. Time to turn a little more inland."

They continued until they reached the 405 highway and drove straight to Sunset Boulevard. By the time they reached it, Saria was all smiles and had her makeup fixed and looked like her usual self. All signs of the sudden and deep emotion was gone. She held her hands up in the air as they drove down Sunset toward the club. Rick smiled as he drove; Saria was such an optimist. What was it that bothered him so much?

Rick saw the club ahead. He pulled into a parking lot and parked the car. He helped Saria out then latched the top and locked the doors. He grabbed her hand and they headed for the club. The garage was well lit. Rick noticed out of the corner of his eye movement in one of the few shadows. He remained alert as they walked over to the elevator. While waiting for the car to arrive, he again noticed the movement. Saria seemed oblivious to it. After what seemed like an eternity to Rick, the elevator car arrived. He pushed the button as they stepped in and the door closed. He waited impatiently as the car traveled to the street level.

Rick remained alert but did not see the movement again. They walked over to the line and waited for their turn to get in. The bouncer at the door smiled at Saria and she promptly ignored him. After a few more minutes and the departure of a few more patrons, the bouncer let them in. A young woman stood by the door.

"There is a ten dollar cover each and a two drink minimum."

Rick gave the woman a twenty and she stamped their hand. They walked into the pandemonium of the club, noting that it was aptly named. They found a booth off to the side in a shadowed area so it was less likely for anyone to see them. They both ordered a drink, and the server soon brought them over. Rick sipped at his and leaned over to Saria.

"Are you ready to dance?"

"You know it!"

They walked out to the dance floor and started dancing. They moved around in the crowd. Every time a young man tried to dance with Saria, she would move back closer to Rick until he got the message. Rick dodged young women just as frequently. Soon, everyone got the idea the two were a couple and was less frequently trying to move in. Rick and Saria smiled at each other. Depending on the song, Saria would move up to Rick, press her body against his, and move her hips back and forth. She would sometimes run her hands along the sides of his face and into his hair.

Rick would respond by taking her hands down and holding them across her body and moving his hips in sync with hers. They danced for several hours. When they were in their latest close position, Saria whipped around and kissed Rick deep and passionately. When she pulled away, she looked at him. She bit her lip as she waited for his response. He looked at her, pulled her back toward him, and gave her the response she'd hoped for. She closed her eyes and enjoyed the closeness she felt with his lips pressed against hers.

He slowly drew back his head and looked at her, still standing in the position of the kiss with her eyes closed. She slowly recovered. He looked at her with different eyes. He no longer saw his coworker. He saw a beautiful woman—his woman. He reached forward and kissed her again. Rick opened his eyes, glanced over her shoulder, and saw movement in the shadows. He broke off the kiss and moved her toward the table.

"I think it is time for us to go," he said quickly.

"What's wrong, Rick?"

"Nothing," he lied. "It's just getting late."

"All right," she said, confused. "Let me run to the ladies'."

"All right. I'll be here waiting."

Saria walked over to the ladies' room and Rick strained his eyes to look for the movement he had seen. He saw nothing. He pulled out his cell and dialed Taiga.

"Taiga, I have movement. I think we have a problem. Let the team know."

"Hai," Taiga responded.

Rick hung up as he saw Saria stepping out of the bathroom. He quickly slid his phone into his pocket. As she walked up to the table, he dropped a twenty on the table for the server, took her hand and started to lead her out. He placed her in front of him, holding her by the waist to direct her more quickly as he moved them skillfully through the crowd. Saria kept looking over her shoulder at him.

"What is going on, Rick? You are acting really spooked," she finally asked.

"I am just trying to get us out so we can get out of here,"

he lied again.

Finally, they reached the parking garage elevator and he pushed the button. The door opened. They got in and he punched the button for the floor above where they'd parked. The door opened and he led her to the stairs. He listened for a second and then led her down to the level with the car. She kept looking at the intensity in his face. He did not appear afraid, but concerned and intense.

He moved out of the stairwell and saw the route to the car was clear. He kept himself between her and the shadows across from the car. He moved her quickly to the car and opened the door. She sat and he quickly moved to the other side, and jumped in. Once the car was started and they were pulling out, he started to relax. He saw movement in several shadows, then everything was still. He drove cautiously out of the parking structure. Once they were on their way back to his house, Saria turned to him.

"Tell me the truth: what was that all about? We were having a moment and the next thing i know, you are rushing me out the door. Not very romantic if you ask me."

"Sorry, it's an old habit. I saw something out of the ordinary and wanted to get you out of there. I wanted you safe."

"Safe from what?"

"My past. I was a gang member when I was younger. After I quit, they tried to kill me. I'm just overly cautious now."

"So you saw gang members, or what?"

"No, not gang members specifically. Something out of the ordinary."

"All right, you just scared me; I thought I had done something wrong. I would hate to know I blew it on our first date."

"First date? Okay, we'll call it that," he said absentmindedly while still looking in the rearview mirror.

She rolled her eyes at him and took his proffered hand as they drove the remainder of the way to his house in silence. He pulled the car into the garage and closed the door. He led her into the house and over to the couch to sit down. He took Saria's hands in his.

"I really enjoyed tonight. I'm sorry I got spooked. I would like to continue this relationship to see where it goes, But I have to take it slow."

"I understand, Rick. How about I come over tomorrow and we go and see a movie or something?" she asked.

"Sounds great. See you tomorrow, then," he answered.

"What time?"

"Let's make a day of it. Come over early—say, ten or eleven?"

"Sounds good. See you then."

"Great, let me walk you out," he said, taking her hand.

Rick led her to the garage door. Just the touch of her skin on his was electric. He kissed her, walked her to the car and waved good-bye to her as she got ready to pull into the street. She waved back, pulled out into the street and drove into the darkness. Rick closed the door and went back into the house. Standing in the kitchen was Taiga.

"Taiga. Report."

"Lord, they did not find anything. I am afraid it is the last Hand."

"Shinto? My god, I certainly hope not. I don't know how I can protect Saria if it is, without revealing who I am. I'm not sure she could accept it."

"Lord, I would not be so sure. She seems very . . . interested in you."

"Taiga, you know what happened with the last relationship. I am still looking for that one. She is the only one to have ever escaped. Though if I was looking for a relationship Saria would be the candidate."

"Yes, lord, I will have them sweep the city. Get some rest."

"Be here early in the morning. I need to hone my skills if Shinto is here. Bring Amaya with you."

"Yes, lord," Taiga stated, bowing. He left the house and disappeared into the night.

Rick walked into the bedroom and collapsed.

***

As Saria drove back toward her apartment, she hit the "mom" button on her navigation system to dial her mother. She waited as the call routed to Romania. After a couple of rings, Ecaterina answered.

"Hello, Saria?"

"Hi, Mother. How are you this morning?"

"Good. You are calling kind of early this morning. Is there something wrong?" her mother asked.

"No, nothing is wrong; everything is absolutely wonderful. I have met this guy and we had our first official date. You and father were right. When you find the right one you know," she admitted.

"Wait—you have found your mate? In America? Tell me more about him. Is it the psychologist you work with that you have been going on about?"

"Yes, Mother, the very same one. He is intelligent, witty, and a pleasure to be around. He can cook, he is polite, and you can tell father he has perfect teeth. I checked. The only thing is he is human and claims to not believe in vampires."

"So I take it he doesn't know. Saria, you have to tell him. If he is the right one he will accept it. This is not something that can wait."

"Come on, Mother, I don't want to scare him away thinking I am deluded. He thinks vampirism is a delusion. He wrote a paper about it."

"What is his name again, Saria?"

"Richard Smythe."

"I have read his work. It is brilliant but comes to all the wrong conclusions. Are you sure he does not believe in vampires? His papers almost read like disinformation."

"He says he doesn't. What do you mean by disinformation?"

"It takes factual information and comes to the totally opposite conclusion than he should. It almost reads like he is intentionally pointing away from vampires. And, young lady, what have I told you about that gutter speak?"

"Contractions are laziness of the tongue and proper ladies

avoid them," Saria recited.

"Correct. So tell me more about him."

"He is perfect. He laughs at my jokes and makes me feel all happy inside. I am not as thirsty around him, either. He makes me feel good about myself without flattering me. I feel like I can be myself around him. When we touch, I feel an electric shock. Just the feel of his skin on my skin turns me on so much."

"Saria, don't let your loins get you into trouble again. Like I have told you before, if you need to put out a fire just borrow the hose; do not buy the whole fire truck. We live too long to let our base desires rule our lives. You remember the last time—although he does sound pretty nice. The lack of thirst is an important factor. I will talk to your father about him when he gets up. I know it is late there so you get some sleep. Keep us informed."

"Yes, ma'am, I will. I love you and will call you soon."

"Love you too."

Saria hung up the phone and drove into the darkness toward her apartment.

***

Shinto stood at the door to Nickolea's rooms. He looked at the mansion around him. He found its opulence and excess offensive. He had waited for Nickolea for only a few minutes but those minutes seemed like hours to him. Finally, Nickolea walked out with a beautiful blonde woman. He sat on his "throne" and waved his hand at Shinto to begin. The woman sat at his feet. Nickolea stroked her hair.

"I was correct. The man is Dr. Richard Smythe. He was the investigator who tracked down my clan, and the Shadow killed them."

The woman jumped at the sound of Rick's name.

"What's wrong, Siobhan? Is that him?"

"Yes, lord, it is," she hissed. "He tracked down our coven in New York. Those creatures he worked with—the Shadow, I guess—killed them all. Only Sigmund and I escaped. I had him in bed and I thought he was asleep but he woke as I was about to rip his throat out. He shoved me away so quickly I couldn't kill him, so I leaped out the window to escape. He is deadly with any bladed weapon."

"Shinto, I want you to kill Saria's new 'friend.' She needs to learn that humans are sheep to feed upon. She also needs to learn that I control this city and she must bow to me. I also want you to kill him for Siobhan." He continued to stroke her long blonde hair.

"This one will be free, Nickolea. I owe him," Shinto snarled. Suddenly his expression changed when the totality of Nickolea's words struck him. He began to laugh. "You expect your dame to bow to you?" His laughter brought up Nickolea's ire.

"Why are you laughing? She needs to suffer before I kill her and take her place as the Elder. Then I will show all the weaklings in Romania where the real power lies." Nickolea curled his lip into a toothy smile.

Chapter III

Saria pulled through the open gate and into the garage. She hit the close button on the wall by the door as she walked into Rick's house. She could see him in the backyard sparring with two other people. Rick held a wooden sword and the other two held naginata. She watched as he moved swiftly. He dodged the blows coming at him, then attacked, forcing them to quickly recover to block his blows. Then she noticed the blindfold around his eyes. Rick's movements seemed to be ahead of his sparring partners by milliseconds. Their movements were almost a blur as they moved to attack him again. Still he was moving before they did. Saria watched in amazement for a couple of minutes before they noticed her. Once his opponents knew she was there, they changed their style of movement and their speed. Saria knew it was for her benefit but she could not decide why. She let that pass and headed out the back door, being sure to keep out of the way.

She pulled out a chair from the patio table, sat and watched. She was amazed at how a human could move like Rick. He was faster than some vampires she knew. She looked at his rippling muscles. She did not see a bit of fat on his long, lean musculature. She absorbed everything she could see: she watched the way his feet moved, the way he moved his arms. She had never been as interested in anyone as she was Rick. After a few more minutes of practice, Rick signaled a stop and walked over to the table where she sat. He picked up a towel from the chair next to her and a sports drink out of the cooler next to it.

"You're a bit early," he said, slightly out of breath, smiling at her.

"I came early to hopefully catch you with your shirt off. I have to say I am not disappointed. It was definitely worth the wait," she said playfully.

"I'm glad. I would hate for the experience to be anticlimactic. Let's go in and let me get a shower." Turning to his sparring partners, he said, "Thanks for the workout, Taiga, Amaya."

"Yes, sensei," they responded in unison. "We will return to our duties."

"Oh, before you do, let me introduce you to Saria. Saria, this is Taiga. He is my gardener and sparring partner," he said, indicating Taiga. "And this is Amaya; she is my housekeeper and babysitter."

Amaya ducked her head and giggled. "He is an easy ward to manage."

"Taiga, Amaya, this is Saria. We work together and are now going out."

"Greetings, Lady Saria," they said together.

"Just Saria, please. I am very glad to meet you both. I knew he couldn't manage this place alone." She winked at them and they smiled back.

"They came with me from Japan, when I moved back. I couldn't tell them no." He smiled at them. "Let's go in."

"Sensei, I will finish the yard first," Taiga said. "I have a question about the garden."

"Okay, Taiga. Amaya, take Saria in and make her comfortable, please."

"Yes, sensei."

Amaya led Saria into the house while Taiga led Rick to the garden. Once the women were in the house, Taiga spoke.

"Lord, something is not right with her. She cares for you; that is certain. Her pheromones tell me that. But there is something else about her. The way she moves, the way she carries herself, it is not normal for the people in this town." The last he said with a little disgust. "Please be careful."

"Of course, Taiga. If you can pinpoint what's bothering you, let me know. I would hate to know I have invited another rogue into my house," he said, patting his companion on the back.

"Lord, I do not think it is that. I would have known that immediately, as Amaya would have. I will try to divine what is wrong. It could be nothing, but just be careful."

"Taiga, I have worked with you too long to dismiss your instincts."

"Thank you, my lord," he said with a slight bow.

Rick returned the bow and headed for the house. Once inside he turned to Saria.

"Give me a little bit to shower and get dressed."

"Can I watch?"

Rick cleared his throat nervously. "Not this time," he responded with a slight quiver in his voice.

"I'll take a rain check."

Saria turned back to the TV Amaya had turned on for her. Amaya walked toward the bedroom to lay out Rick's clothes but he waved her away. She nodded and went into the kitchen. She moved around and started pulling out pots and pans. She took out eggs and bacon and set them on the counter.

"Lady Saria, are you hungry?" she asked.

"It's just Saria, and yes, I actually am. Can I help?"

"No, I have it. You just sit and watch the TV. It is about time for the news."

Saria switched channels. The weather was on and the forecast was for clear skies. She switched back to an old movie. Amaya watched her every move. She glanced out the patio doors and saw Taiga using hand signals to her. She understood his message loud and clear: she was to watch Saria very closely. Taiga did not think she meant Rick ill, but they could not take any chances with their master's life. After about thirty minutes, Rick walked out dressed in shorts and a button up short-sleeved shirt. The top several buttons were open. He rubbed his hair with a white towel.

Amaya set out two plates for Rick and Saria. She took two more out to the patio for Taiga and herself. Rick pulled out the chair for Saria, and once she was sitting, he seated himself. As they started eating, he noticed that Saria precisely cut each piece to a certain size, stabbed it with the fork upside down, and placed them in her mouth, pulling them free with her teeth, not her lips.

Rick watched her eat with increasing curiosity. He had not noticed her eating technique before. He had seen people eat after having etiquette lessons, but hers was to the extreme. He watched as she slowly chewed each bite. He intently watched her mouth and her lips move. Each movement was exact but was so conditioned they were pure reflex. She noticed him staring and covered her mouth.

"What?" she asked. "Why are you staring at me?"

"Your eating technique—it is absolutely superb. Every single movement is so precise, yet so automatic it appears natural. It is like you grew up in a royal court or something."

She giggled. "That is ridiculous. You know my family has lived in California since it was a Spanish colony. My father was very particular about appearances and etiquette, that's all."

They finished eating and Rick put the plates into the sink. Within a few minutes, Amaya walked back in with Taiga and her plates. She cleaned up the kitchen and excused herself. Saria watched the two with a keen interest. As soon as Amaya was out of the room, Saria turned to Rick.

"Why are they so deferent to you and why does she insist on calling me Lady Saria?"

"They are both very old-fashioned. They follow the old traditions of loyalty and deference to the lord of the house and his guests. It is purely out of respect."

"So where would you like to go today?"

"Since I've been here, I have basically gone to work and come home. What would you recommend?"

"The beach," she replied, pulling off her shirt to reveal a bikini.

"Saria, that's more like two bandages and a piece of thread than a bikini."

"It is the latest style. Besides, it covers the important parts."

"That is *all* it covers. Don't get me wrong; I like it."

"I can always take it off," she said, reaching behind her back to untie it.

"No, it's good the way it is," he said, reaching to grab her arm.

She shifted her body and his hand landed on her breast. Rick jerked his hand back and turned a beautiful shade of red. Saria laughed loudly, and when Rick frowned at her, she only laughed harder. He rolled his eyes and walked over to the counter to pick up his keys.

"Aren't you going to change?" she asked.

"No need; these shorts are swim trunks. Let me grab a couple of towels and a blanket."

"Well, I need to," Saria said reaching in her purse.

"Why is that?"

"I would not be caught dead in this thing in public."

"So it was purely for my benefit?"

"Of course it was. I have already seen me naked and it is a sight I wanted to share with you," she said as she pulled off the skimpy bikini top.

"Saria," Rick said, covering his eyes.

"What, haven't you seen breasts before?" she asked walking up to him. She kissed him, brought his hands from his eyes, and laid them on her nipples. He jerked his hands away as if he had touched a hot stove. Saria looked at him with a hurt look on her face. She was still holding his hands and had a tear in the corner of her eye.

"Do I repulse you that much?"

Rick opened his eyes and saw the pain he had caused her.

"No, Saria. You are the most beautiful and sexually attractive woman I have ever met. I have a . . . personal problem. Come sit with me," he said as he rotated the grip and took her hand. She weakly tried to pull away but then walked with him. Once they had sat down on the sofa. Rick continued, "Saria, the last relationship I had ended badly. I mean, really badly. As a matter of fact, she tried to kill me."

Saria looked at him in disbelief. "She tried to kill you? How?"

"She was going to stab me in the chest, I think, or slit my

throat. I didn't wait to find out. I woke up with her over me with a large knife in her hands. As she was bringing it down, I pushed her off the bed while propelling myself to my sword. She landed on the floor and turned to go out the window, grabbing her clothes on the way out," he said in a matter-of-fact way.

Saria had a look of abject horror on her face. She grabbed him by the cheeks and kissed him. Tears ran down her cheeks for both of them. He grabbed her and held her close. He had never shed tears for the fact that he was almost killed. Her shedding tears for him allowed him to grieve himself. She buried her face into his shoulder and cried. They held each other for a long time until Saria finally released him. Rick could feel a release of tension in her as if she'd released something she had held in for a very long time. Her release of emotion had caused an unexpected release in himself. She kissed his lips several times.

Rick looked at her, and her makeup was running and smeared. She looked at him with a vulnerable look. He felt as if his secret was much greater than any she could hold. Even if she was a vampire, his secret remained much more terrible. His admission was on the tip of his tongue. He moved his lips to speak and she placed her finger over them and softly spoke to him.

"I am sorry to have accused you when you held such a terrible memory so close to your chest. I will wait as long as necessary for you to be intimate again. I can wait for millennia if necessary. You tell me when you are ready."

"Saria, give me another six months. I will make myself ready. I had not realized until this moment how much pent-up emotion I had regarding this incident. Britney had taken something from me I had not realized. She had taken my ability to be intimate, my ability to be open and truthful, and my ability to share all of myself with someone."

"You tell me when you are ready to move to the next level. But I am going to keep trying."

She leaned over to kiss him and put on her bikini top.

"You are right. Your breasts are a sight worth sharing. I think they are quite nice. Not that I am a professional judge of breasts," he stated.

"Why, thank you. I understand I come from a long line of nice breasts," she said.

"I think they are nice and hope one day I can feel comfortable enough to touch them. For now this will have to suffice," he said, kissing the top of each one.

He could see the gooseflesh appear across her body and her muscles tense with each kiss. The smile on her face turned to a look of ecstasy. A soft moaning exhale escaped her lips. He was amazed at what that single contact had done to her. She was no danger to him. He felt it in his heart. However, his brain told him a different tale. It told him a tale of pain and death. *Which should a man follow, his heart or his head when they are both such an integral part of who he is; and are at such odds with each other?* he thought. *That is what I am going to have to figure out. Until then, her presence, her closeness will have to suffice.*

He decided to side with his heart and he began to speak. "I have one more thing to admit to you."

"What is it?"

"I believe in vampires. Actually, I know they really exist."

Saria sat up and looked at him. "What do you mean, you *know* they exist?"

"Several of the cases I worked on in New York were cases of actual vampire attacks. From things you have said, you know they exist also. What is your connection?"

"I have no connection. I have come across the truth in my research, just like you did. What is your connection?"

"I track them."

"Track . . . them?" Saria said nervously.

"Yes, I work *with* the Clan of the Divine Shadow."

"You work with the Shadow?"

"Yes, are you familiar with them?"

"Distantly. I discovered them through my research. They are vampires who hunt vampires, correct?"

"Yes. They kill rogue vampires."

"That makes more sense. Are Amaya and Taiga members of the Shadow?"

"I have told you all I can without putting you in danger. I wanted to tell you to explain my strange behavior over the last couple of days. With the increasing intensity of attacks lately, I'm afraid things are going to get stranger. I want to keep going with our relationship but I thought I should let you know what you would be getting into."

"So does this . . . job . . . make you a target?" she said cautiously.

"It has in the past. I'm afraid they are following us. I don't want to endanger you."

"I am not worried. I know everything will be fine. Have you found many here?"

"More than I'd like," he replied. "I will protect you."

"Is this why Britney attacked you?"

"I feel it is. I believe she was working with the rogues."

"So she used your emotions to get close enough to kill you? What a bitch. I can understand your hesitation. My ex was abusive and betrayed me in a similar and violent way. He left me for dead."

"Oh my god, what happened?"

"He shot me and left, thinking I was dead. After he walked out, I was able to reach my cell phone and called 9-1-1. They arrived before I bled out," she said in soft tones.

Rick looked at her and saw her in a different light. She was no longer the happy-go-lucky woman he knew. He now saw someone who had overcome the ultimate betrayal and was still able to be the eternal optimist he saw every day. He saw the incident with Britney as less of an obstacle. He leaned over and kissed her and she returned the kiss.

Saria quickly stood. "Where is the bathroom so I can freshen up? I certainly can't go to the beach looking like this," she said brightly, lightening the mood.

"You used it yesterday. You don't remember where it is?" he said, standing. "Follow me."

She followed him down the hall. After showing her the way, he headed for his own bathroom to freshen up himself. When he had finished he walked to the living room and Saria sat on the sofa in a more modest bikini top and a pair of shorts over her bottoms. Her makeup was once again perfect though her eyes were still a bit red from crying.

"I see you have put on a bit more clothes."

"Just enough to be decent. Are you ready to go? I can't wait to get in the water. We're taking the convertible, right?" she said rhetorically.

"Of course," Rick said after retrieving his keys and wallet.

He then reached in a closet just inside the garage door. He pulled out two large towels, a blanket, and a beach umbrella. He dropped the top of the Jag and put everything in. He looked back at Saria and noticed she had not put her shirt back on. She had it tied around her taut abdomen. He grabbed an extra set of clothes from the closet. He tossed Saria one of his shirts and a pair of shorts. She looked at them strangely.

"Just in case—you never know, you may need something extra. Sorry, I don't have women's underwear in my beach closet."

Saria laughed as they got into the car. Rick had backed out and started to make the turn toward the street when Taiga stopped them.

"Sir, there is something on the news I think you should see."

Taiga led them back into the house. The reporter was talking about a murder that had occurred overnight. They had been murdered in the street after leaving the Chinese theater. Their heads had been twisted in an unnatural position with multiple bite wounds. Like all other attacks, there were no witnesses, and the police had no leads. Unlike the other attacks there had been two victims. Rick looked at Saria; she had tears in her eyes. He held her close to his chest.

"They didn't have a chance," she whispered, "and there was no one there to help them."

"Who could have? Looking at the number of wounds, there had to be at least three or four attackers."

Rick glanced at Taiga and Taiga nodded his head. Rick gave

Taiga a look with a slight flick of his eye toward the TV and Taiga shook his head. Rick kissed Saria on the top of her head and continued to hold her close. She slowly turned around to see the blatant image glaring in front of her. She just stared.

"They have to be stopped," Rick said absently, "before they kill again."

Saria looked at him strangely. "What are you talking about?"

"What I think we have here is a rogue coven. These people don't just pretend to be vampires; they truly are vampires. The worst part of it is, they are not acting like vampires should. They are too blatant and out in the open. Even rogue covens have some restraint. These monsters don't care if people recognize them as vampires. That makes them a very dangerous bunch. Taiga, please put the khukuri in the car. They are not a katana, but they will do in case of trouble."

Taiga went into the weapon room and brought out two forward-curved knives. He carried them outside and slid them into the back of the driver's seat. Saria watched as Rick had the car armed. She looked curiously at him. His expression was serious and as cold as death itself.

Rick turned to Saria. "I'm sorry. We can't be too careful with monsters like this on the loose. Are you ready?"

"For what? The zombie apocalypse? A vampire attack? I realize you are good, but this?" she said, pointing at the TV.

"The beach," Rick replied very calmly. "We are preparing for the beach. I told you I could be a little paranoid."

"I have a cell phone. I can call 9-1-1."

"If it comes down to it, that is exactly what I want you to do. Run and call 9-1-1."

"And leave you to whatever fate they deem proper or fun?" Saria demanded.

"I can handle myself. It will be easier for me if I don't have to worry about your safety."

"Like I said, I realize you are good, but who knows how many he will bring with him. I would feel better if you would run also."

"How many who would bring? What do you know about this coven?"

"I meant their leader, Rick. Groups like this always have a leader of some sort. I don't know any more than you do."

"Sorry. I get paranoid, like I said. I will run if the situation warrants it. But I will still feel better with some protection."

"Granted, I would not want you to leave the knives. But I don't want you to get hurt being gallant and trying to protect me. I can be pretty formidable myself."

"No gallantry. I got it."

"Wait; that is not what I said. I like you being gallant. Just run with me is all I ask."

Rick could see tears starting to well up in her eyes again. In those tears, he could see a faint shimmer. Just as quickly as it appeared, it was gone. There was more to this than she would admit. Rick shook his head, then grabbed and lightly kissed her.

"No heroics. I will run with you if we need to. It is broad daylight and they should not be out. The knives are for just in case."

"All right," Saria said calming herself. She lightly kissed him again.

"Let's go," Rick stated.

"Okay." She took his hand.

"Sir, I will take care of that errand you asked about this morning."

"Excellent idea, Taiga."

Rick led Saria back out the front door and into the car. They pulled out and drove to the beach in Redondo. He parked and put a handful of coins into the meter. He walked to the trunk and pulled out a bag, put the spare clothes and the khukuri in the bag with towels, covered with the blanket. Saria watched as he packed everything. He pulled out a cooler with some water bottles in it, set it and the bag beside the car, and then put up the top and locked the doors.

"I am ready now," he said finally.

"Wow. That is what I call prepared."

"Let's head to the water. I need to clear my head."

They walked down to the beach. Saria placed the umbrella in

the sand until it stood on its own. Rick spread out the blanket in the shade of the umbrella and set down the cooler. He stripped off his shirt, kicked off his shoes, and ran for the water. Saria stripped off her shirt and shorts and headed in right behind him. Rick ran in until he was waist deep and then dove into the cold water. Saria stopped when she reached waist deep. She watched as Rick disappeared into the surf. He was under for what she felt was a long time when he finally surfaced several yards away. He waited for a larger wave, dove into it and let it carry him back to her, then stood and picked her up. She squirmed out of his grip and ran back onto the sand.

He jogged up to her. "What's wrong?"

"I am nervous in water deeper than my waist."

"Why is that? Can't you swim?"

"No, not really. I never learned. I actually almost drowned one time, so now I only splash around in waist-deep water. I really enjoy it."

"I'll stay close to you. You might need protection from these rabid teenage boys."

Saria looked around and saw several teenage boys walking slowly by. They were quite obviously looking at her. They were leering at very specific traits she possessed. She was not the only one garnering looks. Several young women walked by and looked over their sunglasses at Rick's chiseled abs. They watched as the over-muscled steroid addicts walked by, trying to gain the attention of the women ogling Rick. After a little while, the women and males drifted off to another area of the beach.

Rick put on his shirt and lay down on his side on the blanket. Saria reclined, supporting herself on her elbows. They looked at each other for a few tense seconds before Rick finally spoke first.

"I'm sorry if I upset you at the house."

"I was more worried."

"I can take care of myself. I had to do it for many years after I left the gang when I was a teenager. Then when I went to Japan to study a deluded serial killer who thought he was Miyamoto Musashi, I studied under a Japanese sword master. The detective I was working with, Kinoshi Kimura, introduced me to him. I studied with him for many years. I lived in Japan for about five years and helped Kinoshi break several rogue covens. So I am quite capable of taking care of myself."

"I understand, but these people appear very dangerous. Wait—did you say you worked with Kinoshi Kimura?"

"Yes, I did. Do you know him?" Rick inquired intently, watching her body language.

"I know of him," she replied. "He is also into vampire research. We have exchanged ideas by email, but I have not actually met him."

"When he comes to visit, I will have to introduce you. He's almost as fixated on vampires as you are."

Saria leaned up and punched Rick in the shoulder. "I am not fixated. I just have a healthy interest."

Rick rubbed his shoulder. "Okay, a healthy fixated interest."

Saria smiled. "I don't know if that's any better."

She looked around the beach and saw several groups playing volleyball not too far away.

"Rick, do you play volleyball?"

"Yeah, I was on the Columbia beach volleyball team. We took division my senior year. Why? Do you?"

"UCLA beach volleyball champions. We won state three years in a row. How did you play beach volleyball in New York?" she asked, changing the subject.

"There are beaches in New York. It is the EAST COAST, for heaven's sake. California doesn't have a monopoly on beaches or sand."

"Ok, let's teach these guys how to play," she said, competition in her eyes.

"Sure," Rick said, pulling off his shirt.

The games were a short walk from their beach site. Rick walked up to the closest court.

"Hey, can two more join?"

"Sure," one of the men said. He looked Rick and Saria over

for a couple of minutes, sizing them up. "How about you two play us?" he asked, pointing between himself and another tall man.

"No problem. Can we have a few minutes to warm up?" Saria asked, grabbing the ball from the man's hands.

"Sure, why not? We are ready to go when you are," he said, smiling as he and his teammate walked over to sit while Rick and Saria warmed up.

Saria looked at Rick as she bumped the ball to him; he easily bumped it back to her in a perfect lateral. They did that for a few minutes before Saria signaled their opponents that they were ready. The two men walked over. They flipped for the serve and the two guys won. They served toward Saria, she popped it up and forward where Rick had just moved to, and he leapt up and slammed it into the ground just on the other side of the net.

"I believe it is our serve," Rick said, picking up the ball and tossing it to Saria.

Saria jumped and served the ball just over the net. One of the guys dove and popped it back up in the air and his partner jumped to slam it down on Rick and Saria's side of the net. As the ball came down, Rick slid underneath it and popped it back up into the air and Saria slammed it over the net. One of the guys dove for it and missed as the ball slammed into the sand.

Rick and Saria did a high-five and Rick grabbed the ball to serve it to the back of the court area. The guys popped it easily back over the net. Saria hit it and dropped it in the middle of the other side. The taller of the guys popped it up just short of the net and his partner spiked it on Rick and Saria's side. Rick was already moving and dove just above the sand to bump it in the air—high enough for Saria to pop it for him to jump up and spike it later-ally toward the center of the sand. One of their opponents hit it, it popped back into the air, and the other slammed it over the net and toward Saria's face. She put her forearms in front of her face and the ball ricocheted across the court. Rick moved in front of it and drove it to the opposite side. Both of their opponents missed it. The game continued for a while and finally Rick and Saria won with a score of six to five.

Their opponents came over and shook their hands.

"How long have you two been playing together?"

"A while," Rick lied.

"You guys are tough opponents—and you, man . . . you were everywhere the ball was. Are you professionals or what?"

"I was a college championship player at Columbia in New York. My girlfriend here was a championship player here at UCLA." Rick said and Saria nodded her head.

"No damn wonder," the man said he paused then inquired, "You played beach volleyball in New York? Really?"

"Come on now, there are beaches in New York. I know you have heard of the Hamptons, Jersey Shore. Technically the Jersey Shore is in New Jersey but you get the point. It is the EAST COAST. What is up with you California people?"

Rick and Saria played several more games, and they won most of them. After a few hours, Saria looked up at the sky. "Wow, I didn't realize how long we have been here. It is getting late. We'd better get back. What else would you like to do this evening?"

"How about dinner, a movie, and more dancing?"

"Sounds good; let's pack up and go back to your place."

They said good-bye to their new friends, packed up all their stuff and headed back to the car. Rick packed it all in the trunk and put the top back down. He looked over at Saria. She had put on the shorts he had given her, had her shirt back on and tied. She looked beautiful. He thought she could be someone with whom he could spend the rest of his life. He felt the hair stand up on the back of his neck and turned around to see a man across the street, leaning against a parking meter and staring right at him. Once Saria was in the car, Rick got in and started it. The man started walking toward them as Rick sped away. Saria noticed the man as they were leaving.

"Who was that?"

"I have no idea, but he was staring right at us as we were getting in the car."

"Weird."

"Yeah, definitely weird."

They continued to chat as they headed to Rick's house. They soon arrived and pulled into the waiting garage. After exiting the car, Saria turned to Rick.

"I hope this doesn't sound weird or anything. I brought my clothes and a dressing bag. Would it be all right if I got ready over here? It wouldn't be too much of an imposition, would it?"

"Of course you can get ready over here. You can use the spare master suite. It has its own bathroom with shower, and it's no imposition. But I have a question: What if I'm a perv and look at you through a crack in the door or on a hidden camera?"

"A girl could only hope. I have no problem getting into my pants. Yours, not so much," she smiled and put her thumbs in the straps of her bikini and pulled it off her shoulders. "I'm sure your shower has plenty of room for two," she said while shimmying her shoulders.

She smiled as Rick rolled his eyes at her and opened the door to the spare master suite. She walked in with her bag and clothes and slowly started closing the door. She watched Rick walk away into the living room through the sliver of a crack she held open until he was out of sight. She grimaced, finished closing the door and headed into the bathroom. She took her dressing bag with her into the bathroom and started the shower. After showering, she stepped out in a towel and dried off. She put on her red satin, slinky one-shoulder maxi dress and enough makeup to make her pale complexion appear halfway normal.

She stared into the mirror, sighed and decided she was ready, then finally stepped out into the hall. Rick was sitting in the living room. He had already showered and changed. He was now wearing a pair of nice slacks and a tight-fitting polo with a sport coat. He smiled when he saw her. He stood and walked over to her.

"You look beautiful. I like that dress on you. Red is definitely your color," he said.

"Why, thank you, sir. Am I too overdressed?" She smiled.

"Not at all. You look amazing. Where would you like to eat?"

"How about Italian?"

"Sounds good, and I know just the place."

Rick led her to the door and they headed to the restaurant. As they drove through the near-darkness, the headlights cast shadows around them. For a few minutes, they drove in almost absolute silence. Rick was starting to get nervous. Saria was never silent. Something was bothering her.

"Saria, what is bothering you?" Rick asked.

"Nothing," she replied quickly.

"Something has to be; you are sometimes quiet but never silent. What is bothering you?"

She sighed deeply before continuing. "It is Amaya and Taiga. Who are they, really?"

"What do you mean?"

"They are constantly at your house. They spar with you. Taiga acts as if his very life hangs on your every word. Amaya sizes me up every time she sees me. It is just plain weird."

"They are my companions. I do not just own a residence in Japan. I am the daimyo of a house. I inherited it from my former master. He had no children and he left it to me when he died. Are you familiar with ancient Japanese tradition?"

"A little."

"This tradition is similar but has many different traits. As the lord of the house, I must have two companions with me all the time. They are my confidants, assistants, and my bodyguards. Taiga is my lieutenant. Amaya is like a sergeant. My house is part of the Shogunate, meaning we were once answerable to the Shogun who was in charge of the military. I would have been a territorial governor in feudal Japan. We learn and maintain a multitude of combat skills. Those include things like swordsmanship; armed and unarmed hand to hand combat; marksmanship with both archaic and modern weapons; stealth; and also less combat-oriented skills such as customs and courtesies, and sewing."

"So, why are they not with us now?"

"They are. They are in a car behind us. They are staying back a comfortable distance. We also have more of our house spread throughout town. Don't bother looking for them. You will not even notice them. I considered not even introducing them to you but you would eventually have met them either by happenstance or by their design."

"Oh, so I had to be checked out by your security team?" she asked, looking at him through one narrowed eye.

"I didn't require it, but they did it anyway. I trust you. However, they are not so trusting. Especially after what happened with my last girlfriend."

"Tell me more about that situation." Saria was now very interested.

"Other than she tried to kill me?"

"Yes, a bit more than that."

"I was working on this case with the NYPD. One of the less gang-related ones. We had been dating for a while. She was a receptionist in the building where I had my office. I told her about the case. She seemed interested. I thought it was just an act to show interest in my work. One night in bed, as I was getting ready to close the case, I woke up to find her over me with a large knife. You know the rest. I kicked her away from me and she took off. She fled the apartment and I have not seen her again."

"What was her name again?"

"She told me it was Britney. I doubt it was now. That is why I have had trouble with our relationship. That and the fact that my side job can be quite dangerous and I don't want to put you at risk."

"Don't worry about putting me at risk. I guess I can tolerate your bodyguards. Amaya is a good cook."

"So it won't weird you out when I give Taiga updates?" Rick asked.

"What do you mean, updates?"

"I let him know when and where I am going if I am going to be out for an extended period. Like tonight."

"So he can put us under surveillance?"

"Something like that." Rick smiled with that answer.

"Since we are a couple, I guess I take them part and parcel

with you."

"Oh, so we are a couple now, are we?"

"Yes, we are." She smiled with the last as she snuggled into his arm.

Rick smiled down at her and she looked back at him. He felt better telling her that part of his past. The rest he did not think she would understand or accept. He knew he would not have if he had not lived it. He continued driving toward the restaurant. He felt a peace he had not felt in a very long time. He could smell her hair, her perfume, even her skin. It was all fresh and flowery. The lights cast shadows around them as he pulled into the parking lot.

"Is this it?" she asked.

"Yes, Leonardo's."

"I don't think I have ever been here before. It looks nice."

She sat up and looked around. The parking lot was brightly lit and full of cars. They could see all around the cars and even into the area around the lot itself. Rick went to open the door and she stopped him. She leaned over and kissed him. They lingered there for several heartbeats, their lips still in contact. The kiss was over but they were both reluctant to acknowledge the fact. She opened her mouth a little, and he did the same. He gently pulled her lip into his mouth and sucked on it. Saria froze with anticipation. He explored her mouth with his tongue, caressing her tongue with his. He realized she had not been breathing as she pulled in a gentle breath of air. He could taste the sweetness of her lips and was reluctant to leave them but knew he must. She pulled away and started to open the door. Rick moved quickly and stepped out to open her door.

He reached for her hand. She gave it to him and he assisted her from the car. He held her hand as they walked into the restaurant and waited to be seated. The hostess led them to a small booth where they sat across from each other and waited for their server. It was not long and Rick ordered a bottle of red wine. Saria smiled at him and they looked into each other's eyes. Rick saw the glimmer once again but still could not place it. He thought it might have been a flicker of the candle on their table reflected in her perfect eyes. The dining room was dim and each table had a single candle. Rick leaned over and kissed her again, stroking her jaw and cheek with a light touch. Again, he lingered during the kiss. Her presence pleased his senses. The feel of her skin, the smell of her perfume, the taste of her lips. They were all perfect. He felt he had finally met the one.

However, he had to take it slow. His memory of his previous relationship burned in his memory like a hot coal. The pain he felt was still an open wound that needed more time to heal, though being with Saria made it burn much less. He hoped his attentions would give her enough encouragement that he continued to be interested in, if not ready for, something more than an intimate friendship. However, they had already passed that point and he knew it. It was not far enough to demand a physically intimate relationship but they were both too invested for it to end. The gentle touching of her lips was enough to tide him over and he hoped it was the same for her. Only time would tell. Soon the server arrived with the wine, opened it and poured two glasses. Rick looked and smiled a little smirk as he noticed the red wine sat in two white wine flutes. He did not say anything. He took them and handed one to Saria, who took it and placed it to her ruby-red lips.

"Are you ready to order?" the server asked.

"Pasta primavera," Rick said. He had not even opened his menu.

"Shrimp scampi," Saria said, not taking her eyes from Rick's face.

"Very good. Would you like anything else?"

"No, thank you," Rick responded absently.

The server walked away and Rick took Saria's hand. He kissed it once tenderly and Saria felt the tingle run up her arm. She leaned in for another kiss and he obliged. He could not get enough of the taste of her lips. Apparently, she liked the taste of his. She leaned into the kiss and did some exploring of her own.

"Saria, I need to take this slowly. I don't want to run headlong into something and then figure out we're not right for each other."

"I understand, but haven't we already done just that?" she

asked and then continued. "I have had some bad relationships myself. But the rest of that story is for another day."

Time passed while they were engrossed with each other. The server returned with their order and grated cheese onto their plates. They slowly ate. Rick looked around the restaurant. No one looked suspicious but he could tell something was wrong. He could not quite place the disquiet in his head. Rick continued to watch the room. Then he saw a shadow move. He knew someone was watching them, but was careful not to alert Saria. They continued to eat and he continued to watch for trouble. Their meal went without any other problems. He paid the check and they left. He let Saria in and then got in himself. He watched closely as they left the restaurant. Once they were back on the freeway headed for Pandemonium, Rick turned to Saria.

"I think we were being watched in the restaurant."

"Why do you think that?"

"Just a bad feeling. Well, not really bad, even. It was more a sense of disquiet. Let's head on to the club unless you want to do something different."

"No, the club will be great. I love that place. It is our spot."

Rick smiled with the emphasis she put on "our" and continued to the Pandemonium. They made it there quickly because traffic was so light. This time Rick stopped out front and handed the keys to the valet. The valet handed him a stub and they walked up to the door. The guard let them in and they paid their cover. They walked in and discovered it was karaoke night.

"Oh my god, I love karaoke," Saria said.

"So do I," Rick said, excited.

Rick found it interesting how thrilled he was to find out something else they had in common. Saria ran up to the stage and started looking through the song lists. Rick did not notice anything out of the ordinary other than Saria's extraordinary interests in the song lists. Soon she found several and gave them to the DJ running the show. She handed him a one hundred dollar bill and he nodded his head.

"Come on, we are up next," Saria said.

"We? I don't even know what songs you picked."

"Oh, just some older bands, like Aerosmith and Steppenwolf."

"Good, I know most of their songs," Rick replied.

The first song was "Born to be Wild" by Steppenwolf. They sang it followed by "Sweet Emotion" by Aerosmith. Saria's voice was pure and beautiful and a stark contrast to Ricks more raspy tones. Soon Rick got a break, as the DJ had to play other choices. They sat at the same table as the last time. The server came over and took their drink order. Saria grabbed Rick's hand and pulled him out on the dance floor. Rick discovered Saria had an extraordinary endurance. He would start to run out of energy and she would still be going strong. However, she would sit with him when he needed a break. On the dance floor, she ignored the young men trying to dance with her, giving her attentions only to him. He did the same for her. They alternated between singing and dancing until late into the night. Saria looked down at her watch.

"Oh, my. It's midnight and I need to go to the halfway house tomorrow. We should go."

"Let's get out of here, then."

They picked up their stuff and headed onto the sidewalk. As they stood there waiting for the car, Rick felt his pocket move. He whipped around and did not see anyone out of the ordinary. He reached into his pocket and pulled out a note. It read, *That's one time I've let you live.* Rick slid the note back into his pocket. Minutes later, their car was brought up. They got in and Rick headed back to his house. As soon as they got there and Rick had closed the door, Saria turned to him.

"So how about I come in for a bit?"

"Sure. Don't you need to be going so you can get some sleep?"

"Nah, I am good."

Rick and Saria headed for the living room and turned on the TV. The news broadcast was talking about another vampire murder. Rick flipped channels until he found a movie. They snuggled on the couch and watched the movie. After the movie, Rick reluctantly saw Saria out. He watched as she drove away and a slight tear welled up in his eyes. He turned around. Taiga was standing directly behind him.

"Do you have a report?"

"Yes, lord. Shinto is here in LA and we believe he is working with the rogue coven."

"Excellent work. Next, tell me how Shinto got this into my pocket." Rick handed the note to Taiga.

Taiga scanned the note and replied, "I do not know, lord, but I will find out."

He disappeared out the back door. Rick walked into his bedroom and looked around at the lonely darkness as he changed and went to bed.

***

As Saria drove home, all she could think about was what he had told her. He had admitted he had worked with vampires hunting rogue vampires, but there had to be more than that. It was obvious that Taiga and Amaya were members of the shadow. Why was he hiding the truth. Why would he omit something like that? What if he was a hunter and thought she was the leader of the rogue coven? That was a thought she didn't even want to consider. She had to tell him and soon. Since he was involved with the Shadow then Amaya and Taiga were definitely vampires and she wouldn't be able to hide who or what she was from them for long.

She pushed the button to call her mother. She waited a short time for the call to be routed and her father answered the phone.

"Hello."

"Hi, Father, how are you today?"

"I'm good. Your mother said you have found a proper man with good teeth? Tell me about him."

"Actually, Father, that is why I called. I found out he works with the Shadow. I am afraid to tell him I am the local elder."

"Hmmm, afraid he will hold you responsible for Nickolea's

actions? The Shadow doesn't work quite that way. But this is an interesting development. A human who works with the Shadow. He did not say he was a member of the Shadow, correct?"

"No, he actually emphasized the word *with*. Father, I love him. I know I have said that before and regretted it. This is very different. I haven't even told him I was a vampire. Now I am afraid to."

"Saria, you have to tell him. If he thinks for a second you are hiding that, then he will think the worst."

"Mother said the same thing."

"Listen to your mother. She is the wisest person I know."

"Thanks, Father. I am sorry for not listening before."

"You were still very young, an adolescent as it were. Now you are an adult; make your decisions like one. We both love you very much and want what is best for you. If he is it, then we will support any decision you make."

"Thank you, Father. I love you both very much, and I will call again soon. Good-bye."

"Good-bye, baby girl."

Hanging up the phone, she thought about what her father had told her. She couldn't let this secret drive him away. What would be worse, telling him and losing him forever, or not telling him and losing him forever? She drove into the night with the question as much on her mind as the taste of his lips.

Chapter IV

Rick woke to Taiga shaking his shoulder. He rolled over and looked at the clock. It read four a.m. He looked through the darkness and saw a concerned look on Taiga's face. Rick sat up.

"What is it, Taiga?"

"Lord, we have a problem."

"What is the problem?" Rick asked, concerned since Taiga did not typically use those words.

"A team disappeared."

"What? A team of Shadow does not just disappear."

"They went on patrol and have not reported in."

"Where were they patrolling?"

"Downtown."

"Get my gear," Rick ordered as he got up and grabbed a uniform out of the closet.

Rick was changed by the time Taiga returned. He slid his katana into his belt and tied his mask around his face. He stashed the throwing knives in easily accessible places. He grabbed the bag with the remaining gear and headed for the door. He jumped in his car and headed for the area where the team had disappeared. Taiga knew what to do and already had a new team dispatched to meet him there. Rick knew the perfect place to park so he could quickly get to an observation perch. He knew the downtown area like the back of his hand, and he had an idea where they could have been ambushed.

Rick parked in an out-of-the-way parking structure and headed for the roof of a nearby structure. He took a running jump and landed on the rooftop, moving from roof to fire escape. He would then jump to a window-washing scaffold or whatever else was at the right height. He soon arrived at the area he had suspected and was correct. He could see several members of the Shadow bound in the alleyway. The remaining members were lying dead on the pavement. A figure was standing in the shadows holding another Shadow and seemed to be interrogating him.

Rick had just moved to a place where he could drop on the figure when he suddenly felt the need to duck. He bent backward at the waist until his torso was horizontal. Three shuriken flew over him. A person in a ninja uniform appeared behind him, charging with a ninja-to. Rick popped upright, drew his katana and spun on the attacker. The ninja swung at Rick. He stepped quickly to the side, letting the sword pass. Rick flipped his wrist and brought the sword across the hands of his attacker. The ninja dropped the sword and quickly recovered it before it hit the ground. The wound closed rapidly.

The ninja dove into a roll and sliced at Rick's ankles. Rick leaped straight up, grabbed the edge of the roof and flipped onto it. The ninja leaped up beside him and swung again for Rick's lower legs. Rick leaped vertically and tried to land on the ninja's sword, but it was moving too fast. Rick brought his sword down toward the ninja's neck, but the ninja easily moved out of the way. Rick reached into the back of his belt and threw the weighted end of a rope toward the ninja's neck. The ninja brought his blade up and the rope sliced itself in two when it started to encircle the ninja's neck. The ninja dove into a roll and sliced at Rick's lower legs. Rick did a forward somersault, landed on his hands, and flipped back to his feet, twisting to face his opponent, who was already charging toward him. He leaped over Rick, trying to land behind him. Rick spun and brought his katana down across the ninja's back; the sword barely missed his neck.

The sword bit deep into the ninja's back. He twisted, trying to wrench the sword from Rick's grip. Rick quickly freed the sword and swung again. The ninja leaped over the side of the building and disappeared from sight. Rick moved over to the edge and looked. The ninja was gone. Rick worked his way down to the pavement. The second figure was also gone. A few minutes later, Taiga showed up with the second team. Rick was already checking the remaining Shadow. He said a Japanese blessing as he piled the bodies and lit them on fire. The pyre flared for a few seconds then everything was dark again. The Shadow untied their brothers and collected the equipment. Rick, with all the adrenalin burned from his system, stumbled as he stepped forward. Taiga ran forward and caught him, looking down to discover that Rick had a large slice in his left leg. Taiga took a bandage and wrapped the leg, then took Rick's keys and tossed them to one of the other Shadow to drive the vehicle home.

"Come, lord, I will get you home and suture that. It is not too deep—should I heal it?" Taiga asked.

"Once we are home, I will consider it. That was Shinto."

"Yes, lord, I thought it might be. There is not another vampire who could match you with the blade."

***

The ninja hid in the shadows until Rick and his team left. Shinto had never seen a human move that fast—faster than many of the vampires he had defeated and bound. The pain in his back was mostly gone. Enough remained, though, to act as a reminder to not underestimate a foe. The nearby bum had been a quick fix. He walked around the corner deeper into the alley and arrived at the car, finding his partner already behind the wheel. Shinto could tell Sigmund was upset; his Viking heritage did not allow him to hide it well. The fire of his anger flared in his eyes.

"Damn it, I would have gotten something from one of those Shadow, I know it, if he had not shown up when he did. So that was this Lord of the Shadow, was it? He seemed to be quite the warrior."

"He is one of the greatest to ever hold that rank. He moved faster than many vampires do. He is one of the fastest humans I have ever seen. I know I sliced his leg, but he kept pressing the attack. If I am to kill him, I have to distract him. I have to break his iron concentration somehow."

"We have to get back to Nickolea and report this failure. He will not take it well—but that is his problem, not mine."

The two drove off into the night.

***

Taiga led Rick to a car, drove him home, and helped him hobble into the house. Amaya was standing at the door; she gave Taiga an inquisitive look and they both led him to the bedroom. Amaya started to pull off his pants while Taiga went for the emergency bag. When Taiga returned, Amaya had already licked the area around the wound to clean and disinfect it. It was deeper than Taiga had first thought. He reached into the bag and brought out a suture kit and a jar of salve. Rick started to refuse but Amaya put her finger on his mouth, stopping him. With the area already numb from Amaya's saliva, Taiga applied the salve and sutured the sword cut closed. Once he had applied a bandage, Rick stood up.

"Our first priority is to find that bastard. He has a second vampire with him. Since we destroyed his entire Clan, it has to be someone local, and I am sure it's someone from the rogue coven. I just realized something. Why have we not heard from the elder? LA is supposed to have an elder. Kinoshi thinks there is, anyway. He said she was a powerful vampire. I hope she's not the rogue we are looking for. That would be very bad. But, if she isn't, then why are we not getting help from the rest of the coven? This is more confusing by the day."

"Maybe she is powerless against the rogues. Maybe they are the remainder of the coven. I have seen it in the past," Taiga replied.

"Maybe; that's another avenue we will have to pursue."

"Get some rest, lord. Will Saria be coming over?"

"Probably later; she has to go to her halfway house."

"Good, you are . . . different . . . around her, less intense. She is good for you and I can sense no malice in her."

"Well we'll see how this goes. I do like her quite a bit." He appeared to give himself a mental shake. "Back to the matter at hand: Shinto is actively pursuing me. I am going to have to go underground. He does not know who I am, so only the Lord of the Shadow has to disappear for a while, not Dr. Rick Smythe. Although, he seems interested in either Saria or me. That note in my pocket could have meant me or us as a couple. Taiga, I need you to run all the operations. Amaya will stay here and provide security for us. I need him found and destroyed."

"Yes, my lord. It will be as you say. Should I call Lord Kimura?"

"No, he's still running the rest of the operation. Once that is complete, I will bring him here."

"Yes, lord. I will leave immediately to start the search for him."

Taiga bowed and left the room. Rick lay back down and tried to go to sleep, but his sleep was fitful and broken. The rising sun woke him. He got up and walked into the kitchen to find that Amaya had his breakfast ready. He walked over to the table and sat down. His leg was sore but he could walk comfortably on it. He would be able to remove the sutures later that afternoon. Kinoshi had warned him many times about the dangers of hunting alone. That is why he'd brought Taiga and Amaya with him. He could not let his Shadow be killed by Shinto, not when he could do something. Taiga was right about one thing: Saria seemed to make everything better. Maybe he would text her and invite her to come over later. He grabbed his phone off the counter and texted her the invitation.

Rick worked out most of the morning. The healing cut on his leg bothered him but did not stop the workout. Amaya watched closely as he moved, to make sure things were as they should be before she went about her household tasks. Rick pulled out his gear bag and dug in it until he found the cut weighted rope. He went into the back of the garage where he had a small shop set up, and pulled out a small steel cable. He unwound the rope and rebraided it with the steel cable as part of the stranding. Once he got to the end of the rope, he braided in another weight he pulled out of a drawer in the workbench. He then pulled out his throwing knives, felt their weight, and removed bits of the steel until they were balanced once again, making sure everything was sharpened and ready for use so he would be ready for Shinto when next they met.

He continued putzing around until early in the afternoon. When he had finished his prep work; he checked the wound and found that it appeared closed and mostly healed. After pulling out a kit from the bathroom cabinet, he removed the sutures. The skin was still red at the site of the wound but otherwise had healed with no sign of infection, thanks to the salve Taiga had applied. He had formulated it himself from vampire saliva and silk protein. He got into the shower and started getting ready for Saria's visit.

It was late in the afternoon when Saria arrived. Rick walked up and met her at the door, kissing her as she walked in. He turned a touch too quickly and winced with the pain in his leg a little. Saria noticed and looked at him curiously.

"What happened, Rick?"

"Scraped my leg on the coffee table earlier. It's just sore."

"Let me look at it."

"It's nothing."

Saria pulled up his pant leg and saw a line of blood across his calf. She frowned and wiped at it. It appeared to be a small scratch. She lowered his pant leg and kissed him, then led him over to the couch. Rick adjusted so he was lying the length of the couch. Saria moved so she was snuggled to him, spooned together. Amaya had made herself conspicuously absent from the room. Rick turned on the TV, and they watched for a bit before Rick leaned a little forward to talk to Saria.

So I thought we would stay in this evening and watch TV or something."

"Sounds good. No news, though; all this vampire attack stuff is getting to be too much," she said with a bit of relief.

"I agree. No vampires tonight. Just two regular people enjoying a night in."

"Yeah, no vampires," Saria said with a crooked smile.

She turned back and snuggled against Rick as he turned the television to a movie. They snuggled together for several hours, their only interruption being Amaya bringing drinks and snacks to them. Amaya smiled at Rick, giving her approval of Saria.

Saria could feel the tension leave his body. She enjoyed the warmth of him, which she thought was a little warm for a human; his scent, an intoxicating fragrance; and his calming demeanor. It seemed to her that even in the most stressful situations he remained perfectly calm and was formulating a plan. She had to tell him. If she didn't he would feel she was hiding it and possibly a threat. She wondered how she would ever be able to tell him she was a vampire elder, since they had been hunting down the rogues in the area, which was her problem—a problem she could not resolve on her own. Maybe destiny had a way of righting itself. It certainly had put the right man in her way for both her loneliness and her problem with Nickolea. She started fidgeting with her building anxiety. Rick looked at his watch and started to get up. Saria moved to allow him.

"It is getting late and we have work in the morning," he started.

"I could always stay here," Saria said hopefully.

"Not tonight, but soon," he responded.

"I take that as a promise," she said with a touch of sadness in her voice.

"Like I said, a little time," he said reassuringly with his own touch of regret.

"Walk me to the door then," she said, resigned.

"Of course," he replied, smiling.

Rick walked her to her car and helped her in. He watched as she drove away and felt the loss as she left. He knew he would see her in the morning but he would have loved to have her spend the night. He had to resolve that nagging in the back of his head; until that was gone, he could not take any chances. He had ignored that nagging once and almost paid the ultimate price for it. He could not risk that again. He hoped he had not gone too far with his admission of knowing about vampires and working with the Shadow. He'd felt that if she was working with the rogues, that info would have elicited a response. The only thing he'd caught was a touch of nervousness, which was a noncommittal reaction.

"Taiga is out hunting Shinto so I guess I should get some sleep."

"Yes, lord, get some sleep," Amaya answered from behind him. "You should have let her stay. I am afraid you might regret this decision later."

"Why is that, Amaya? What have you seen?"

"Nothing, lord, just a feeling. As a matter of fact, I have seen nothing regarding you for several weeks now. It seems your fate is in flux, my lord. I do have a feeling Lady Saria is involved somehow. Not in a bad way, though. You should let her stay next time."

"Why, Amaya, you have never pushed me toward a woman before. What is so important about this one?"

"Her fate and yours are intertwined, just as Taiga's and mine are. That much I do know. Keep her close, my lord. She may be the key to saving your life."

"I will keep that under advisement. I must go to bed now."

"I have it turned down already for you, lord. Rest well."

"Thanks, Amaya. Feel free to use the guest room. I don't want you too far away. Shinto is tied to this whole thing; I just have to figure out how. I think Saria is, too . . . I still have that discord in the back of my head. But I respect your counsel and will keep it close at hand."

"Thank you, my lord. I do not want you alone while you sleep. Shinto may have other agents. You wounded both him and his pride; he cannot have a human best him in combat. Not even you, lord. He will be looking for revenge. As you have said, he also seems to have an interest in Rick Smythe. Maybe you should go underground and take Saria with you. Taiga seems to think he knows you were instrumental in the purging of his coven. He may want revenge on Rick Smythe for that. If he has joined forces with the rogue coven, that bitch who tried to kill you may have identified you as the tracker of her coven. That makes you very dangerous to them and they will want you eliminated. Taiga and I will figure this out, lord."

"I think you're right. Thanks for being my lookout in more ways than one."

"It is my duty and my pleasure, my lord."

"Have a good night, Amaya. I'm heading off to sleep."

Amaya bowed, moved off to the living room and turned on the news so she could monitor the rogue activity. Rick went into the weapons room, grabbed his katana, and placed it within easy reach beside the bed. Amaya had never given him bad advice. Her sense of the future was uncanny, but that was her talent. Taiga's talent was sensing vampires; if anyone could find Shinto and the coven, it was he. They were the best companions he could have. He also knew that they had volunteered. Kinoshi had tried to hide that fact when he'd recommended them. He also knew that Amaya had seen that they would be necessary for him to succeed. Rick tried to clear his head to go to sleep. Too much was coursing through it for a simple relaxation, so he went into a deep meditative trance. Once his mind was at peace, he fell asleep.

ChAPTER V

The next morning he started his workout routine, like every morning since the Lord of the Shadow had stopped patrolling. After his shower, he got ready for work and drove in. When he walked in, Saria was already there. Her face lit up and she smiled when she saw him, and he smiled back. He pulled out his files for the day, looked at his schedule, and slowly thinned out the cancellations. He also had to see the police chief today. He shook his head.

"What's wrong, Rick?" Saria asked.

"Oh, nothing. Just not enough hours in the day. This afternoon I need to go see the chief. Hopefully, he will have more information. Why don't you come with me? Your research would give you an insight I would never have."

"I don't know . . ."

"Come on. What, you afraid of cops?"

"No, silly, I just have so much work to do."

"That's not it. Come on, spill," he said.

"It's my ex, Nickolea. I don't want any of his agents to see us together."

"Agents? What is he, a spy? He does have a name. I'm sure they already have. Besides, you can tell me more about him."

"Fine, you convinced me. I'll come with you. Besides, I know the chief and a few of the officers, so it will be good reason to visit them again."

"Good, it's settled, then. Let's meet here at 2:00 p.m."

"We have to be careful, though."

Rick shrugged off the last comment as he walked to the door

to call his first patient. Saria looked worriedly at him. Rick was oblivious to her look of concern because he was in deep contemplation. The attacks were the most vicious and violent Rick had ever seen. It was as if the attackers wanted everyone to know they were real vampires, which was very uncharacteristic. Rick was becoming very concerned about the vampire threat in LA. *It is the most blatant display I have ever seen. Maybe I should call Kinoshi and bring in the rest of the Shadow,* he thought. He shrugged the thought off and went to work.

The day passed as any other. Soon it was approaching 2:00 p.m., and Saria walked back into their office. Since they were alone, he gave her a kiss. He felt an attraction to her unlike any he had felt before. Her beauty filled his every thought. The scientific part of his brain told him love was only a set of biochemical reactions that caused an emotional response. However, she entranced even the analytical part of him. The fact remained that he was being hunted by a dangerous vampire, and because of that, he had to keep a small amount of distance, at least until he could decide how safe he could make her.

She returned the kiss. They left together in Rick's car and traveled to offices of the LAPD. As they approached the door, the officer buzzed them through. He led them to the desk and made nametags for them, speaking first to Saria.

"I'm sorry, but we are under a high security alert. We had a bomb threat. But I know you are okay, Saria. Is this the vampire expert we've been hearing about?" he asked, pointing at Rick.

"It is, Tom. Dr. Richard Smythe is a world-renowned vampire psychosis expert. We are very lucky to have him. He moved all the way from New York to help us with this problem."

"Dr. Smythe, I hope you can fix this mess we are in."

"Please call me Rick, Officer Williams."

"You can call me Tom. All right, you two. The chief is expecting you. I think you both know the way."

"Yes, we do, Tom. Tell the wife hi for me."

"Will do, Saria."

They walked down the hallway to the elevators. The officer standing in front of them turned a key and pushed the button for the floor of the police chief's office. After a couple of minutes, the elevator door opened, and they walked into the squad room. The chief saw them across the room and signaled them over. They walked over to the chief, and he pointed to a map of the US.

"Doc, you sure know how to pick them. There have been thirteen murders across the country in the last six months, all with a similar MO. Apparently we have a nationwide epidemic of crazy going on, and LA seems to have the biggest case of it."

"I was afraid of that," Rick responded.

"Oh, by the way, Saria, I was not ignoring you. How are you today?"

"Good, Chief. How are Rhonda and the girls?"

"Good, thanks for asking. She loves that recipe you gave her."

"Good to hear. I have a lot more if she ever wants any." She turned to Rick. "The Chief and I go way back. Back to when he was a sergeant."

"Yeah, she's been a real benefit to the department."

They continued to discuss the findings and decided to revisit it in a week. Saria watched every officer who walked by and did not see any Gluts that she knew. They said their good-byes and left. Once in the car and headed back to the office, they started talking.

"So let's get some dinner. We can discuss this over a meal, maybe even catch a movie."

"Sounds good. There are several new ones I've wanted to see. Just no movies about vampires or werewolves, please. They are so droll."

They both laughed as Rick agreed. The mood lightened a lot in the car. After dinner and a movie, Rick took her back to her car and waited until she was safely in it and was pulling away. He felt much better after talking with the police chief and the familiarity they shared. He felt more confident she was not a rogue. He was not even sure she was a vampire. That was a relief on his mind. Now just to see to her safety.

Over the next few months, they spent more evenings together

and more trips to the police headquarters. They continued to go out almost every night. They talked and shared more about themselves. Rick discovered they had many things in common. They both loved to dance, sing karaoke, and listen to a wide spectrum of music. Rick decided that she was his soul mate, though he never let on that he felt that way. He hoped she felt the same. They were always smiling when they were together.

"Saria, I want you to spend the weekend with me," Rick stated on the way back from their most recent trip to the police station.

"Of course. I have been waiting for that invitation," she said emphatically.

"I have a surprise for you on Saturday. I am going to share one of my passions with you."

"Awesome. I don't have any cases this afternoon, so when we get back I'll go right home and pack."

"I don't have anything this afternoon, either. So I'll see you in an hour or so?"

"Definitely."

Rick drove Saria around to her car and waited until she was in it before driving straight home to make sure everything was in order for the evening. He parked and walked into the house. It was spotless. He took out a bottle of champagne and put it in the refrigerator to chill. He pulled out candles and decided to make a small dinner for them. As he was moving around, Amaya came out of the guest room.

"What are you doing, my lord?"

"I am preparing a dinner for Saria. I invited her to spend the weekend and I wanted to start it off with a nice little dinner."

"I will take care of that," she said, taking the pans from Rick. "You get ready."

Rick turned and went to his bedroom. He took a shower and shaved. When he got out, Amaya had laid out his clothes for him. She'd laid out a simple silk black kimono, haori jacket, and hakama pants. She also had laid out his black belt with gold trim. He dressed and walked out to the living area. Amaya looked him over and nodded in approval. She had almost completed the dinner. Rick went to the living room and put on some soft ambience music. When Amaya was finished, she put the food in warming dishes and waited for Saria to arrive.

Saria arrived a short time after all the preparations were complete. She showed her in and sat her at the table. Rick moved to the table and sat next to her. Amaya made up plates for them and poured the champagne. Once she was finished, she excused herself. Saria looked at Rick and he waved his hand, inviting her to start. She took the first bite. The taste shocked her; it seemed to be a combination of many different flavors. Rick was eating slowly, watching the look on her face.

"Amaya is an amazing cook. I have never tasted anything like this."

"Her cooking is delightful, especially when she's making traditional dishes like these."

"So what is up with the outfit?"

"Amaya's idea also. She felt it was appropriate. I am a Japanese lord entertaining a young lady. I think she is designing our wedding invitations as we speak."

"So is that a proposal?"

"Let's see how this weekend goes first."

Saria smiled as they finished their dinner. They moved to the living room to watch movies, and she snuggled into his chest as usual, spooning to him. This had become her permanent seat at Rick's house. Rick took the remote and turned on a movie, but they only watched about half of it before Saria turned onto her back and kissed him. As he responded, she kissed him a bit more passionately. He returned the intensity. She continued to kiss him, and embraced his tongue with hers. She reached into his shirt and ran her hands across his chest, wrapping her fingers into his chest hair. Rick ran his hand under her shirt and discovered she was not wearing a bra. He massaged her breast.

"I want you," she whispered in his ear, nibbling on the lobe.

Rick stood up and she wrapped her legs around his waist as he carried her into his bedroom. He sat her at the foot of his bed and she lay down, keeping her eyes fixed on his. He lay down beside her, continuing to kiss her while he unbuttoned her blouse. She worked her hand into his clothing and loosened any ties she could find as he unfastened her skirt and pulled down the zipper. Within just a few minutes they had each other's clothing sufficiently loosened to have access to each other's bodies. They caressed and stroked each other. Rick slowly pulled away and shed his loose clothing and Saria did the same.

Saria scurried up to the top of the bed, grabbed his hand and pulled him back to her. Rick started kissing her abdomen, making his way up her body. Her body shuddered with each successive kiss. The anticipation of his next touch was heightened by the sensitivity of her skin. Each of his touches exploded throughout her body in a kaleidoscope of sensations. The smell of his pheromones heightened her excitement. The seconds between each kiss were an eternity followed by the explosion of passion.

He finally reached her mouth, and the previous kisses were nothing compared to the sensations and explosion of colors once he wrapped his tongue around hers. He rubbed her body with his free hand and supporting all his weight on the other while he continued to kiss her. She was in bliss as his nude body rubbed against hers. She could feel his body near hers even when he was not in direct contact with her. She closed her eyes in order to focus on the sensations and his caresses. What she felt, she had never felt before with anyone else. When he nibbled her neck, the explosion was incredible. The tension had built up as tight as a watch spring and when his teeth scraped across her neck, the dual sensations exploded within her, and she screamed.

***

She lay next to Rick, both of them covered with sweat from their exertions. She snuggled up to him with her head in the pocket of his shoulder and he instinctively curled his arm protectively around her. She nuzzled deeper. She could smell the scent of their passion, the fragrance of their exertion. Both of their energies were spent. Rick was asleep; she could tell by his rhythmic breathing pattern. With her heightened senses, she could hear every noise in the house, even the creaking of the seismic foundation. She slowly slipped out of bed, trying not to awaken him. Her legs were weak. She could barely stand as she walked over to his dresser and slid open a long drawer. She was lucky: her first guess had been successful. She slid a T-shirt out of the drawer and closed it while she slipped the shirt on. It fit like one of her nightshirts.

She walked into the bathroom. She looked in the mirror; her carefully applied makeup had run across her face. She looked in the cabinet for a colored washcloth, found one, and gently washed off the runny mess. Her milky-toned skin was a stark contrast to the darker foundation she used. She looked and saw Rick still sleeping. She slipped out to the living room. It was early morning; the sun had not even started to rise. Amaya had closed all the curtains the evening before. All the lights were dimmed but there was plenty of light for her to see around the room. She looked for her purse and found it in one of the chairs by the island. She grabbed her makeup bag and crept back into the bedroom and eventually to the bathroom. She pulled out her remover pads, removed the remainder of the smeared makeup, and quickly applied a new foundation coat, enough to darken her skin so that it did not appear so pale. Once she was finished, she stood up and started checking it when Rick walked in behind her.

"It looks fine, baby," Rick said.

She turned around, wrapped her arms around him, and kissed him. He returned her embrace. He had a towel wrapped around his waist. His muscular chest was still glistening from sweat. The sight excited her and she ran her fingers across his chest. He moved his hands to under her buttocks, pulled her close to him, and lifted her out of his way as he moved past her to turn on the shower. She gasped at the sensation, which was both strange and stimulating. He dropped the towel and stepped in the shower. After a second, he stuck out his head.

"Are you coming?"

She pulled off the T-shirt and climbed in the shower behind him.

Chapter VI

R ick woke with the sunlight in his eyes. He turned over and saw Saria was still asleep. He smiled remembering their shower experience that sent them back to bed exhausted. He quietly climbed out of bed and put on a pair of sweat pants before heading to the kitchen to start cooking a couple of steaks. The coffeemaker Amaya had set the evening before buzzed, and he poured two cups of coffee. He looked up to see Saria standing next to the bar in one of his T-shirts. He smiled at her and turned back to the stove. She walked up to him and hugged him from behind, laying her cheek against his back while he cooked. She reached up, grabbed a cup of coffee and the chocolate creamer he had placed on the counter.

"Mmmm, chocolate coffee. Yummy," she said, trying to pull away.

"How do you like your steak and eggs?" he asked, grabbing her arms and pulling her close to him for a second.

"Steak very rare and eggs over medium. I hate it when the whites look like snot," she said playfully, pouring the creamer into her coffee. "How about I make the toast? It is my specialty," she said, putting the creamer back in the cabinet.

"If it is your specialty, then by all means. I am glad you're here. Thank you for your patience with me."

"I am really glad to be here," she said as she turned him around and kissed him, exploring his mouth with her tongue.

"Now, that's a good morning," he said as she turned him loose. "Breakfast will be ready soon. Why don't you turn on the TV so we can catch some news? I'll go ahead and do the toast."

"Sure. I want to see the weather anyway."

The newscaster was talking about another murder during the night. She switched channels until she found a weather-only channel, sat, and watched until they got to Los Angeles. She watched as they reported clear skies and moderate temperatures. Rick soon came over with breakfast. Saria sat on the couch with her legs folded beneath her with her cup of coffee nestled in her hands, sipping it. When Rick handed her the plate, she sat up straight and set the coffee on the table.

"This looks good, baby," she said, cutting her steak.

"Thanks. So does it look like we are having good weather today?"

"Clear and moderate temperatures. Why?"

"It will facilitate my surprise."

"What surprise?"

"I'll tell you in a bit," he said with a grin. "I cannot believe they are still talking about those vampire murders," he said, changing the subject.

"Yeah, apparently there was another one last night. That makes, what? Twenty or thirty now? The police are no closer to solving it than they were when we started trying to help them. It's like someone on the inside is intentionally derailing the investigation."

"You're right; we had a similar instance in New York. Turned out one of the cops was a vampire in the rogue coven. Could be happening here. No place is immune. The rogues can infiltrate any system, any organization. All they have to do is turn a detective. I had a research lab in New York where they turned a research assistant to get access to the chemist and his lab. We never did figure out what they were trying to do with that."

"You never know. I need to get my stuff out of the car," she said standing and heading for the garage.

Rick watched her. She moved as gracefully and silently as a cat. When she came back, she headed for his bedroom. She emptied the contents of her bag on the bed and refilled it with necessities. He watched her as she took her bag to the bathroom to get ready. While she was dressing, he looked at the stuff that was lying on the bed. He noticed a strange-looking silver-colored object about the size of her hand. It was large and D shaped. She came back out and saw him looking at the object.

"Find anything of interest?"

"Actually I did," he stated, holding up the object. "This thing caught my interest for some reason."

She took it from him and slid her hand in. With a snap of her wrist, a three-foot-blade unfolded and snapped into place. She then snapped her wrist again, and it collapsed once again into the D-shaped object. She handed it back to Rick. He looked it over and could not tell where the blade came from. It was perfectly smooth.

"Neat trick. Where did you get that, and why do you have it in your purse?" he asked.

"It was given to me, and a girl has to be able to protect herself in a big bad city like LA."

"Point taken—and you're less likely to get hauled into a police station than if you have a sword on your hip. But most women carry a pistol."

"I am not much for pistolas, and once you give someone a batty-fanging with that, they tend to leave you alone. You know, I might have another one, if you would like it for your collection. I can look when I get home."

"A batty-fanging? What the hell does that mean?"

"Oh yeah," she said, covering quickly. "It means 'a thorough beating.' My grandmother used it all the time, so I picked it up."

"Nice. You know, I was thinking we should go sailing today," he said.

"Sailing, like on the water?" Saria said a little nervously.

"No, like on the snow. Of course, on the water. If it bothers you too much, we can do something else. I know you don't swim well," he said, concerned.

"Uhh, no not really. We won't get out of sight of land, will we?" She sounded a bit less nervous.

"We don't have to if it would make you feel better."

"It definitely would."

"We can definitely do that. I keep the boat docked at the ma-

JT Buckley

76

rina in Pedro. Let's go."

He grabbed his wallet and keys, as they headed to the garage. They pulled out and headed toward the marina. As they drove, she reached over and slowly ran her tongue around the outside of his ear and across his earlobe,then gently bit it. A couple of drops of blood came from the bite, and she licked them off. She sucked his earlobe a little. He felt the sensation travel down to his loins. He wriggled a little, and she snickered a bit. She licked the couple of drops of blood on her lip.

"Wow, okay, can we not do it when I am trying to drive? It felt really good, but it wouldn't look too good if we were to have a wreck with your tongue halfway to my brain."

"Yeah, that would look bad," she admitted. "Deal. No nibbling on your ear while you are driving. You said the boat is in San Pedro?" she asked, changing the subject.

"Yes, it is, and it is a thirty-five footer, too. There is no need for you to be nervous. I am an excellent sailor."

"I am just very nervous around water. My parents took me on an ocean voyage, and I had to stay below the whole time."

"If it bothers you that much, we can go somewhere else."

"No, I want to try especially since you are so passionate about it. But, not out of sight of land, okay?

"Deal."

They continued down the hill toward San Pedro and the Port of Los Angeles. Saria snuggled into Rick's side and fell asleep. Rick ran his hand through her hair. He did not understand why the feelings he had for her were so strong. He had been attracted to her from the very first day, but he felt like he'd known and loved her all his life. He was not one to believe in love at first sight. However, something was definitely happening. It had always been more than sexual attraction, even though that had been there. He really did like her, maybe even love her, which could be a problem if she turned out to be one of the rogues. He could even take it if she turned out to be a vampire. *You're being paranoid. Not every beautiful woman you meet and like is going to be a rogue vampire,* he thought to himself.

He watched the scenery as he drove off the peninsula and onto the mainland. Rick thought it was hard to believe that the peninsula had once been an island like Catalina and was constantly pushing into the mainland. He looked at the cracked roadway. He smiled at the "Road Work" signs. It was the second time they were repairing the roadway since he had moved there a year ago. As they entered the City of San Pedro, he woke Saria.

"We are almost there, Saria."

She yawned, ran her arm under his, and snuggled into his shoulder. He moved his arm around her to make her more comfortable. Her closeness made him both a touch uncomfortable and complete at the same time. He smiled as they passed the grocery stores and gas stations. After a few more twists and turns, they could see the Port of Los Angeles and just short of it the marina where he docked his boat. The masts in the marina stood shadowed by the sun, a stark contrast against the bright blue sky. As they approached, Saria's look of apprehension slowly turned into a look of awe.

"It looks like a painting. All these years, I have lived here, and I have never seen it like this before. I am seeing lots of things in a new light," she said, looking at him, smiling.

He wondered if she felt the same as he did. She seemed to, but it could be a façade. It would not be the first time he had been fooled, especially by a vampire. He knew she had to be one even though he didn't want to believe it. The way she moved, her mannerisms, her etiquette, everything was anachronistic. If she was, why didn't she admit it to him? Why was she keeping it a secret? When he looked in her eyes, which he could do all day long, he just melted. He sighed a minute sigh. Everything else would have to wait until he knew for sure if she was a vampire and why she was keeping it a secret. He glanced back at the road to make sure he was not going to run into anything.

Soon they arrived at the marina, Rick swiped his card across the reader, and the gate opened to the sailing club lot. They parked in the private lot and walked down the dock to his boat, an old thirty-five-foot sloop that he had painstakingly renovated. Saria walked around looking at it. Rick opened his deck box, pulled out two life vests, and tossed one to Saria.

"Put this on. My one rule is everyone wears a vest. I don't care how seasoned you are or how good a swimmer."

"Oh, don't worry, since a flat rock swims better than I do, I will wear it till you take it off. Just like the rest of my clothes," she said, smiling.

He laughed as he jumped onto the boat. He began uncovering sails and preparing the boat to cast off. As soon as everything was ready, he reached out of the boat to Saria. She hesitantly took his hand. He pulled her aboard and sat her down in one of the cockpit seats. She sat like a stone statue and did not move unless he leaned her out of the way. He removed the mooring ropes, started the engine, and started backing the boat out of its slip.

He maneuvered it into the main channel. He looked at the wind finder on the top of the mast while he walked over to the mainsail to raise it to its full height. He then moved to the front of the boat to raise the genoa to its full height. Both sails luffed in the wind awaiting his command. When he was ready, he set up the winches behind him to move the genoa so he could tack the boat. When he had everything else ready, he tightened the mainsail so it started to catch a little wind. Saria watched with intense concentration. She had never seen any single person command a boat like Rick did.

"Are you ready? We will be sailing against the wind until we make our first turn. So, I have to tack the boat. That means I adjust the front sail to grab the wind, so we will be zigzagging."

"Sure. I think I am ready," she said in a nervous voice.

"Here we go. First, we will tack to port, which is left."

Rick pulled the left rope, pulled the genoa tight to the left, and spun the wheel as quick as he could. The sail caught the wind and gave the boat a slight jerk. He shut off the motor; the ship went silent except for the sound of the wind in the sails and the water rushing beside the boat. He grabbed Saria's hand and pulled her next to him. She grabbed him by the waist and moved close. With her head on his shoulder, she felt the cool sea air hit her in the face. Suddenly Rick started pulling on the right rope, released the left one, and spun the wheel in the other direction. The wind held the genoa in its caress as the boat began moving in the other direction. The tacking continued in a smooth rhythmic pattern. The boat heeled up on its side some but not much with each tack. Saria started looking toward the water, but she clung tightly to Rick. She saw a couple of dolphins racing beside the boat.

"Look at the dolphins."

"Yeah, they follow the boats. Some fishermen will throw cull fish overboard, and the dolphins will grab them. Just wait until we get to the main channel and are running with the wind. This boat is old enough and big enough that it produces a decent bow wave. They love to play in it. Prepare to come about. Have a seat."

Rick tacked the ship one more time and sharply turned the wheel to move them into the large main channel. He released the traveler on the mainsail, and it caught the wind. It whipped to the side, and the boat took off. The boom slid over Saria's head, and Rick simply ducked as it passed over him from behind, without even looking at it. Saria watched him move and react to the sail boom that was invisible to him. Each time the boom moved, he ducked just as it got there even if he was looking in the other direction.

"You can move forward to the bow and watch the dolphins now, if you would like."

Saria crept forward, looked over the bow of the boat, and could see the dolphins leaping and playing in the wave of water pushed ahead of the boat. She reached down, and one bumped her hand. She smiled. She watched them as they danced in front of the boat.

"Hold tight. We are making another turn."

She grabbed the line in front of her and looked up in time to see them turn to follow the breakwater. Once again, Rick began tacking the boat. She slipped back to the safety of the cockpit to be next to him. He had secured the traveler of the mainsail again. He smiled at her, and she smiled back as she moved beside him again. He placed his arm around her and only moved it to pull on the ropes. She turned and leaned against him. He moved his arm around her waist.

"You want to steer?" he asked.

She looked at him as if he was insane. "Steer?"

"Yeah, take the wheel. I'll work the front sail. When I say, 'Tack to port,' just turn the wheel to the left. When I say, 'Tack to starboard,' turn the wheel to the right. It's easy. Do you know why they use 'port' for left?"

"Not really."

"The real nautical term for left is larboard. It sounds too much like starboard, the term for 'right.' In the day of the tall ships, they had a door on the left of the ship to load and unload cargo. It was the side next to the dock. The doors were called 'the port'. That is also, where the term 'pulling into port' comes from. So, they adopted the term port for the left side of the boat to decrease confusion. Tack to port."

"What? Oh," Saria turned the wheel as hard as she could to the left. The boat jerked.

"Oh my god, what happened? Did I break it?"

Rick smiled. "No, I got the front sail into position before you did the rudder, so the ship pulled sideways against it for a second. It is fine. I refinished this boat myself and she is one tough lady."

"How long have you been sailing?"

"For about as long as I could walk, I would say. My dad was an avid sailor. The first time he brought me on the boat and I heard the water against the hull and the wind in the sails, I was hooked."

"It is a wonderful sound. I guess I was so afraid the first time I was on a ship, I didn't even notice. We are getting a bit away from the shore, huh. We aren't going much further out, are we?"

"Nope, just a little past the breakwater. Once we get there, we will be in the open ocean but still in sight of land. Then we will sail up the coast a bit. I want to show you something."

She looked a little nervous but agreed. Rick took the wheel back and continued sailing the boat up the coast. She stood behind him with her arms around his waist and her cheek to his back. After a little while, he dropped the sails and started the motor to position the boat. He stopped the engine and dropped the rear anchor. Soon the boat pulled against it. He dropped the front anchor. The boat moved very little against the waves.

"Look at the top of that hill. That is my house. I have filed a permit to build a dock right here with a stair from here to there."

He pointed out the path of the stairway down the hill to the area where he pointed out a dock as he continued. "The previous owner had already started the permit process. I just had to file a petition to assume the permit request as the new owner. The county approved it last week. He had already completed the due diligence doing research for rare fish that may spawn here. He even completed an environmental-impact study. I had a hearing last month to get a preliminary authorization to submit a construction plan. I had a contractor out here for an estimate last week. My blueprints and site plan are on file."

"Wow, that is nice. It would be nice for us to sit on the dock and watch other boats, huh?"

"Yes, it would."

Saria looked quickly at him with her comment. He was smirking but did not betray anything else. She smiled too. He pulled her close and kissed her. She felt faint as his tongue caressed hers. His mere touch made her heart race. She closed her eyes to take in everything that made him who he was. She focused on his smell, the warmth of his skin, even the sound of his beating heart. She could feel his presence even with her eyes closed. Her skin tingled with his nearness. She wrapped her arms around his neck and held him. She kept him in the embrace and he did not pull away. After what seemed like an eternity of bliss she let him go and slowly pulled back. They both stood motionless. He moved first by reaching down in the hatch of the boat and pulling out two folding chairs. He set them up on the deck of the boat. He went below and came back with a bottle of wine and two glasses and a small table to sit between them. He then brought out an ice bucket for the wine. Saria smiled as he kept pulling things out.

"What else you got in there?" She looked over his shoulder.

"A galley, salon, and two berths. That is a kitchen, a sitting area, and two bedroom areas for you landlubbers."

"A bedroom, huh? I don't think I have ever seen a bedroom on a boat. Does it have a waterbed?"

"Nope, a memory-foam mattress. You want to check it out? It is pretty comfortable."

"Nice." Saria removed her top to reveal her bikini top and wriggled out of her shorts to reveal the rest of the outfit. "I thought it would be beneficial to wear this instead of undies. Or maybe nothing at all is better still," she said as she pulled off her top walking through the salon and into the closest berth. Grabbing his hand, she pulled him behind her.

Rick followed her. She curled on the bed, lying on her side. She rubbed her thigh in a provocative way. Then she patted it. He smiled at her and lay down next to her. Again, he felt an uncanny calm with her. It was more than familiarity. However, there was a feeling of strangeness too. She looked at him. He seemed to be looking through her again. She reached over to kiss him, and he did not resist. She gave him a light peck. He did not resist again, so she reached forward and kissed him deeply.

He tenderly massaged her bare breasts. He ran his tongue along her arm and across her neck. She could feel his teeth as he ran them along her tense neck muscles and her jugular. His warm breath rolled across her skin. She rolled her head back to allow him better access to her neck. He continued to run his tongue along the taut lines of her neck muscles. She began to moan as the sensations ran throughout her body. She gently moved his head and ran her tongue around his lips and into his mouth in a gentle kiss. She reached down, unbuttoned his shirt, and slipped it off his shoulders so it fell to the boat's deck. He slipped his hands along her hips and slipped her bikini bottoms off. He then loosened his pants and slipped everything off. He took her into his arms and she felt his skin as he moved across her bare breasts. He adjusted her position on the bed and kissed her again. This time he started sucking on her upper lip. She repositioned to give him better access to her body.

***

He spooned her. He buried his face in her hair. He smelled the wonderful fragrance she wore. Her hair smelled like the simple shampoo and conditioner she used. He could smell something else though a gentle floral fragrance unlike anything her had ever smelled. He ran his hands along her soft supple skin. He nibbled at her ear. He decided it was time to move to the next level.

"Saria," he said as she turned toward him and he looked deeply into her eyes.

He stopped as he saw a familiar tinge of gold fire deep in her eyes. He pulled back and sat on the edge of the bed.

"When were you going to tell me?" he asked quietly.

"Tell you what?" she asked.

"That you're a vampire, dammit," Rick responded angrily.

"I thought since you tracked them, you already knew. How could you not? I took your silence about it as a sign you didn't care about that. I thought you just liked me for who I am, not what I am," she said.

Rick sighed. "I guess I did already know. I have been preparing myself for this eventuality. Why were you hiding it from me?"

"I wasn't. I didn't admit it to you before because I was nervous. Ever since you told me you worked with the Shadow and hunted rogues I was afraid of how you would react."

"To you being a vampire? Well, this is it. I feel a touch betrayed, especially after I told you that I had already been almost killed by a vampire in my bed."

"You never said that woman was a vampire."

"Oh."

He realized that he had, in fact, not told her Britney was a vampire. Rick watched her every move. Within them, he saw the movement of a vampire. He was not sure why he had not realized it before. Maybe he just had not wanted to see it. She was right. She had not tried to conceal it. The only one concealing anything was him. All he could do was hope she was not a rogue. They had been together for six months now, she knew what he did, and she had not tried to kill him. She couldn't be a rogue. If she was, he would be dead.

"If not that, then what?" he finally asked.

"I was afraid that if you knew I was the local elder that you would think less of me or even hold me responsible for what has been going on."

"Wha. . . you're the elder? You have been feigning concern with me and all the while you have let this madman run loose?"

"Hold on now, Rick. I have not been 'letting him run loose.' I have tried to stop him on many occasions. You have only been dealing with this a year. I have been dealing with it since I made him."

"You're his dame, too? So you made this monster and turned him loose on an unknowing city. How long has this been going on?"

"About forty years. I have stopped him in the past and he waits a decade or two, then starts back up. I haven't been able to kill him because I thought I loved him and somewhere deep inside he loved me too. That is, until I met you and learned what real love is. I have asked the Colony for help and all I get is that I created him, so I have to take care of it. I have gotten no support. About thirty years ago, he took control of the coven. He forced the members to swear a blood oath to him or die. Many vampires loyal to me were hunted and killed by him and his minions. I tried to stop them but was unsuccessful. As more vampires in the surrounding area heard his rhetoric, they joined him. I could not fight that many alone. When the Shadow showed up, I thought help had finally been sent. Then I find out you are following an escaped ex-girlfriend and her leader. How do you think that makes me feel? To know that someone that I care about and I thought cared about me would jump so quickly to judge."

"If he took control about thirty years ago then that means either he or one of his minions killed my parents in cold blood. So your inability or unwillingness is the reason for the death of my parents. How do you think that makes me feel?" Tears were running down Rick's cheeks.

He threw on his pants and went up on deck. He sat in one of the chairs and poured himself a glass of wine. It was still cold though the ice had melted. It was not as cold as the shiver that ran down his spine. She quickly put her bikini back on and followed. She sat next to him.

"What the hell, Rick? Don't just leave me like that. How could you say I was responsible for your parents' death? Just because they were killed by a vampire in the same town as my rogue ex? I tried my best but I was outnumbered."

She could see that he was conflicted. She felt like he was analyzing each of her words and movements. He'd never told her his last girlfriend was a vampire, and he had never told her his parents were killed by vampires. Now he thought she was responsible for his parents' death. How was she going to fix this? He was a very frustrating man. She knew she should have told him before they went to bed together. She should have told him months ago. *But it shouldn't matter. I love him and he loves me. At least he did,* she thought.

Rick looked out to sea. She knew he was trying to calm his mind and process. He saw a fishing charter boat anchored close by. Rick watched the tourists as they moved around the boat, catching some of the local ocean fish. His face lit up as he stood and flagged the captain.

"Ahoy there, anyone have any sea bass that they would like to sell?"

The captain asked around the deck. A couple of the tourists nodded their heads. "How many you want?" he shouted back.

"Just a couple. It will save us a bit of time and effort."

"Sure. Just come over and get 'em."

Rick nodded as he walked over and lifted his small launch off the back of the boat while Saria watched. He climbed in and motored out to the charter boat. He handed the captain $100 and took the two fish. The boat crew had already cut them into four large fillets. He waved to everyone and motored back to his boat. He climbed back aboard and stowed the launch. He went below, lit the gas stove and brought out a pan. He covered the bottom with olive oil and pulled out a small pie dish. He emptied the contents of a zipper bag into the dish, cracked two eggs, and quickly whipped them. He dipped the fish in the egg wash, then in the flour and seasonings mixture, and then placed it in the pan. He started all four fillets cooking. He reached in the small fridge on board, grabbed some vegetables, chopped them into large pieces, and placed them in another pan. He did everything in silence, not speaking a word to her. Saria watched with amazement as he quickly made a meal. She also felt the tension in the boat.

She sat down at the salon table as he plated their lunch. He stepped out onto the deck and started to retrieve the wine and glasses. He stopped and put them back. He stuck his head in the hatch.

"Bring the plates. Let's eat on deck."

"Sure," she replied and grabbed the plates.

He took them from her as she reached the hatch. He put them on the little table, helped her out onto the deck, and then stepped back inside to grab some flatware and napkins as she sat. He brought those out and sat next to her. He handed her the flatware and placed the napkins next to them. The fishing charter boat was still sitting there with the gulls grabbing all the remains of the fish processing. They waved to the tourists.

"So this is what sitting on our dock will be like," Rick said, warming back up to her a bit.

"This is beautiful, and you know, I have not been that nervous out here on the water. I think it has something to do with you. I just feel safe with you. That is not something I can say I have felt with any man, ever. I know you feel like I have betrayed you, but I haven't. I don't understand how you didn't realize it—you are a vampire hunter. I took your silence on the subject as your acceptance of it. I am sorry about your parents. I do understand your anger about it. Please don't take it out on me. But, all that shouldn't matter, should it? If we love each other?" she asked. He looked down. She continued.

"I thought that you being distant for so long was you deciding to accept me or not. I didn't freak out when you told me your secret. How do you think it makes me feel that you hunt my kind? It scares me to death. I thought you had accepted me. Accepted me as I am," she finished.

"I understand. You were afraid I would react like an ass . . . like I just did. Sorry," he said, still looking at the deck. "How is your fish, by the way?" he asked, looking up and changing the subject.

"Delicious. Where did you learn to cook like this?"

"The—" he started.

"—Internet," she finished.

They both smiled. The tension eased a little. Saria could still tell he was working through everything in his head. She would have to give him more time and possibly be away from him, which ripped her heart apart. She looked up and in the distance; she could see large container ships as they passed between the peninsula and Catalina Island. The island was clear as a bell. She could see every tree on the hillsides and even a few boats.

"We used to buy fish like that on the coast when I was a kid. It is as fresh as you can get," he finally said.

"You are an interesting man. I have been meaning to ask you, when the boom was moving back and forth, you would duck as it got to you even if you were not looking in its direction. How did you know?" she asked, trying to change the subject.

"I just did. I knew where it was at all times. It is like that when I fight too. I always seem to know where my opponent's blow is going to land, and I just make sure I am not there. It helps me to fight vampires. With their unnatural speed, it gives me an edge. It is just a knack. I just watch my opponent's movements or listen to the traveler on the boom. It isn't magic or anything. Well, I don't know, maybe it is. It woke me up an instant before Britney murdered me."

"Maybe it is a touch of magic, then. It sure seems like it when watching you do it."

"When you're finished, we will head back in. It is starting to move into evening. We should get back to the marina."

"Let's finish off this bottle of wine."

Rick offered his glass and she refilled it. She poured the last into her glass. They sat watching the water and each other. Soon they finished eating, and Saria took the dishes and went into the galley to wash them as Rick took down the chairs and table to prepare to get under way. Once they were stowed, Rick picked up the anchors and motored out to where he could get wind into the sails. He raised the sails and moved to the wheel. He pulled the genoa into the wind, and the boat began to move.

Once she had finished with the dishes, Saria came out to the cockpit. The wind was with them, so Rick had let loose the traveler, and the boat was heeling into the wind. She stood behind him and grabbed him around the waist and rested her cheek against his back. He stiffened and after a few seconds relaxed. She frowned. However, she realized that might be his reaction for a while. He had to readjust to their new dynamic. She closed her eyes and felt the sea air blowing in her face. It had a very different feeling than the first time. This was a different day and a different ship, and this wind felt good on her face.

Soon they were motoring the boat back to its slip. They moored it, and Rick reconnected the power, sewage, and waterlines and hit a pump button to empty the storage tanks. He clicked it back off, and they headed for the car. The drive back to the house was quick. Saria remained snuggled against him the entire trip. He kept his arm around her. Soon they were pulling into his garage and the door was closing behind them. They went into the house. Rick turned on the TV as they sat on the couch. The news was still talking about the couple who was murdered.

"Gosh, I can't believe they are still talking about it. They don't need to give these murderers all this sensational attention. I bet they are eating it up," Rick said.

"Yeah, I bet he is," she replied.

"Your ex?"

"Yeah, Nickolea."

"Tell me more about this ex. He is the new leader of the coven, correct?"

"His coven, yes."

"I don't know why you bother to differentiate. It is just you and them. I have one question, though. Why did you not destroy him?"

"I don't know. Love, pity, fear, I just don't know. As I said on the boat, I think I thought I loved him and could save him. But, instead I have doomed my entire coven to death."

"I don't think we would have to kill everyone once we get him."

"You are not who I am referring to. You are much more merciful."

"Well, who are you talking about, then?"

"If you don't know, then I have said too much already. Your life could already be at risk."

Rick looked at her inquisitively but she would not reveal any more. Saria switched channels on the TV. All the news channels were carrying the same news report. She kept flipping channels until she found an old movie from the eighties. She laughed as she watched. Rick leaned back into the couch and she leaned against him. They snuggled and watched TV. Rick grabbed the phone and ordered a pizza. Saria smiled. After the pizza arrived, they watched another couple of older movies.

"Rick, will you come with me tomorrow to the halfway house? I would like to show you around."

"You mean show me off. Sure, I would love to. Maybe I can find some time to help out too, once this Nickolea thing is resolved."

"Hopefully you will before then. We will go early in the morning."

"Should we go to bed early, then?"

"I am always ready for bed. Are we sleeping in the same bed?" she asked cautiously.

"I don't see why not," he replied.

Rick stood up and headed to the bedroom. Saria stood smiling at him and followed him. She walked into the bathroom and walked out in a thin silk nightgown. She jumped in the bed and covered up.

"I had a very good time today. Good night, Rick. Pleasant dreams."

"What do you mean pleasant dreams," he said as he dropped his clothes and climbed into bed next to her.

She looked at him seductively. He reached down to kiss her. She did not stop him. She leaned up to meet him. They kissed. She ran her hands across his chest. She sat up, pushed him onto his back, and started kissing his chest. Rick had never noticed the roughness of her tongue until she started licking his abdomen and kissing her way up and down his chest and abdomen. As her tongue ran around the sensitive portions of his body it sent him into a sensory overload. He finally just closed his eyes and let the sensations pour over him.

***

She turned away from him, smiling. Rick cradled her in his arms. She had never felt so comfortable or safe. She slowly drifted off to sleep. Saria dreamed peaceful dreams. She dreamed of walks with Rick through the beautiful Spanish gardens of her youth. She dreamed of them being side by side forever.

Rick, however, had dreams of darkness and creatures in shadows. He saw Shinto attacking Saria. He felt a sharp pain in his side, then nothing. He awoke in a cold sweat. He was standing in the middle of the room. Saria was standing next to the bed with a look of fear on her face.

Chapter VII

aria walked over to Rick, pulled his head to her chest and sroked his hair. Rick shook in her embrace. His hair was soaked with sweat from his fear. He calmed as she stroked him. Finally his shivering stopped.

"What's wrong, Rick? You screamed and leaped over me," she asked, in a consoling tone.

"Oh, sorry. I had a nightmare. It was nothing."

"Nightmares are never 'nothing.' What did you dream?"

"I just dreamed of darkness and shadowy creatures. I think it has to do with the case we're working on. This happens to me at times. It is nothing to worry about. Let's go back to bed."

"Rick are you sure you're all right?" she asked, concerned.

"Yes, let's go back to bed."

They went back to bed. He spooned her and wrapped his arms around her. He could smell her hair. Her mere presence made him more comfortable. All his angst slowly flowed out of him. He could not be mad at her for what had happened. He snuggled closer to her. He knew that she was the one. However, the gnawing feeling inside him remained—his deep-rooted fear she was a rogue. He drifted off to sleep.

Rick slept peacefully, but Saria could not sleep at all. She was full of worry and of hate. There were many meanings to his dream. None of them were good and she knew Nickolea was at the core of each one. She would do whatever was necessary to protect the man next to her. She turned enough to kiss him and whispered in his ear, "I love you." He mumbled something and fell deeper into sleep.

His touch felt good to her. She knew deep inside that she had found her mate. She now knew what her father had meant when they had talked those many years ago. She understood why Nickolea had so easily fooled her, why he was able to escape with his life each time she'd meant to kill him. Now she knew who her mate truly was, and Nickolea would not fool her again.

She lay in the bed, alert the rest of the night, watching for danger. Soon morning came and she slid out of his embrace, got up, dressed, and went to the kitchen to make breakfast. She could feel the first tinges of pain around the edge of her consciousness. She looked in the refrigerator and pulled out the vegetable juice bottle she had placed in there the morning before.

She took a sip. The deep, rich flavor caressed her senses. She could feel the pain recede into the background. She took a long drink and finished the remainder of the small bottle. She was wiping her mouth and getting a glass of water as Rick walked in. She took a big drink of water, swished it in her mouth, and swallowed. He walked over and kissed her.

"Good morning, Saria. How are you?"

"Good morning. I am very well," she replied.

"You finally drank your juice, I see. You know I have plenty of all kinds of juice. You did not have to bring your own."

"Well, it is a special brand with a particular combination of vitamins and minerals. You know, blood. I am on a special diet, you know."

"That is what you said."

"So what would you like for breakfast?" she asked.

"Hmmm, maybe eggs Benedict? Or maybe pancakes."

"Pancakes it is. I saw the tastiest recipe on the Internet."

They both laughed as she pulled out the ingredients and started mixing them. He watched as she deftly made the pancakes. She was quick and skilled in the use of the whisk and skillet.

"Syrup?"

"But of course."

She reached behind her back, grabbed the maple syrup, and

poured some on both stacks. They sat at the breakfast bar and enjoyed the food. Afterward, Rick took the dishes and washed them. Saria walked toward the bedroom and the shower. Rick looked at her shapely body, and she almost seemed to glow.

They got ready to go to the halfway house. She came out in a T-shirt and jeans that hugged her every curve. She then pulled out a pair of leather riding boots. She slid them on and zipped them. They contoured over her calf muscles, making them more pronounced. She tossed her raven-black hair, and then pulled it back into a ponytail. She then moved over to his closet and Rick stopped her.

"I need to tell you something. But I need to start from the beginning," he said, taking her hand.

Rick walked over to a locked chest. He produced a key from the nightstand. It creaked loudly as he lifted the lid. Lying on top was a forty-caliber automatic pistol. He lifted it and set it on the bed. He moved away a switchblade and picked up a few pieces of material, a couple of them with rips and bloodstains on them. He also set those on the bed. He lifted out a leather jacket. It had spikes and chains on it. He handed it to Saria.

"What is this?" she asked, looking at the jacket.

"It's from my not-so-happy years. I was angry with my parents for dying and I was lashing out at everyone. So, I joined this gang. A few months later, there was a fight. Six of my fellow gang members were killed. I killed two or three of the rival gang myself. I was almost shot a couple times, as you can see." He pointed to the holes. "You noticed there are no bloodstains on the jacket." She nodded her head. "I was not hurt."

He walked over to the bed and picked up the bloody material. She could see it was two shirts. He handed them to her. "My best friend was wearing these. He joined the gang because of me." He held up the bloodiest one. She could see a knife cut right where the wearer's liver would be. "And he also died because of me. He died in my arms, bled to death. I quit the gang that day. They tried to kill me a couple times after that. When everyone they sent was unsuccessful and ended up in the morgue, we reached an agreement. They would leave me alone and I wouldn't kill any more of them.

"We moved to another part of New York, and I straightened out. I got my shit together and finished high school with a 3.8 GPA, got a full scholarship to Columbia, and majored in psychology. I pursued my master's degree and did my thesis on gang violence and the gang mentality. That caught the NYPD's attention, so I started working with their anti-gang unit. I ended up in my old neighborhood, and somebody recognized me.

"That is when I decided it would be best to take my studies abroad. I went to Japan to research the 'Katana Killer.' That is also where I found the first clues about this worldwide vampire cult, or so I thought at the time. I met a police detective there, Kinoshi Kimura. He also seemed very interested in the vampire cult. We worked together and stopped a few cult members. He introduced me to my master. I studied under my master for five years, learning to hunt and kill vampires. That is how I became the leader of the Shadow. So once my research was over, I returned to the US and went back to helping the NYPD and opened an office in Manhattan catering to rich parents who thought their kids needed 'therapy' as a cover."

"Wait a second; did you just say you are the leader of the Shadow?"

"Yes, I did. Why?"

"You are the leader of the Shadow, the largest organization hunting rogues today? But you're a human."

"Yes, for the last thousand years, the Clan of the Divine Shadow has been led by a human. Let's see . . . where was I? Oh yeah, so the money started rolling in. I was not very happy with what I was doing. I met Britney and we developed a relationship. After a couple of months, I revealed who I was and she tried to kill me. The Shadow and I eliminated her coven and she and her leader fled to Los Angeles. I sold everything and moved out here to hunt them. After we arrived, I discovered the blatant activity and called for a team and we started hunting the rogues. I am now here with you."

"Damn, never a dull moment. Here I thought you were just

a regular guy. Turns out you are the most famous person I know. Your title is whispered in dark corners among vampires. It is whispered for fear they will summon you and you will punish them for some long-forgotten crime."

They started digging through his clothes. She instinctively jerked her hand back as it brushed across his Shadow uniform. She reached back in and pulled out an old concert T-shirt that had a few tears, a pair of faded jeans, and a pair of biker boots. She walked over and put them on the bed. She looked over at Rick expectantly. He walked over and looked through the clothes she had picked out.

"The last thing these kids need is a hoity-toity, rich bitch social worker and her stuffed-shirt psychologist boyfriend trying to 'help' them. I have built trust with these kids by approaching as one of them. I brought the biker boots because I didn't expect you to have any grunge clothes. The T-shirt and the jeans pleasantly surprised me. Where did you get those, the 'I am old and think I am cool' store? Though the band is cool."

"First of all, that was the bitchin'-est concert I ever went to, and if you looked in the back, you would have seen the half ripped-up hikers. I used to wear those to raves back in the day. Back when I tripped on "E" and smoked my fair share of pot. That was much to my uncle's chagrin."

"I would never have spotted you as an ex-stoner. Nice. You will blend in well. And bring this jacket; it will give you a lot of street cred with these kids. What about the streets?"

"East NYC baby, some of the meanest streets when I was growing up."

"So, why did you reveal all this to me now?"

"Well, you showed me yours so I figured I should show you mine. It is only fair."

She rolled her eyes at him.

"Well, I felt it necessary, especially after last night, and to establish my credibility with you." He continued while putting everything back in his trunk. "So you understand where I am coming from, since you are sharing your protected clients with me. I wouldn't want you to think this was all a ploy. I can see these kids mean a lot to you."

"You're right, they do. We have kept several of them alive. Quite a few have reached the end of their rope. We have a couple of severe cutters. I have had to rush them to the hospital a couple of times."

"Well, I will need to see them first. I have to determine their need for self-destruction."

"Well, I need to tell you the rest about myself."

"If you feel you need to, I am ready."

"Well, you probably aren't as ready as you think, but here we go." She took a deep breath. "I am a seventeenth-century Spanish princess who was turned into a vampire by a man who wanted to usurp my father's throne. King Felipe IV of Spain, House of Habsburg." she rattled off quickly. She took another deep breath then bit her lower lip, awaiting his response.

"Seventeenth-century Spanish princess? So you're a cougar, then?" he said questioningly with an emotionless look on his face.

"We are long-lived . . . What?" she said, halting in midsentence.

"Well if you are a seventeenth-century princess, that makes you what? Three hundred fifty years old? I am thirty-eight. You are over ten times my age. So by definition you are a cougar," he explained. "Go ahead where you left off. I was just making an observation."

"Uhhh . . . oh, yeah." She stumbled across her words until she finally got her wits back. "Rapidly healing flesh and blood creatures. We love and we hate, we cry and we laugh."

"How much blood do you drink?"

"Only what is necessary to live. I am what they call a Thin Blood, or Thin for short. The other kind of vampire is a Gluttonous Ravager, or a Glut for short. Gluts drink blood for the power they receive from it.

"However, what I am doesn't change my feelings for you. Around you, my thirst is less. The pain it inflicts upon me when I haven't fed is less around you. That is very important because it has never happened before."

"Wow. That is a lot to absorb. Well, you have had plenty of opportunities to drink my blood, and you haven't. I do care for you a lot, Saria. So is that what the sword is for? Killing vampires?"

"Yes, a vampire heals so quickly, the only way to truly kill one is to behead them. But of course you already know that."

"Is that why you wanted me to be careful around the police? Have the Gluts infiltrated them too?" he asked leadingly.

"Yes, but not all Gluts are bad, only ones that don't follow the Law. The Law is simple: take what you wish, but do not expose the race to danger and never raise more than you can put down."

"Why are the ones here so blatant?"

"They are led by Nickolea. Enough of this—the kids await us. You will still help me, won't you?"

"Of course, but you have to answer one more question."

"Fire away."

"How do the kids fit into this?"

"I was sent away from my family to live with an uncle. I felt deserted by my family because of a single bad choice I made—which I made up for by killing the man who made me into a monster. He killed my brother to open the way for me to succeed to the throne after he killed my parents. I felt so lost and different at that point, and someone helped me, so I wanted to help other lost kids."

"One more very important question. Do you feed on them?" he asked flatly with a piercing stare.

"Only if we have a severe cutter; vampire saliva has a healing factor that causes the tissues to close. By licking the wound, I start it to heal, and I drink the blood that has already come out. That is why the two severe cases we have had survived to make it to the hospital. I have never bitten any of the kids and never will."

"Good enough. Let's go," he said, a bit more relaxed.

Rick reached over and kissed Saria on her soft, ruby-red lips. They headed to the halfway house. Rick was quiet on the drive over. He was having a hard time deciding if the information she had given him was accurate. Yet his feelings had not changed. He still saw her as the beautiful young woman she appeared to be.

He desired nothing else other than to be with her forever. Was that part of her power? Was she making him love her? Probably not. Their powers did not really work that way as far as he understood. Could he love her after finding out she is a few hundred years old and an elder to boot?

Soon they arrived at the halfway house. They parked in the back and walked to the front. Once inside, Saria introduced Rick to the kids as a friend. The young girls looked at him, sizing him up. The young men were doing the same but in a different way. They walked to the back, and Saria introduced Rick to the housemother, Cheryl.

"Cheryl, this is Rick. He is a psychologist from the county."

"He looks more like a rock-and-roll wannabe."

"Saria said to dress casual," he said, smiling.

"I bet she did."

"I guess you need a private area to talk to the kids?"

"Yes, I do. I like to give them as much privacy as possible."

"I have just the place."

Cheryl led them to the old library. It was in a mostly deserted area of the house. Rick looked it over, counted the exits, and looked outside each door. When he was satisfied, he walked back to Cheryl.

"Yes, this will be perfect. I will set up in here."

They went through the day talking with the kids and getting them familiar with Rick. He told them his story and showed them the jacket. A couple of the boys looked at the gang markings and the holes and shook their heads. They were looking at him with a new respect. They were whispering excitedly among each other. The group passed the jacket around.

"Those memories pain Rick, especially since he feels responsible for the death of his best friend. He is willing to relive them to help prevent you guys from making some of the same mistakes." Saria explained to the boys catching the feeling starting to go around.

"We're sorry, Rick. It is just so strange to see someone like you with this kind of history," one of the boys answered for the rest.

"Apology accepted. Like Saria said, I am here to help you to avoid the same regrets I have," Rick said.

Rick went to the library, and several of the kids came to see him and talked about some of their problems. Rick explained to each of them that their circumstances were not their fault, but their decisions were a choice, and to always make decisions based on fact, not conjecture. By the time they were finished, it was getting late.

Rick and Saria told everyone good-bye. They were getting ready to leave when one of the young men told them to be careful because it was dangerous at night. They thanked him and headed out the door. They walked around the corner and got into the car. After they drove off, Rick turned to Saria.

"These kids need a lot of help, and I would like to help them."

"I sure hoped you would," she replied.

"I would also like to see more of you. But I have to get used to the thought that you are older than me by several hundred years. It is a little disconcerting."

"I understand. I would like to see more of you too."

"Good. It's decided, then."

They drove back to Rick's house. He watched Saria gather her things, then walked her to her car, kissed her goodnight, and he watched her drive away. He pounded his fist into his hand.

"I can't believe she is a vampire. I am in love with a vampire. I cannot believe this. Please, God, let her story be true. Please don't let her be a rogue. I would regret forever having to kill her."

He turned around to see Amaya behind him. Her head was bowed. Within a few seconds, Taiga entered from the garden. He stood also with his head bowed. Rick walked around them looking at them. He finally stopped in front of them.

"Who wants to start?"

Taiga stepped forward. "Lord, Amaya sees her not only as part of your future but as your future. We decided that you needed to be sure of your own feelings before you discovered the whole truth."

"It is clear that she loves you. I can also see that you love her. I have seen that your survival is dependent on her presence. Your fates are intertwined, as I have already told you. If you'd known the whole truth too soon, you would have cast her aside. Our job is to protect you. Even if we have to protect you from yourself," Amaya said.

"We knew from the second day that she was one of us. We monitored her closely. Lord Kimura told us to allow your relationship to continue. He said it was paramount to our mission and your happiness," Taiga continued.

"I should have known you had cleared it with Kinoshi," Rick said, turning to Amaya. "So you have seen my survival is dependent on her presence. What does that mean?"

"I do not know. As I have told you, your fate is unclear and your fates are as intertwined as is mine and Taiga's. Just as intertwined as Taiga's and mine are with yours and now hers. I am ashamed to have kept her secret but it was a necessary omission."

"I know you have my best interests at heart so I do not blame you for your silence on this issue. Taiga, did you know Saria's ex was the leader of the rogue coven?"

"I did not, my lord."

"Now that we have his identity, we must find him and kill him. I am sure where we find him we will find Shinto. There is no time to waste. Notify the teams; we start tonight. No patrols—we are hunting."

"Lord, we cannot risk you."

"Fine, I will stay here. Leave a guard if you like. You need Amaya with you. Her abilities will help."

"Yes, lord, I will leave a single Shadow to watch over you."

They bowed as he dismissed them and they turned to leave. Rick walked back to the bedroom. It was going to be cold and lonely tonight.

Once Rick was in the other room, Taiga turned to Amaya.

"Are you sure this is the only way?" he said, pulling out his phone.

"Yes, Taiga, it has not changed. In order for us to succeed, our lord must die."

***

Shinto walked into the laboratory. Nickolea was looking down into a pit. Shinto could see leathery-skinned, skinny, bat-like creatures below. They were milling around, and occasionally one would attack one of the others. Then the rest would attack the same one and tear it apart. Shinto walked over to Nickolea.

"You called for me?"

"Aren't they beautiful?" Nickolea asked absently. He offered Shinto a vial of green liquid. "Yes Shinto, I did. I have a present for you," Nickolea said without taking his eyes from the Reapers.

"What is it?" Shinto asked.

"It turns humans into those," Nickolea said pointing into the pit.

"It turns humans into Reapers?"

"Once they drink vampire blood, it does."

"Ah, so if I stab Smythe with a knife coated in this . . . When that girlfriend of his tries to save him by changing him into a vampire . . ."

"He will turn into a Reaper and she will have to kill him herself. Kill two birds with one stone, you could say. Once she has to kill him, she will want to take her own life. I'll arrive and do it for her," Nickolea finished.

"Very devious, Nickolea, very devious. There is no antidote, I take it?"

"None, and the change is irreversible."

"Wonderful," Shinto said as he walked out of the lab with the green liquid.

Chapter VIII

ick was closing out his cases for the day when Saria walked in. He kissed her, finished placing his files in the cabinet, and locked them. He turned to Saria. "You ready for dinner, baby?"

"So what do you want to do after dinner, Rick?" Saria asked.

"I think we should go out dancing. I really enjoy dancing with you."

"How about we go to the Pandemonium as usual?"

"Sounds good. Let's go."

They grabbed a quick dinner and drove to the club. They could hear the music outside while they were waiting to get in. A man walked out of the club and saw them in line. He walked out and moved them to the front of the line

"No charge for Rick and his guest."

"Two-drink minimum, you two," the man told them.

"No problem, Donald."

The man let them in.

"I have really enjoyed being with you for the last few months," Rick said. "And this last weekend was the best."

"Me too. I have not had this much fun in a long time. Maybe even ever," she said, smiling at Rick.

He leaned over and kissed her deeply. She was surprised at first and then returned the kiss. After they finished their drinks, they went out to the dance floor. They did a bit of bump and grind on each other, dancing with each other and with a few other people. Saria was enjoying herself when she saw someone looking toward her from the door of the club. She quickly made sure they could not see her or Rick through the crowd.

"Rick, I think someone is looking for one of us."

"Why is that?"

"Do you see the guy at the door? The guy with the trench coat."

Rick looked toward the door. He saw the man. He was taking off his coat and handing it to the bartender, who put it behind the bar. The man was scanning the room. Rick spun them behind a column. He glanced around the column with one eye. The man was still scanning the area.

"I think you are right. I think it is Shinto. Kiss me."

"What?"

"Just kiss me."

Saria kissed him. He watched the man while they kissed. He recognized how the man moved. He was sure it was Shinto. He had to protect Saria. After a few minutes, the man disappeared into the crowd. Rick quickly scanned the room and could not find him. He looked to Saria and broke off the kiss.

"I lost him. He is hunting someone. I can tell that by the way he is scanning, and I think it is us. Grab your stuff and let's go."

Saria grabbed her small bag from the table, and they stealthily and anonymously moved toward the door. Soon they had made their way out. Rick watched the door as he pulled out his keys. He did not see the man follow them out of the club. Saria went to the passenger side of the car. Rick turned back to look again, and the man was standing in front of him. He bumped into Rick and jumped back around the corner. Saria turned to chase him, but she could not see him anywhere. She turned around and saw Rick holding a knife.

"Oh my god, what happened?"

"He bumped into me and stabbed me in my gut with this knife. Damn it, I was a fool. He was after me. I thought he was after you. Damn vampire ninja." Rick looked at his hand. "There is a lot of blood," he replied shakily.

Saria ran to his side, looked, and saw blood pouring from his right side. She looked around. Seeing no one, she licked the wound. It failed to close as it should. Tears began to well up in her eyes as she licked it again. It continued to refuse to react. Rick started coughing up blood and became very pale. He dropped to his knees and finally collapsed to the ground. Saria took his head into her lap.

"Rick, my darling. The wound refuses to close. The bleeding is profuse. Only one thing will save you," she said through her tears.

"He lacerated my liver, which means I'm going to die. Kind of poetic, don't you think? I would've liked to live longer to be with you. I wonder where the Shadow is? It's getting dim, Saria."

"Rick, I can turn you and save your life. But, you have to ask me to. You have to give me permission, my darling. Please give me permission."

"Please, all I want is to be with you. It is okay as long as we'll be together," he whispered as he lost consciousness.

"Forever, my darling."

Saria pulled out her bladed ring. She gashed her arm as deep as she could. She screamed in pain as it tore deep into her flesh. She held her arm so the blood ran into his unconscious mouth. Several drops hit his tongue. He instinctively licked them. Her arm healed quickly. She ripped it open again to drop more blood into his mouth. Rivulets of blood ran down her arm and into his mouth. Soon he licked all she could squeeze out of the cut. His breathing stabilized, and the bleeding began to decrease.

Once she was sure the change was taking hold, she loaded him into her car and went as quickly as she could to her apartment since it was closer than his house. She grabbed Rick's phone and dialed Taiga. She told him to meet them at her apartment and gave him the address though she knew it was unnecessary. She rushed as fast as she could. Taiga and Amaya met her at the front door. They helped her carry the unconscious Rick up to her apartment and put him in her bed. She undressed him. She could see the wound slowly closing. The blood was only seeping. She bandaged him and covered him up.

"We should not have left him. He is going to die and it is our fault," Taiga said.

"Taiga, he ordered us to hunt Nickolea and Shinto. It is his *unmei* and we cannot change it. If we had tried, everything would fail. Lady Saria has this under control. We must inform Lord Kimura, so he can make the preparations."

"Preparations for what?" Saria asked.

"He must take leadership of the Shadow until our lord is able to resume. The Shadow can't be without a lord. We could become Ronin," Taiga explained.

"But Rick is not dead. And I am not going to let him die."

"We do not expect him to. We need a war leader and Lord Kimura will assume that role. But he must be informed."

"You do what you need to do. I will take care of Rick."

"You will have a member of the Shadow with you at all times. Our lord needs to go to the Colony. We must go. You will be safe here. Just keep his phone close and take care of our lord. We entrust his life and safety to you."

"I will, Taiga. You have served him honorably and faithfully. Continue to do so. Catch the bastards who did this to him," Saria said as she started to cry again.

Taiga and Amaya bowed to her and headed out the door. Saria closed the door and went back to Rick. He was sleeping quietly. She cuddled up next to him. He flinched as she bumped his wound. She looked at her unscarred arm and then to his bandaged abdomen. The bandage already had red seeping through. She cut the bandages away and looked at the wound. It was still open instead of healed as she thought it should be; however, it was not bleeding anymore. She walked downstairs and opened her refrigerator. She pulled out a bottle of blood and poured it in a glass. She bit her lip and sliced her arm open once again. She added her blood to the glass of blood and carried it back upstairs. She woke Rick and handed him the glass.

"What is this?" he asked weakly.

"It is life and love. Drink it all, my darling."

Rick sipped at it. He continued sipping until it was gone. She kissed him, licking his lips clean. She looked at the wound. It was starting to close again. She put the glass beside the bed, cuddled to Rick, and drifted off to sleep.

***

Shinto walked in to Nickolea's "throne room." Nickolea sat on his throne dozing. Shinto slammed the door and Nickolea jolted fully awake. Shinto gave a mock bow.

"Nickolea, it is done. I killed the human. She just sat with his head in her lap crying. Then one of those foul Shadow appeared and I had to depart. His blood was pouring onto the pavement. He did not even know what happened. You got what you wanted. I got part of what I wanted. His death was free but his discovery was not. I want the Reaper program."

"Sure, you can have the program. But it is still my program; you are just in charge of it."

"Agreed. I will run the program for you. I will make sure they produce the most terrifying army this world has ever seen."

The two men smiled and shook hands. They heard screams down the hall. They stood and followed them. They entered the lab and saw a Reaper strapped to the table. Its claws reached for the closest technician. Nickolea saw a man in the corner with a large rip in his side. Blood gushed onto the floor as the man quickly died. The doctor stood against the wall and moved toward Nickolea as he entered.

"Lord Nickolea, I increased the dosage as you ordered and I got this beast. He is ten percent larger and stronger. His aggression seems to be significantly higher than previous ones. I am about to put him into the pit with the others. We'll see what happens."

"Very good, doctor. Oh, how did the surgery go?"

"Excellent; the candidate is exactly as requested. The bandages come off in a couple of days."

"Excellent, doctor. Now let's see what this creation of yours is capable of."

The doctor pulled out a remote control and pushed a button. The beast's gurney began to roll out the door and down a short hall to the pit. Once they arrived, the doctor flipped a switch, the gurney positioned almost vertically above the pit, the straps came loose, and the beast slid into the pit. Everyone walked over to see the beast land on its feet. The other Reapers attacked the newcomer. The beast ripped through the others quickly. Nickolea watched with a sadistic glee as it tore the other Reapers apart.

"Excellent, doctor. This looks like a perfect formula. Make sure it is all logged so we can repeat it exactly."

"It is already done, my lord. I logged and programmed everything into the injection computer as you asked. Everything is prepared for stage two."

"And you said the other project is complete?"

"Yes, the subject will be ready in a couple of days. The nurse already has all the orders she needs."

"This is great news, doctor," Nickolea said, patting him on the back. "So I do not need you anymore, do I?"

Nickolea picked up the doctor and threw him into the pit. He watched as the beast ripped its creator apart. It then sat and began to consume the pieces, sucking each one for the blood in it, then eating the flesh.

"Oh, I should have turned him first. What a waste," Nickolea stated as he and Shinto walked back to the throne room.

"Phase two is mine?" Shinto asked.

"Yes," Nickolea answered, grabbing a goblet full of blood.

"Then I will take my leave."

Shinto turned and walked out of the room.

"I need to see how a vampire lasts against him," Nickolea said and turned to a vampire close to him. "You come here."

***

The sunlight woke Saria. She looked at Rick. He was still asleep. She looked at the wound. It was closed and healing but not nearly as fast as a vampire should. She walked downstairs and retrieved another glass of blood for him. Again, he sipped it until it was empty. She collected the other glass and walked downstairs. She heard a knock on her door and was shocked to see Nickolea standing there as she opened it.

"Ah, Saria, how are you this morning? And how is Dr. Smythe? I heard he had a terrible accident. Did he not make it? I'll bet you are heartbroken. I bet you tried to save him." Nickolea smiled a vicious grin. "You are a miserable failure as a vampire and a mate. Your softness for these sheep makes you weak. That is why you couldn't save him. You just let him die with his head in your lap, didn't you? Crying to infinity about how unfair it all is. You are a vampire, you stupid whore. Your happiness should be in bringing misery to these sheep called humans."

Saria had angry tears in her eyes. "You'd better get away from my home, or I will take your head as you stand there, you son of a bitch. If I find out you had anything to do with this, I will hunt you down and kill you. You will not be able to find a hole deep enough to hide in."

"Oh, but I did have something to do with it. I had that flea exterminated. He was bothersome. You can't do anything to me. You are too weak. Otherwise, you would have killed me long ago. But I will take my leave."

Nickolea turned and left. Saria slammed the door. She slid down behind it and started to sob. All the angst of the last twelve hours had taken its toll on her sanity. She walked straight to the phone and called the police chief. She waited patiently for him to pick up his private line.

"Chief Brown," the man said finally.

"Chief, it is Saria," she stated.

"Yes, what do you need?"

"Rick was attacked last night and almost killed. He is recovering at my house, but he is in grave danger. I need everyone to think he is dead. Can you do that?"

"Of course, Saria. I will let Detective Stevens know—" he

started as Saria interrupted him.

"No one can know he is alive. Only you and a few friends in high places will know. It is necessary for my ruse to work. Do not trust the information to anyone else."

"But Stevens is my best man."

"Cedric, do this for me. You are not naive enough to think your department doesn't have any dirty cops in it. With the money available in this town, there has to be dirty ones. So no one must know."

"You've got a lot of balls, Saria, to talk to me like that. All right, no one knows. Are you leaving town?"

"Yes, I have to get him out of here."

"Have a safe trip."

Saria hung up the phone. She called the Department of Health and Human Services and told them their office was to be closed due to an emergency. She made sure everyone they knew heard that Rick was injured. She made an anonymous call to the Times about a knifing and that the police had named the victim. She called the CEO of LA General Hospital and informed him of the injury and death of Rick Smythe and that it was a necessary fabrication. He agreed. She made two more calls. She called an old CIA friend who owed her favors and had him create false IDs and credit cards for them. Then she called her father and alerted him of Rick's condition and their soon arrival at the colony.

Once her web of deceit was spun, Saria packed a suitcase, got Rick to her car, and drove to his house. His suitcase was packed and laying on the bed. She wrapped the knife and placed it in his large suitcase. She packed a laptop and all the records she could find. Soon her cell rang; her friend told her the documents were ready. She loaded everything and took off for downtown. She pulled up to the garage of the CIA headquarters. She walked to the front desk. The agent was waiting for her with a visitor's pass.

"I have a friend in my car downstairs. He needs help," she told her friend.

"Agent Richards, Agent Simmons, go look after him."

The two agents headed for the garage. Saria and her friend boarded the elevator. Saria remained silent the entire trip. She was still shaking.

"What is up, Saria?" her friend asked as they entered his office.

"I have to get my friend out of the country. He is sick, and only my father, Stefan, can help."

Realization appeared on his face. "Saria, is he the one this time?"

"Yes, he is. My world has been totally different since he came to town."

"Good. You deserve some happiness, Lady cel Tinar."

"Cel Tinar? 'The young?' What a touch. So are we lord and lady?"

"Yes, you are Stefania cel Tinar. He is Alexandrel cel Tinar. Lord and lady of the Moldavia region of Romania. They are political documents, so you should have minimal interference from the TSA. If you have any issues, ask for the supervisor and give him this card."

"Thanks. Hope this is not a problem."

"Saria, with all the help you have provided this and other agencies over the years, this is a minor repayment. Besides, it is an honor to serve an elder. Oh, I took the liberty of booking you first-class tickets. Aristocrats of your stature shouldn't travel any other way. I am very sorry I couldn't free up a Lear. So first-class commercial will have to do. Your friend and your new suitcases have been loaded into a visiting dignitary limo, and all your personal items have been repacked. Agent Lansdale will be your American attaché until we get you on the plane. He will take care of everything. Oh, and you will find some appropriate refreshments in the car."

Agent Lansdale walked into the room.

"It is my honor to serve, Lady cel Tinar," he said bowing to her.

He picked up their identification and led Saria to the waiting car. Romanian flags flew on the front of the vehicle. She got in the back and noticed Rick was dressed differently. He was a pale green color and had developed a fever. Saria opened the small refrigerator and pulled out a carafe of blood. She filled a glass and held it for Rick to drink. He slowly sipped until it was empty. She reached to his wound, and he flinched as soon as she touched it, and whispered it was sore. She pulled Rick into her lap and held him close.

"Is he your husband, ma'am?" Agent Lansdale asked, seeing the worried look on her face.

"Not yet, but I hope soon. He is very sick and I have no idea why."

"I didn't think vampires got sick, Your Grace. What happened?"

"We had a run in with a rogue coven and he ended up like this. That is why we are headed back to Romania."

"Well, there will be a wheelchair waiting with your entourage. You should change now. We will be arriving at LAX soon and you need to be ready. Everything you need should be in here."

Agent Lansdale handed her a garment bag and closed the window between them. Saria opened the bag and found a beautiful regal dress. The CIA really knew how to put on a show. She changed clothes and put on the jewelry they'd provided. Almost as soon as she was finished changing they arrived at LAX.

The driver stopped the vehicle and a team of both CIA and FBI agents deployed around the car. Agent Lansdale opened the door and helped them both out. He set Rick in a wheelchair and pushed him in. A team of skycaps came, unloaded their luggage, and rolled it into the terminal. She helped Rick to sit up straight and to adjust his disguising sunglasses. The media had been rushing to get pictures of the couple as they passed through the airport. She moved with the grace of a princess and followed Rick's wheelchair to the security checkpoint. Agent Lansdale presented their documents, and the TSA agent passed them through after making a phone call to his supervisor. The entourage continued through the airport. Once they reached the gate, the agents waited until they were finished boarding. Agent Lansdale handed a cooler to the flight attendant, saying that the Lord cel Tinar was on a special diet and the contents were to be kept cold. She accepted it and told him they were expecting it because they had already been informed. They rolled Rick onto the plane and settled him into his seat. Saria looked around as she sat next to him and held his hand. First-class was empty except for a couple of other passengers, but none were seated close to them. Once the plane was airborne, she felt much better. She raised the arm of the seat and reclined both of their seats. She snuggled to Rick and got some much-needed sleep.

After several hours, the flight attendant came and asked them about refreshments. Saria asked for her husband's special drink. The attendant pulled out an insulated bottle from the chilled section of her cart and handed it to Saria along with two cups. Saria poured two cups of the cool blood and gave one to Rick, who drank it a little faster than he had been. She drank the other one. She felt the energy course through her. Her enhanced senses could hear Rick's racing heartbeat. She felt him and he still had a high fever. She knew something was terribly wrong. Could it have been the green gel residue on the knife?

She poured them both another glass. She closed up the bottle and handed it back to the flight attendant to put away. She laid the seats back down and snuggled up to Rick. She heard him weakly say, "I love you, Saria." Then he fell back to sleep. She cried herself to sleep.

She had been asleep for a long time when the flight attendant told her they were landing in Romania. She sat them both up. She took her cup to the bathroom, cut her arm, and ran blood into the cup, along with the fresh blood the attendant had poured before she woke them. She brought it out to Rick and helped him to drink it. He drank the blood a little stronger than before, but he was still visibly weak. Soon she felt the plane start its descent. The attendant came to help her adjust Rick's seat and seat belt. Not soon enough, the plane landed in the main airport in Budapest.

Chapter IX

Once the plane parked at the gate, Saria helped Rick up, and she and the attendant got him into the waiting wheelchair. Then Saria pushed him up the ramp. Once in the airport proper, she could see the entourage waiting for them, led by her father. After someone took Rick's wheelchair, she ran up to him, then gave him a hug and kiss on the cheek.

"Thank you for meeting us, Father," she stated with angst. "Alex is very sick."

"Don't worry; we will get him help right away."

He led them to a waiting car. Their luggage was loaded in the limousine. Once they were settled, Saria explained what was going on to Stefan. He rubbed his head and was at a loss. They drove a long time to reach the Colony. After what seemed hours to Saria, the limo finally pulled through the gate. The driver stopped the car in front of a very large hospital.

"The hospital as ordered, sir," the driver said.

"Thank you, Radu," he said to the driver. He then turned to Saria. "Let's get him inside, and bring that knife."

Saria opened the luggage and rummaged until she found the wrapped knife. She let the luggage be moved to their residence. She carried the knife inside, with the staff watching her with caution. She carried it swiftly to where they had Rick and handed it to the doctor. He looked very closely at the knife. He scraped some of the gel, smelled it, and sent it to the lab for processing. He had them draw several tubes of blood and sent them to the lab.

"So this is the man, is it? Your CIA friend felt it was very important he come straight to the hospital."

"Father, he is only partially turning. Look at this wound," she said uncovering the wound.

"And you have been feeding him blood, both donor and yours?"

"Yes, I have probably given him a cup or two of mine and several pints of donor. I was afraid he wouldn't tolerate fresh. Otherwise, I would have tried that. Help him, Father."

"How am I to know he won't turn out like the other one? Since you are here, there has been an enclave called to decide what to do about Nickolea."

"Rick makes my thirst less, makes the pain better, and without him I could not survive. You used to tell me I would know when I found the one, and I have."

"Stefan, listen to the child; she knows her mate just as you do," her mother said as she walked up. "How are you, my child?" she said, kissing Saria on the forehead.

"My heart is breaking, Mother. He is the one and I cannot live without him. Please help him," she said with tears streaming down her face.

"Stefan, make it so. Our child cannot be heartbroken. The Enclave will have to accept my decision."

"Yes, my wife," Stefan said, calling for the doctor. "Heal him, no matter the cost. The mistress orders it."

"Yes, Lord Stefan." The doctor bowed and immediately went to work on Rick.

"We will make him well, baby. Let us leave the doctor to his work. You need some rest."

"No, I cannot leave him. What if he wakes up? What if he needs me? What if—?"

Saria's parents dragged her out the door with many more questions still on her lips and put her in the car. After a short drive, they arrived at the house that Saria had lived in for fifty years of her life as she was learning to be a vampire. The neighborhood had not changed a bit. She jumped out of the car and ran upstairs. Her room was still the same as she had left it. She could tell it had a new occupant, though. There were pictures on the desk of a young woman and her parents, and the smell was wrong. She walked back downstairs.

"We adopted another wayward waif," Stefan told her. "Now that you are to be married, you should have your own home, not live with your parents. Come with me."

They ran into a young woman as they were headed out the door. She stopped them and spoke to Stefan.

"Father, is this my older sister?"

"Yes, it is, Esmeralda. This is Lady Stefania cel Tinar." He stated.

"Welcome to the family little sister," Saria said hugging her weakly.

"Her mate is very ill and in the hospital. So to cheer her up a little, I am showing her their new home. You go on upstairs and start your homework, I will be home soon."

"Yes father, good to meet you Saria."

"Good to meet you too."

Esmerelda headed on into the house and up the stairs. Stefan led Saria out the door and down the road. They made two turns, and in front of her stood a seventeenth-century Spanish-style villa. They walked to the front door, and Stefan slid in a skeleton key to unlock it. Saria reached past him and pushed the door open. It reminded her of the family vacation villa in southern Spain. She looked at the marble floors and all the fixtures. While she was looking, Stefan received a call on his cell.

"Saria, come along. The doctor has news about Rick," he told her, pulling on her arm.

"Let's go, then," she responded, passing him almost pulling him through the door.

They raced back to the hospital. As soon as they stepped into the lobby, the doctor met them, led them to an elevator, and took them to the critical-care unit. He showed them to a conference room in the back. Inside the room were two other people. Stefan recognized two of the Colony's council members. They turned and smiled at Stefan and Saria.

"I have everyone here now," the doctor stated. "We have an issue. The knife that Saria's mate was stabbed with was coated with

RX-34. This was an agent developed for the immunization against vampirism. I can see by the look on your face that you know what this is. He said to Stefan.Just to catch Saria up, RX-34 was used to inoculate a group of human subjects. But instead of protecting against vampirism, it caused an incomplete conversion, and they mutated into monsters."

"The Reapers?" she asked.

"Yes, that's where they originated. We scrapped the entire project, and all the materials and notes were destroyed, or so we thought. Apparently, Nickolea has gotten his hands on some. What has saved Rick so far is the fact you have continued to give him your blood mixed with the donor blood. It is slowly overcoming the effects of the RX-34."

"Rick mentioned the rogues had turned a lab assistant to get access to the lab and the scientists. I wonder if that has anything to do with this?" she asked.

"It could, but we have to focus on saving Rick right now. We need to give him a transfusion of your blood. Since you turned him, he needs your vampirism viral cultures. A pint of whole blood should do it."

"Well, let's get started," she said, starting to pull her bodice off.

"The nurse will help you," the doctor said as a nurse walked in. The nurse led her away. He turned back to the group.

"Gentlemen, the reason you are here is the issue of the RX-34. All the logs state everything was destroyed, including all notes and research surrounding it. Either he has somehow recreated it, or some was missed. We need to check all the logs again to find that remaining RX-34. As you remember, some batches were worse than others. We also need to check into this lab the rogues gained access to, and see if it was one of our research labs."

"We must get a handle on this very quickly," said Stefan. "But right now, I must see to my daughter."

The other men excused him, wished him well, and went back to talking about the RX-34. Stefan walked out and over to the station, and a nurse led him to Rick's room. Saria lay on a cot with a needle in her arm, next to Rick, removing the pint of blood Rick so desperately needed. She had made them place her close so that she could hold his hand.

"Saria, how is he?"

She looked up at Stefan. "He is not waking up, but they say he is in a healing coma. His body is trying to throw off the effects of the RX-34, and my blood will save him. The doctor said so."

Stefan looked into her pleading eyes. "Yes, it can, he said. But be prepared in case it doesn't."

"But Father, it has to. He is my everything. I have never felt this way about anyone. You were right; I knew from the first moment I saw him."

The nurse looked at the bag connected to her arm, pulled out the needle, and disconnected the tubing. She then reconnected a new set and started the blood dripping into Rick's arm. Saria had the cot moved and pulled a chair to his bedside. She sat holding his hand in both of hers. She could feel his fever had broken. Stefan tried to get her to leave the room, but she absolutely refused. She would not leave Rick's side again. Stefan had blood brought to her along with food. She ate and drank very little. After a couple of hours, Rick started to move and groan. The nurse left to get the doctor. Within a few minutes the doctor came in and had them draw more blood and check his lab work. Within the hour, the test results came back.

"Saria, the transfusion worked. His cultures are where they should be," the doctor said, looking at the results. "He is fully turned. He should be able to leave this evening and will be much better tomorrow."

She leaped up and kissed the doctor. "Thank you, oh, thank you. That is the best news ever. Please call my father and let him know."

Rick was groaning and calling her name. She ran over and kissed his lips over and over again. He cracked his eyes open. She could see the pain in them; however, she could also see the joy in them that she was there. She climbed in the bed with him and snuggled close. The doctor and nurse left them alone as they both fell asleep.

After a couple more hours, Rick woke up. When he did, Saria snapped awake. She opened her eyes, staring into his. "Hello, my dearest Saria. How are you today, love?"

The biggest smile grew on her face. "Wonderful, my love, now that you are recovering."

"Excellent. What has happened to me? Where are we? I don't remember much after getting stabbed—except I do remember you made me drink the most terrible-tasting stuff. What was it?"

"Blood."

"Blood? So you made me a vampire?" he asked, drawing in a breath. "I asked you to, didn't I?"

"Yes, you did. You said as long as we could be together."

"I did not say anything as corny as that, did I?"

"Oh, you did, and you said later that you loved me."

"Oh my god, I didn't. You must have some kind of drugs in your blood," he said, reaching over to kiss her.

The doctor walked in with Stefan. "All right Saria, he can go home, but you have to make sure he gets plenty of blood. He shouldn't need any more of yours, but if he isn't progressing, feel free to feed him more. Stefan has informed me that your fridge has been properly stocked. Do you have any questions?"

"No," Saria responded. "Baby, do you have any?"

"What about strenuous activity?"

"No sex for a week, no swordplay for a couple of days."

"No—"

"Rick, don't even ask. I'll explain that later. Everyone get out while I help him get dressed," she interrupted.

They looked at each other and left the room. Saria looked in the mini closet and pulled out one of his Lord cel Tinar outfits. She looked at the wound; it was completely healed. Only a thin red line remained of the jagged rip. She rubbed her hand across it, and he did not even move. She smiled as she rubbed her hands playfully across his abdomen. He smiled at her playfulness. He continued getting dressed. He was a bit stiff but otherwise felt good. He kissed Saria, and she held him in the embrace.

As soon as he was dressed, she opened the door. Everyone came back in. The doctor had headed on to his next patient. The nurse helped them collect all Rick's belongings and brought a wheelchair for his ride out. They exited the hospital to a sports car at the door. Saria helped him into the passenger's seat and got in the driver's seat. She drove him around the Colony and pointed out different things from her youth. After several minutes of driving, she pulled up to their seventeenth-century Spanish-style villa. She pulled into the garage and closed the door.

They walked into the house from the garage entrance. The pristine white marble floors gleamed. Greek, Roman, and Romanian statues circled the walls in art nooks. Carpathian columns were scattered throughout the room. They walked through the entry and arrived in the family room. A seventy-inch LCD TV mostly filled one of the walls. She led him through the halls and into the master bedroom. A king-sized four-poster bed dominated it. The linens on it were of a fine silk. She rang a bell, and a servant came out and brought them a change of clothes.

"Welcome home, Lady Saria, or should I use cel Tinar? It is your choice. Dinner will be ready at 5:00 p.m. Will you need assistance changing clothes?"

"No, we are fine. Please make sure we have sufficient beverage. Lord cel Tinar requires a little more than normal during his recovery."

"Yes, ma'am. Will there be anything else?" she asked as she curtsied.

"No, that will be all."

The young woman curtsied and left the room. Saria turned to Rick and helped him change to house clothes. She then changed herself. He took a deep breath. His enhanced sense of smell filled with the fragrance of her. Then he noticed something, walked over to the window, and looked out over a fragrant garden of flowers. He turned to see Saria changing clothes, and he could see her smooth skin with much more definition. He could hear her heart beating; it was a soft, comfortable pace. He walked over to her. He could hear it increase in rate as he touched her. His sense of touch was so enhanced he could feel the bumps in her skin as the tiny muscles connected to the hairs on her arms started to contract, causing the gooseflesh to appear at his soft touch..

"Learning about your new senses, my love?"

"I understand what you mean about the fragrance of the flowers. They have the most wonderful scent. As for my senses, I feel so much more . . . alive."

"This is only the beginning. Wait until you smell the blood coursing in a human's veins. It is a very unusual experience the first time. Now it is time to go downstairs—time for you to taste blood for the first time fully conscious. Oh, you are now Alexandrel cel Tinar when outside the Colony. We are Lord and Lady cel Tinar, and that is how everyone will address us until we get used to it. You received a Romanian identity upon arriving at the Colony. It is how the Romanian government interacts with the vampire community. So I will be addressing you as Alex, and you should address me as Stef or Stefania unless you are using a term of endearment."

"Wow, this is a lot to absorb after coming out of a coma."

"This will have to be a crash course. Father will present us to the populace tomorrow. Follow me down the stairs. Nobles do not walk. They glide. No bouncing."

He watched as she approached the stairs. She glided down them like a spirit. He followed trying to imitate but failed miserably. Saria laughed at the sight. Rick looked at her, a bit cross. She came over and kissed him. He felt the softness of her lips. She put a large book on his head and told him to walk and not to let it fall. Rick took one step, and the book fell. She giggled. He looked at her and smiled. He put the book on his head, then bobbed and weaved to keep the book on his head. He then took it off and handed it to her. She laughed and took the book and placed it on her head and glided across the room. She went to the bookshelves, took a book off an upper shelf, and walked back. The book on her head never moved. Rick shook his head.

"Actually, men strut, women glide. I just thought it would be cute to watch you," she admitted.

"You," Rick was shocked how quickly he darted to her and had her in his arms. He leaned her back, and kissed her neck.

"Wow, that was fast," Saria said, a bit surprised herself. "You are getting the hang of this enhanced-human thing."

They continued to the dining room. As they entered, the staff escorted them to the seats both at the head and at the foot of the table. Rick looked at Saria strangely. She returned the look with a shrug. She seemed as confused as he did. After they were seated, the butler escorted their guests to the table. First were Stefan and Ecaterina, who were seated next to Saria and Rick, respectively. Then each of the members of the city council and their wives were welcomed in. Each alternately placed with each member seated next to either Rick or Saria in a gentleman-lady way. Soon all the guests were seated.

"Sorry for the intrusion, Alexandrel, Stefania, but the council wished to meet Alex, and I thought this would be the best way: an informal dinner," Stefan started.

"Father, this is not really informal," Saria stated.

"No one is dressed in formal state attire, therefore it is informal. Besides, we have some things to discuss before the Enclave in a week. It is being called because of the attention Nickolea is causing to all of us. He is instigating Gluts all over the world to throw off the mantle of secrecy and expose us to the world to take over. As you know from history, Stef, that does not work very well. The humans get scared and kill anyone they think might be a vampire. The problem is since you created him, you are responsible for him. The Enclave is being called to determine what is to be done about both of you."

"What? What are you talking about? Stef has nothing to do with what he is doing," Rick stated.

"Alex, I am sorry, but Father is correct."

"What? What kind of crazy rule is that?"

"One I helped write and pushed through an enclave about three hundred years ago. It is called Saria's Rule, or the Law. We had a period of irresponsible behavior by vampires creating other vampires—my sire was one—and they were attacking so many people, it was almost disastrous for everyone. The Colony was attacked, and many homes were burned. We had to kill many young vampires to satisfy the people that we were not to be destroyed. That is what Father was referring to earlier. I could lose my life. If not, I may lose the right to make vampires, and if I do, all vampires I have created could be destroyed."

"Like me?"

"Yes, and Nickolea and any he has created. It destroys an entire line. Since I killed my sire when he tried to usurp my father's throne, I am the head of the line, and as such, I am ultimately responsible for the entire line's actions. I also inherited all my sire's lines. Thankfully, it was only a couple. However, because I am a line head, it makes me an elder. Therefore I am held to a higher standard."

"But how can you be responsible for his actions?"

"If I had not made him a vampire, he would have died long ago, and there would not have been this issue. If I had done what I should have when he started this and killed him, we would not have this issue. I am, as Father said, responsible. But I thought there was some hope for him. I thought I still loved him, but after meeting you, I now know I just pitied him."

"So what can we do?"

"She and her line have to prove they are worth saving."

"How do we do that?"

"Well, you and Nickolea are her immediate line, which holds the most sway. We know what they will say about Nickolea. We have to prove your worth, and you will have to make Nickolea no longer a threat. But first, we have to survive this enclave."

One of the council members chimed in about this time. "The Colony is behind both of you one hundred percent. We have to find as many allies as possible to support Alex. Do you know of anyone?"

"The only person I could possibly think of is a Japanese detective I worked with several years ago, Kinoshi Kimura."

Stefan looked at Rick and then Saria. "Oh yes, Kinoshi Kimura.

I had forgotten, Saria. He is the leader of the Japanese contingent to the Enclave. He has been killing rogue vampires in Japan for years. He mentioned a human who was instrumental in breaking his hardest cases. The human was an American psychologist. It was you, but you were more than just helping, weren't you? What exactly were you doing?"

"Yes, I worked with Kinoshi for several years tracking the rogues. I would hunt them, then help them eliminate them."

"Your organization, the Clan of the Divine Shadow, has been very active in eliminating these rogues worldwide. Wait—did you say you helped eliminate them?"

"Yes."

A smile came over both Saria and Rick's faces. Everyone looked at them oddly. Rick looked at Saria pleadingly. She nodded her head. Rick stood and turned to his valet. The man nodded and immediately left. Rick sat back down and held his head in his hands. Soon the man returned with the katana wrapped in the simple bamboo scabbard. He handed it to Rick.

"Gentlemen, this is the sword of the Kensai of the Clan of the Divine Shadow," He pulled it out far enough so that they could see the engraving next to the blade. "This is the symbol of the clan of which I am a sword master."

Everyone looked at Rick, then at Saria. She nodded her head "yes." Rick put the sword back in its sheath and set it next to his place. Saria signaled the butler to start serving the first course. Everyone relaxed and settled into the dinner. They slowly moved through the courses. Rick was required to drink a glass of blood with each course. He looked at everyone else's glasses, and they were half-full, but every time his became half-full, it was refilled.

"I realize that blood is necessary for survival and my recovery, but I really don't want to become a Glut."

Saria laughed. "My dearest Alex, you have to drink much more than this to become a Glut, but we will let you have a break. Finish that one, and Radu will get you a glass of wine."

"Thank you for the mercy. That stuff is tolerable for the first glass, maybe two, but after that, it is hideous. How do the Gluts do it?"

"Well," Stefan started, "have you ever had alcohol?"

"Yes, of course" Rick answered.

"It is kind of like that. It is not that good at first, but you will quickly develop a taste for it. The extreme faction of the Gluts drink it for the effects they get. Once you are well, drink a quart of blood, and you will see what I mean. While you are still recovering, you will not have any of the extreme effects of blood."

"Wow. Is there, like, vampire school or something? There is a lot to learn."

"Stefania can help you. She is probably one of the most knowledgeable of all of us. She has done the most research. She is quite smart, you know."

"Oh, I know that. She is brilliant."

"Don't let him fool you. He would have discovered the Colony in another year or two of casual research. He is very intelligent."

"Oh yes, tell me about this research," one of the council members said.

"It started as a casual interest. I noted an increase in the number of vampire-type attacks about ten years ago. I had done a master's thesis on gang mentality and violence. After that, I decided to do one on delusional criminal behavior. The most common one I discovered was the vampire delusion. Well, now I know that quite a few were not delusional. I continued collecting data from all over the world.

"That is actually where I met Kinoshi. I helped him break several cases of vampire delusional phenomenon, as I called it. It was then he introduced me to his master and I became part of the Clan. I was tracking rogue vampires while I mastered the sword. The increased activity and the escape of the remaining members of the coven of rogues in New York led me back to LA. I was collecting the data in LA and presented a lot of my information to the police chief. A few months later, I was stabbed with a poisoned knife. Well, Saria—I mean, Stefania—did warn me."

"Oh, Alex," Saria started looking at him. "I think Rick Smythe should stay dead. I think it would be better if Alexandrel cel Tinar were to buy his house and Saria de la Rosa should inherit every-thing. It would eliminate any complications and get the assassins off you. Saria will eventually have to die, also to be replaced by Stefania cel Tinar. Once we are married, anyway."

"Stef, I was thinking the same thing. I am going to have to hunt down Nickolea and kill him. I don't need any interruptions, and neither do you. You will have to give up the halfway house. We can always start another one in the cel Tinar name somewhere other than LA. You are too well known there."

"All right. If you can give up the only life you have ever known to save me, I can give up one I only have had for a decade."

Rick stood up. "Rick Smythe is now officially deceased. I will from this day forth be known as Alexandrel cel Tinar."

"Documents will be drawn up in the morning to be filed with the Romanian government. You will have a record all the way back to your birth, including ten years of military service. You retired with the rank of major. That is a requirement of the Roma-nian government. You will have ten years ahead of you of reserve service. If the government needs you, they can call you up. Only a drop in the bucket for someone who will live for hundreds more."

"I will make a couple of calls to make your death permanent in LA," Saria said. "I will send the will to the Los Angeles County Courthouse once it is signed tomorrow."

"It is done. Once I am better, we will return to the US and begin the search for Nickolea Dalakis."

"Remember, we have to get through the Enclave first," Stefan reminded him.

"I think that won't be a problem."

Alexandrel smiled.

Chapter X

lex woke early the next morning. He headed to the kitchen of the villa and was stopped by his valet, Radu, who led him to the family dining room. It held a much-smaller table for simple family meals. He sat, and they brought a simple breakfast of eggs, sausage, freshly baked bread, and a large glass of blood. He ate his breakfast. He went into the display room, took the katana from the wall, and started to do sword kata to warm up his new muscles.

The sword spun faster and more accurately than it ever had. He saw himself in the mirror. He looked like a whirlwind. He flipped the sword from hand to hand. Suddenly he turned and parried a dagger thrown at the back of his head. Standing behind him was Stefania, dressed in full fencing gear. She signaled to Radu, who brought him a full set of fencing gear. Alex quickly changed and took the foil and whipped it around.

"Time you mastered another sword, Lord Alex."

"Ah, the favored blade of the Romanian aristocracy. I cannot wait to learn from a master such as yourself. But the doctor said no foreplay, I mean, swordplay, for a couple of days."

"Let's see. No swordplay. We will do just drills, then. Nothing strenuous."

Stefania started carrying him through drill after drill. He felt his new body respond like nothing ever before. He was so much faster. He knew where blows were going to fall before they struck. He knew where the dagger she had thrown was during its entire journey. She continued the drills until around noon. They took a break and had a glass of wine. He was glad there was no blood this time, although he knew it would be there the next time.

As he continued the drills, Stefania started facing him while they drilled. She started doing attack drills while he did defense drills, and then they switched. Alex started to catch on to how they were interconnected and how they responded to each other. A defense for a strike each had their own, just like in other martial arts. After another couple of hours, they removed the gear and took real rapiers. They walked up to two practice dummies the servants had set up for them. She called out a strike, and they hit the dummy and retreated. She called another strike, and they struck the dummy and retreated. After about an hour of this repetition, they began to move in unison. Soon she stopped calling the strikes, they moved as one. He knew what the next would be.

After another hour, they took another break. This time, they each had a glass of blood. They began once again. Still, their movements were in perfect unison. He knew what she was thinking as soon as she thought it. They moved through each movement in perfect synchronization. Then each movement became more complex. Stefania smiled at him. He could tell she felt it too. She knew his every thought, every feeling. He started to smell that delicious fragrance that was her. He now knew it was not a perfume. It was a scent produced by her body, and it was intoxicating.

***

Stefania continued through the flurry of movements. She felt him in her head, and she knew she was in his. This feeling was something totally new and exhilarating for her. She smelled his scent and it was the most stimulating thing she had every smelled. Each vampire pair knew the other by their scent, and it was something beyond measure. She was amazed at all the new experiences engulfing her. She knew he had been smelling her scent before even becoming a vampire. She was entranced as they continued their dance of death. Attack to parry, they moved in absolute unison.

She looked up. It had been hours since their last break, and neither one felt the least bit tired. They continued locked in that dance. At that moment all doubt was gone from her mind; he was the one. Until now, she had only suspected it, but as they moved in unison, she knew. She looked at him and felt that he knew they were bound together forever and it pleased him. She knew they had to take a break, but she did not want this feeling to end.

They stopped simultaneously and as they stepped together, he kissed her deeply, passionately. She still felt him at the edge of her consciousness, and that provided her with a deep sense of comfort. She could feel it was the same for him. She continued to move with Alex mirroring her. It became a game as they moved synchronously. Stefania reached out, and Alex took her hand. She pulled him close and started to dance. He mirrored her movements.

They moved into a waltz and danced around the room. Their synchronistic movements were perfect. They flowed around the room without music. Slowly, quietly, music started and gradually increased in volume. They continued dancing around the room. The house staff watched as they glided around and around and smiled. They knew from their years with the vampires what had happened. Nothing was more romantic than when a couple bonded to each other. Their actions became one, always in touch with the other.

They also knew what it meant when one of them was killed. The pain and torment the other would suffer. They were very concerned for them with the upcoming enclave. If she was determined to be unsuitable as a dame and her line had to be destroyed, she would have to suffer not only a large amount of shame, but to lose her mate would be unbearable for her. Alex and Stefania continued to dance for several songs. However, they eventually stopped and went to get ready for the assembly that night, where Alexandrel cel Tinar would be presented to the populace of the Colony and the Romanian officials who monitored it.

They took their shower together but were then separated by their staff to get ready. This was not only Alex's coming out, but their first state function together. As Radu and his staff helped Alex dress and get prepared, he also gave him a crash course in court etiquette. Alex quickly absorbed as much as he could. His etiquette classes he had taken in college for his international studies class was a help, but this was hundreds of years of specialized etiquette for a very special people.

The next hours went quickly. Alex wore a Romanian army dress uniform with his major rank gleaming on his shoulder. His gold shoulder boards were a contrast to the dark black of the cloth. A silver tassel dangled from the shoulder board—on it was three red stripes.

"Radu, what is the tassel for?"

"My lord, it is a Hunter's tassel. It is only worn by the elite Rogue Hunters. Each thin red stripe represents a rogue killed and a thick stripe represents a rogue sire."

"Why do I have three?"

"Well sir, the ones you helped stop in Japan count, so the city council authorized them. Plus, when it comes time for the enclave, they will indicate your dedication to the protection of the race. It will go a long way, sir."

Radu looked him over very closely. They trimmed all the loose threads and removed any remaining debris. His highly polished equestrian boots gleamed in the well-lit dressing room. Once Radu was happy, Alex walked to the foyer to wait for the Lady cel Tinar. They waited another twenty minutes, and from the other dressing room emerged the most beautiful woman Alex had ever seen. Stefania cel Tinar was dressed in a flowing white ball gown. Diamond- and sapphire-encrusted combs held back her raven-black hair. Her plump lips were the most beautiful red, a contrast to her pale, milky-white complexion. She stepped forward, gliding across the floor to Alex. He took her hand and walked her to the carriage waiting outside. He guided her into the carriage and then followed with the assistance of Radu. Her maid, Alina, took her place beside her, and Radu took his place beside the driver.

The driver guided the carriage to the assembly hall for the meeting. He stopped the horses with the door above a red carpet. The doormen helped Lady cel Tinar out of the carriage and then

Lord cel Tinar. They entered the large foyer, her hand palm down on the back of his, followed by their staff. As they entered, the courtesan at the entrance announced them. Everyone turned to watch them.

They were the most radiant couple in the room. They walked in and Lord Stefan and Ecaterina met them. They led them through the crowd and introduced them as his daughter and son-in-law. Everyone gave their well wishes as they progressed through the crowd. Toward the door to the inner assembly hall, Alex saw a familiar face. He told Stefan to move toward that face. Soon they walked up to Kinoshi Kimura.

Alex hugged him. "Kinoshi, I am so glad to see you."

"As am I, my brother. Is this the lovely Lady cel Tinar, your dame?"

"Yes, it is. She saved my life in more ways than one."

She blushed. "Welcome, Lord Kimura, to the Colony." She made an all-encompassing sweep of her arm. "Our home."

"Why thank you, Lady, and you can call me Kim or Kinoshi."

"So why did you come early?" Alex asked.

"Well, as soon as I heard that your life might be in danger, I was on the next plane here. I have told you about hunting alone. I thought we needed to talk before the enclave."

"Thank you, brother, and I know. I am very much going to need your support."

"I know this is going to be a difficult battle, but not any worse than we have fought before. Oh, and your tassel is short two red stripes. We killed a total of five rogues with your assistance that you will accept credit for. And you also need a thick one for the sire."

"Wow, my legend grows as we speak. Stefania brought the sword with us. I will wear it during the enclave if you think it appropriate."

"You know better than to ask me. Of course I feel it is appropriate. Really, you should have it here."

Radu turned and spoke to a footman behind the group, and he took off at a run. "It will be here before the assembly starts, sir."

"Thank you, Radu," Alex said.

"It is my honor, sir."

"That issue is solved. How many members are here from the clan?" Alex asked.

"About fifteen, lord. It was all I could get here on such short notice," Kinoshi said, smiling.

"Kinoshi, we are friends. No need for extra deference."

"There is when I am reporting on the status of the clan to one of its lords. When this is over, you should come see the cherry blossoms. Though they are not as beautiful as Stefania here."

Again, Stefania blushed. "Why thank you, Kinoshi."

About that time, the footman returned with Alex's katana. He took it and slid it in his belt. Kinoshi looked at it and smiled. He clapped Alex on the shoulder. They shook hands and moved on to more of the assemblage until they had greeted almost all of them. Kinoshi walked with them, deferring to Alex by walking a bit behind him but within reach of his lord. As they approached the entry to the assembly hall, Stefan stopped Alex and replaced his tassel with one with the appropriate number and kind of stripes Kinoshi had relayed.

"We want you appropriately represented here, because this could mean your life. Lord Kimura is here because your and my daughter's lives are at stake. It does my soul good to see the look of a bonded vampire in her eyes. It is a happiness that has eluded her for many centuries."

Kinoshi looked at them both. "I had not noticed, Lord Stefan. Congratulations, Alex, Stefania. I'd better get an invitation to the wedding."

Alex looked a bit confused. "You can see a change in us?"

"Of course, bonding changes a vampire, although it is a curse and a blessing. As glorious as it is now, should one of you be killed, the consequences are as terrible as the benefits are great. The surviving one will feel a loss greater than you can ever imagine. Imagine losing a piece of your soul, never to return. They can never achieve true happiness or peace again. That is why this enclave is so important, especially to Stefania."

All the blood drained from Alex's face. "I had no idea. Do not worry, my darling, I will not fail you."

"I do not worry. I know you will not allow any harm to befall me. But to matters at hand: it is time."

They walked into the assembly hall and took their places on the stage as all the citizens of the Colony came in and sat in row after row of seats. Finally, the entire hall was full. Lord Stefan stood and welcomed the group. They conducted some city business that required the entire populace vote. Soon they came to the part where they introduced Lord Kinoshi as a special guest, and he proceeded to describe the grand acts of Lord Alexandrel cel Tinar in Japan. He was sure to emphasize the part where he was instrumental to the destruction of at least five rogue vampires and their sire whom the Enclave had decreed destroyed even before it was his responsibility.

When he had finished, Lord Stefan stood and introduced the lord and lady themselves. Everyone noted his hunter's tassel. After they sat, he introduced the local Romanian officials, including the commanding officer of the local post. Alexandrel and Stefania were required to speak for a few minutes each. Finally, after all the pomp and circumstance was over, the entire group moved to the large banquet hall for dinner. After dinner, there was a formal ball welcoming the two newest members of the community and their special guest. Alex and Stefania started the first dance, and then Stefan and Ecaterina soon followed. Kinoshi found an unescorted lady and danced with her. The evening went late into the night. They finally found themselves on their way home.

The next week found them meeting privately with prominent citizens and Romanian officials. Kinoshi and Alex spent many hours developing strategies, and Stefania spent many hours with Alex fencing. Stefania also spent many hours with Stefan and Ecaterina, planning other strategies to use on the Enclave to save their lives. As the days clicked by, they both felt more confident in their destiny, but also more trapped. They frequently took solace in each other's arms, leaving the rest of the world behind them.

Finally, the first day of the enclave had arrived. Representatives from all over the world came to the assembly hall in the Colony. An enclave only occurred for the most terrible and influential of issues that related to the entire vampire race. Mundane proceedings filled most of the first day. Individuals placed their petty problems at the feet of the Enclave. They all received judgments; some were happy, some not. There were even a couple of petitions by individuals to regain their right to reestablish a line. Since once that right was lost it was very difficult to regain, those petitions were summarily denied.

Stefania continued to worry about their fate. She did not worry for her right to make vampires, but worried for Alex's life. However, it would be tomorrow before they could plead their case. She hoped Stefan's plan would work. She knew that Kinoshi and Alex had formulated one with Stefan's help also. They had some of the best political strategists helping them. She just wished Alex could be with her instead of in his own accused's booth. She was alone in the middle of hundreds of vampires.

The Enclave was constituted of one or two members of every major coven of vampires in the world. The assembly hall of the Colony was the only building that was able to hold them all in one room and it was filled to capacity. Many of them were here particularly for Stefania's trial. Since she was known all over, everyone came to see what would happen to one of the most famous and infamous vampires in the world. She had killed her sire as a young vampire, which made her legendary in itself. Most vampires had lived for decades, even centuries, before they would stand up to their sire or dame. She was a mere two years raised.

She was also the dame of the infamous Nickolea Dalakis. He was perhaps the most dangerous vampire to his own kind ever raised. For that crime, she could lose everything. A sire or dame must teach a raised vampire not to put the species at risk, and Nickolea was doing just that. She had stopped him once, right after she raised him. However, she was still too young to keep him under control. Now this put both her and Alex, her love and bonded mate, in deadly peril.

Finally, the Enclave finished with the petitions and was ready to read the charges. Stefania stood straight as the magistrate of the Colony stood at the podium. She could feel Alex's support on the edge of her consciousness. She longed for him to be standing next to her, but that would never happen, at least not on the first day. The magistrate tapped the mike and cleared his throat.

"Ladies and gentlemen, we have been called here to hear testimony in the case of Crown Princess Rosaria of Spain, of House Habsburg, now known as Lady Stefania cel Tinar. She has committed a most heinous atrocity. She has raised a vampire who threatens the entire species to accomplish his personal goals. She is charged with failing to pass to him the importance of not risking the species after raising him, and failing to stop him once he started on the path he is currently on. Now she brings another she raised upon his deathbed. He is another unknown factor. Like her previous failure, she raised him based on emotion, without thought or consideration.

"We must decide the value of this new vampire and whether she will keep the right to raise vampires. This enclave is merciful and will take into account that she and Lord Alexandrel cel Tinar have bonded and the consequences to her if we determine he is to be destroyed. Does anyone stand for the accused?"

Two men stepped out of the crowd. Kinoshi Kimura walked over to Alex's booth, and Stefan walked over to Stefania's. Once they were in position, Kinoshi was the first to speak.

"I, Kinoshi Kimura, stand for Daimyo Richard Smythe, Lord of the Shadow, now known as Lord Alexandrel cel Tinar, Lord of the Shadow. He is well known to me and is a friend and Lord of the Clan of the Divine Shadow."

A murmur went over the crowd. The Clan of the Divine Shadow had spent the last ten centuries tracking and killing rogue vampires all over the world. Rick had led them secretly for the past ten years. They executed the will of the Enclave. Lord Kinoshi Kimura was one of its leaders, second only to the Lord of the

Shadow himself. After a minute or two, ten men walked out to Alex's booth. They spoke with one voice.

"The Clan of the Divine Shadow stands with our lord, he who has hunted rogue vampires beside us before it was his responsibility as a vampire to do so."

With that, Kinoshi continued, "Alex, prior to becoming a vampire and our lord, assisted me and the clan in hunting numerous vampires, specifically in Japan: five rogue vampires and their sire. He was also in command of the contingent in Los Angeles, the group hunting Nickolea's rogue coven. As you can see, he bears the silver tassel of an elite hunter. It bears five small rings of rogue vampires and the thick ring of a renegade sire. It does not include all the rogue vampires he ended in Los Angeles. This all before it was his responsibility as a vampire. He did it because it was the right thing to do. With a heart like his, there is no doubt that he is worth saving."

There was another murmur among the members of the Enclave. The silver tassel glinted in the light. The clan stood in a defensive position around Alex. Kinoshi stood behind his right shoulder. The deference was obvious. Kinoshi Kimura was one of the most revered vampires of his age. The Enclave quieted down as Stefan began to speak.

"Ladies and gentlemen, Stefania is my adopted daughter after her own parents deserted her on a distant foreign shore, for her to never hear from them again. She came to me a broken, lost child. She had to kill her sire in order to protect the family that deserted her. Longing for the love she had lost, she fell for the wiles of a young Romanian servant, Nickolea Dalakis. He promised her love, and once he got what he wanted from her, he tried to kill her and left her for dead. All she got was more heartache. She tried to teach him, but all he could see was the power he imagined he had. She stopped him once, but her feelings for him stopped her from ending his evil. She requested assistance from this august body in correcting the very crime she is being accused of and was denied.

"She has learned from those mistakes and now has a bonded

mate who has filled the emptiness that drove her to raise Nickolea Dalakis. If you should decide to punish her by killing this new mate, you know the consequences. You do not just stop her from making any more vampires, you will destroy her—destroy someone who has served beside you in enclaves and helped you write the laws that you want to enforce on her now. So as you contemplate the fate you will place upon these two, remember that it could have been anyone here to make the same mistake. Remember all the good they have done for the entire vampire race." Stefan stepped up to Stefania's booth and kissed her cheek. Ecaterina walked up and stood on her other side.

The Colony's council walked up and stood between the booths and the president of the council spoke. "We, the Colony council, will stand for both these vampires. Both are Thin Bloods. By decree of this enclave five hundred years ago, Thin Bloods were deemed incapable of being a threat to the vampire race. We, as the ruling council of the Colony, feel there is no threat to our citizens, and our citizens feel there is no danger. We are, by fact, the single largest collection of vampires in the world, bar none. If we have no fear, why should the remaining covens?"

The magistrate stood back up at the podium. "The Enclave shall deliberate. We will notify you when we have reached a decision. The accused are excused to return to their home." Escorts came to the booths and led the cel Tinars out of the enclave and back to their home. They went to bed and snuggled together, spending as much time as they could in case the decision went against them.

The deliberations continued for two days. All the pros and cons were weighed numerous times. Kinoshi and Stefan both presented and represented all that the two had done for vampires as a race. The opposition presented and represented the dangers that Nickolea presented, and claimed that Alex still presented an unknown factor. Kinoshi rebutted with the fact that Alex held five rogue marks and a sire, and was eligible for many more he would never claim, so he was very much a known factor. That made him an asset, instrumental in ending those threats even as a human. As a vampire, he would be an even greater asset. In addition, as Lord of the Clan of the Divine Shadow, he was entitled to all those victories also, though he would never claim them, either.

Stefan reminded them that because Stefania and Alexandrel were bonded, his death would mean a death sentence for her also, because she could never recover. He also reminded them that they'd had Count Cazacul's wife put to death for her crimes, and the rampage he went on had been one of the most deadly in Romanian history. He did not think Stefania would go on a killing spree, but she would most likely become depressed and find a way to take her own life. They could not do that to her after everything she had done for this very enclave and for the entire species.

Finally, the Enclave came to a decision. The escorts brought Alex and Stefania back to the assembly hall. Alex was dressed in his finest military uniform. His hunter tassel glared at the assemblage against the black of the vampire forces. On his head, he wore a gold circlet, indicating his status as a Romanian lord. Today he wore two swords: the katana of the Lord of the Clan of the Divine Shadow and the sword of the Masters of the Dragon Clans. Another gasp came from a section of the assemblage that recognized the second one he wore. Stefania wore a beautiful white gown covered in silks, her hair held by a golden coronet of the crown princess of Spain. They stood in the same booth today, and everyone around could see the difference. Their supporters returned to their sides as they waited for the pronouncement.

The magistrate walked to the podium. "Ladies and gentlemen, the Enclave has reached a decision. It has two parts. First part: Alexandrel cel Tinar, because of his and his clan's extensive assistance in stopping rogues and because of the damage it would invoke on Stefania cel Tinar, will be allowed to live. Stefania cel Tinar will retain her status as a dame but will have her raising rights limited for one decade. She must consult with a member of the Enclave before raising any more vampires. Her advisors will be Lord Kinoshi Kimura and High Lord Stefan.

"The second part of the proclamation is that all parts of their old lives must be eliminated. Dr. Rick Smythe died from his in-juries in LA County General Hospital after a long stay. Saria de la Rosa perished in a plane crash in rural California yesterday. All their holdings are heretofore transferred to the Lord and Lady cel Tinar by way of several intermediaries. The Lord and Lady cel Tinar will be assigned as agents of the Enclave to stop any threats to the peace and safety of the vampire species. Their first task will be to stop Nickolea Dalakis by any and all means necessary.

"You will begin your mission once the Lord cel Tinar has been released by his physician. Once your mission is complete, we will allow you to return to normal lives. However, if needed, we are free to call you back into service at any time. The Lord and Lady cel Tinar will now be made members of the Enclave. Lord cel Tinar will be a representative of the Clan of the Divine Shadow, and Lady cel Tinar will return to her place as a representative of the Colony. Please take your places."

Alex and Stefania took their places with their delegations. Kinoshi gave Alex a big hug when he arrived with the clan. The enclave continued late into the evening, discussing damage con-trol for Nickolea's actions. Alex concentrated on catching up on all the information Kinoshi was feeding into his ear while he paid attention to the proceedings. What really shocked him was that he could do both—split his attention between both the speaker and what Kinoshi was telling him—and he did not miss any of ei-ther. Suddenly he raised his hand to stop the flow of information from Kinoshi. He requested the attention of the Enclave.

"Let's use our greatest ally, disbelief," Alex said. "Humans want to believe it is anything but vampires killing people."

"So what do you suggest?" came from the assemblage.

"We give them a vampire cult. It would take a little work and a bit of staging. We design a 'fang knife,' toss a few in a den or other secret hideout, put some evidence of the killings, such as blood from the victims in bottles or jars and all over the floor. It has to appear they are getting careless. It might actually anger Nicky that 'humans' are stealing his thunder. If he is as much of a megalomaniac as I think he is, that will drive him up a wall. He loves the fear and attention he is getting. I believe that if we don't take some of that away, he will announce himself.

"He thinks he killed me and that Saria died in a plane crash. That means he doesn't think anyone knows he is doing it. He will have to announce himself, so someone will know he is the mastermind of this and that they should fear him."

"Interesting. If we act fast enough, he may reveal himself and be only considered another deluded victim," Stefan replied. "That might disarm him a bit, even make him a bit less cautious."

"The fact he came to Saria and told her he was the one who killed me shows me that he has to have people know."

"Alex, you are as good as everyone says," Stefan replied. "Let's make this a priority. Can the clan handle the staging?"

Alex looked at Kinoshi, and Kinoshi snapped his fingers. One of the clan pulled out a knife shaped like a vampire's mouth with two large protruding "fangs." Alex presented it to the Enclave. "I already took the liberty of having a prototype made."

Stefan shook his head. "Present a plan with a solution in progress. My daughter did choose well this time." Stefan looked at the Enclave. Everyone's eyes locked on the knife. "It needs to be tested. Stefania, stand ready."

Stefan signaled for a human to be brought in. He asked the man if it was okay if they tested this knife on him. He feebly answered yes. Alex handed the knife back, and his Shadow walked up to the man and stabbed his neck. Stefania licked the wound, started its healing, and numbed it. Stefan looked at it, took a picture, and broadcast it on the wall as Stefania finished healing the man's wound by sipping at it gently. Every member looked closely at the picture. They decided the proportions were correct and that it would work. They even authorized killing a few humans in Los Angeles to increase the credibility of the staging.

"Do I have permission to put the plan into action?" Alex asked.

"Permission granted."

Alex raised one hand, and three of the clan disappeared. "It is done."

    The other Enclave members looked on with curiosity. They wondered exactly how involved Lord Alexandrel cel Tinar has been this entire time. The clan members respond to a mere hand movement. He was a lord of the clan, after all, and nothing happens that a lord does not know about. The Enclave members felt he bore more watching. Even Stefan seemed a bit suspicious. Soon they finished all the business and adjourned for the night.

Chapter XI

Alex and Stefania left together for their villa. As soon as they went in and closed the door, she wrapped her arms around him and kissed him deeply. He returned her kiss and carried her into the bedroom, dropping clothes as they went. He sat her on the bed. Sitting behind her, he unlaced her dress and slowly pulled it from her shoulders. Then he kissed them as the dress fell. He continued pulling the dress down, and kissed her shoulder blades as his hands explored her breasts. He slowly unlaced the corset and continued to remove the dress and chemise below it.

"The doctor said no foreplay," Stefania said breathlessly over her shoulder to him. She stood and dropped all the loose pieces to the floor, pulled him to her, and started to undress him, returning his caresses.

"He said swordplay," he said as she removed his coat and shirt.

"Same difference," she said as she threw him on the bed.

***

He lay there and held her sleeping form. He was feeling a bit guilty about ordering the death of innocents in order to cover their existence. Though he knew for most of his life of the existence of real vampires, he had never expected that such a large group would exist semi-openly as the colony did. After ordering Kinoshi to destroy the rogue coven in Japan all those years ago, he felt they had minimized the threat. That was his whole reason for traveling to Los Angeles—to determine if the attacks were rogues and how big the coven was. He now knew the attackers were a large group of rogues—and their sire, a vampire that was now his brother . . . brothers because they shared the same dame, the woman he loved and who had made him a vampire. He snuggled to her and drifted back to sleep. The morning sun shined in Alex's eyes. Feeling Stefania shifting awake, he rolled over and kissed her.

"Good morning, darling. How are you this fine day?" he asked.

"Fulfilled, my dear, very fulfilled." She smiled as she rolled to her feet.

Alex jumped up at the foot of the bed, intercepting her as she headed toward the shower, and pulled her nude body toward him, rubbing against her; she moaned softly as her head fell back and she closed her eyes. Alex looked at her bare neck, and seeing her jugular bulging, he tilted his head back and his fangs moved forward. He bit her neck and her moan deepened and grew throatier. Her blood was a touch sweet and tangy. He pulled his fangs from her neck and licked the wound clean. She tilted her head forward again and licked her blood from his lips.

"Now that is a good morning, darling," she said after catching her breath.

Alex looked at her and suddenly a look of anxiety mixed with fear crossed his face. She kissed him and whispered, "It is okay. I loved it. Almost as much as making love, but not quite."

She led him to the shower and turned on the shower. The steam filled the room and she stepped in and pulled him behind her. She took the cloth laid out for her and rubbed soap into it until it had a large froth on it. She turned him around and scrubbed his back her sharp nails dug into his flesh and he healed immediately. A moan escaped his lips. Alex could not believe the pleasure her nails gave him. The pain was a sweet pleasure and he felt the cool cloth cross the wounds for a slight second before they had healed. She scrubbed harder and Alex moaned louder. He then turned around and grabbed her, pulling her slick wet body close to him. While kissing her, he reached behind her to grab the other cloth and the soap. He worked it to a thick lather and began to wash her. He ran the cloth across and around her breasts. He then ran the cloth across her tight abdomen and around to her back and over her tight buttocks. Once he was finished, they stepped out of the shower and dried each other. They hesitantly parted to their dressing rooms, and Radu and Alina were there to assist them into their clothes for the day. The enclave was over and so was the formality. They had day clothes to wear, and Alex had never felt so glad not to see another formal outfit.

They walked out to the breakfast area and found that the cook had already prepared breakfast. They sat next to each other and ate. Once they finished, Stefania started to stand. Alex stopped her and sent the help away after they had cleared the dishes. He turned her chair toward him and kissed her deeply.

"We have some important matters to discuss," he said as he pulled his chair close to hers.

"I wasn't finished yet. But go ahead," she said with a pout.

Alex sighed. "We have to discuss our new identities in LA."

"Fine. I thought we were going to live in your house."

"Well, I have been thinking about it. I think we should sell that property and buy a different one. Somewhere an old family aristocracy would buy. I don't think the peninsula is it. Besides, it would be too easy for Nickolea and his minions to figure out who we are if we stay in the same house."

"Yeah, you're right. I was looking forward to sitting on our dock, though."

"I was thinking the Bel Air area. It is a large 'old money' area and cel Tinar *is* old money. It is much more distinguished with less flamboyant residents."

"I think that is a great idea. There are some beautiful mansions there and usually one or two are always for sale, especially to vampire couples."

"I never thought being a vampire would have real estate advantages," he said, smiling.

"It will also be easier to hide our identities there. It is not too far out, either," she said.

"I think a Tuscan or Mediterranean style would be most appropriate."

"I definitely agree, something big enough for us and our staff. Nothing too extravagant, though. Maybe in East Bel Air, the gated area. The controlled access will make it harder to infiltrate. That area has some beautiful houses. If I could have explained it on a social worker's salary I would have had a house there instead of downtown."

"I agree, and now that we have an area picked out, we need to send someone to find and purchase the property."

"I know just the person and I think I know just the house. Hope it is still available; you will absolutely love it," she said with a wink. "I'll put him on it tomorrow."

"Now that we have that behind us, I feel I need to tell your father the truth about me."

"What do you mean?"

"Well my actual position in the Shadow, et cetera."

She flinched a bit. "All right, we'll head over there in a bit. I do have another question about the Shadow. If the Enclave had decided to kill you, what would have happened?"

"There would have been a lot of dead vampires. The clan would not have allowed it to happen without resistance. That is why I had two katanas. I might have been able to escape but would have been a rogue myself. But with you so close, I would have stopped them so you didn't get hurt."

"I was wondering, when the entire clan contingent surrounded you during the hearing, why they were doing it."

"I think the Enclave understood that the clan was under my control then and had been the entire time. That is one reason why Kinoshi and your father kept reiterating about how much both of us had done for the species. I think your father knows or at least strongly suspects."

"He probably does. He is much smarter than I am."

"Let's go see him and hope he doesn't cut off my head."

"Yes, let's hope," she said, winking.

They stood and walked to Stefan and Ecaterina's house, followed by Radu and Alina. They gingerly knocked on the door. After a couple of minutes, a servant opened it and ushered them in. The servant led them to where Stefan and Kinoshi were sitting at a table. Stefan and Kinoshi stood as they entered. They all greeted each other and they took the chairs Stefan offered. Stefan and Kinshi sat as the couple was seated.

"So are you here to tell me something, Alexandrel? Something like what is actually going on?"

"Since Kinoshi is here, I take it you have had the basic briefing?" Stefan nodded his head. Alex continued, "Well, since you know about my full involvement with the clan, I was investigating the murders in LA when I met your daughter. I did fall in love with her, as you can tell by our bonding." Stefan continued to look at him. "I had determined that it was the work of a rogue coven and was getting ready to call in Kinoshi when I was killed."

"I knew something was up when you signaled and three of the Shadow disappeared. It was obvious that there was something amiss. I am sure the Enclave suspected too, but had enough sense not to ask. So how are you feeling today?"

"Good and strong, no tinges of pain in my side at all. I am fully healed inside and out. I am just waiting on the doc's okay."

"Well, he'll give it today if I ask. Are you ready to take this to Nickolea's door?"

"He killed me, remember? I am ready to take it to every door in his house, and I'll drag him back in chains to suffer the punishment of the Enclave. After I pay him back a little in kind for how he hurt Stefania. I have special plans."

"Why, thank you, darling. I have a few myself."

"You seem to be ready enough. I'll call the doc to release you. We have your flights set up. You will leave in a couple of days. All your luggage is packed and ready. Enjoy your next few days. Oh, Radu and Alina will accompany you. We will send a cook and housekeeper when you secure a new property. You must keep up the image of who you are, and we can't risk using local help. You also cannot keep using the same help. Kinoshi already tried to win me with that. A Romanian lord and lady would use Romanian help. Stefania, you know the drill."

"Yes, sir, I do."

"I have a report, lord." Kinoshi finally spoke. "We have already set up the 'den' and will lead the police to it in a few days. We want to have you in striking distance should Nicky try something. We have another problem."

"What is that?"

"Nickolea has recruited an Eternal Hand into his organization. I believe he is from the coven we eliminated."

"I know who my would-be assassin was. It was Shinto. I believe he just thought he was killing Stefania's lover and a human who assisted in wiping out his coven. If that's it, then we still have the upper hand. The Hand will still be looking for the human leader of the Shadow. Kinoshi, as far as anyone outside this Colony and the clan knows, you are now a clan lord and the Lord of the Shadow is still underground. Nicky boy can't suspect who I am until it is too late. I will get you the sword when we go back to the house. Take care of it, my brother."

"As you command, my lord. I will leave for Los Angeles immediately to assume command of the operation."

Stefania looked at the two quizzically. "I know who this Shinto is, but who or what is the Eternal Hand?"

Kinoshi and Alex looked at each other, and Alex deferred to Kinoshi. "Well, my lady, the Order of the Eternal Hand is a group of assassins, ninja if you will, that is comprised of vampires and vampires only. We have been trying to eliminate them for the last one hundred years. The coven we destroyed was what we thought was the last of them. Until Shinto appeared.

"They are very dangerous. They are Thins, not Gluts, as you can guess by their nature. Most of them have been honing their art for hundreds of years. Shinto is the most dangerous one of them all."

"This is not good," noted Stefan. "He will make Nickolea

even harder to stop because he isn't a megalomaniac—he is a stone-cold killer."

"He stabbed me in the liver with a knife covered with stuff to turn me into a monster. I think he is looking for payback."

"Well, at least he thinks you're dead."

"Yeah, for now, but he is smarter than that. Well, Stefania, we have a trip to prepare for, and so do you, Kinoshi."

"Yes, my lord. I will depart tonight."

Stefania kissed her father. "I will miss you while I am gone, Father."

"We will miss you too," Ecaterina said as she walked into the room. She came over and kissed Stefania on the cheek. "Be safe, my darling little girl, and call us more often."

Esmerelda walked down the stairs and saw the preparations for Stephania and Alex's departure. She ran up to her sister.

"Are you leaving already?"

"Yes, they are headed back to America in a couple of days." Ecaterina said.

"When will I be able to go to America?"

"I will write to Father when it is safe, and you can come visit us. But we have much work to do right now."

"Does it have something to do with the evil man?"

"Yes, it does, and remember, Father knows best. I had to learn that the hard way. I want you to listen to him so you don't make the same mistake. You will know when the right man comes along. Don't fall for fancy talk and compliments, and if you have any problems, you let Father, me, or Alex know, and we will take care of it."

"Okay, sister, I will. But you be sure to let Father know when it is safe for me to come and visit."

"I will, little sister," Stefania promised.

Alex smiled. "I'll make sure she does, little sister."

She hugged both of them and kissed them on the cheek. Ecaterina walked up, kissed them both also, and led Esmeralda back upstairs. Alex shook Stefan's hand and gave him a firm hug.

Stefan hugged him back.

Alex whispered in his ear, "Thanks for keeping her safe for me for all these years. I will keep her safe for you now."

"I will hold you to that," Stefan whispered back.

Stefania looked at them strangely. They finished their good-byes, Alex led her out of the house, and they walked slowly home. She leaned into him, and they watched as the moon rose into the sky. He cradled her against him. They slowly meandered toward their villa. They were not looking forward to the immense task ahead of them.

As they made the last turn, they could see the villa with its faux torches out front. They walked to the door and walked in. Radu and Alina followed them in and led them to their dressing rooms to help them get ready for bed. Once they had changed, Radu informed them that the luggage was packed for the trip and the chatelaine had already made their travel arrangements. Radu had notified the US State Department of their visit, and all the paperwork was complete. Alex and Stefania thanked them and headed for the bedroom. They both had a fitful sleep, dreaming of meeting Nickolea and Shinto.

CHAPTER XII

T he next two days passed quickly and soon they were ready to return to LA. They dressed in traveling clothes and collected all the personal items they would need for the trip. They had a nice large glass of blood so they would be at their best. Alex had finally gotten used to the taste, so it was tolerable. However, they both felt this was prudent so they did not have to try to carry any on the plane and get it through customs. Once everything was prepared, they had the car brought around and were driven to the airport.

Radu and Alina rode in the front with the driver. Once they were at the airport, they had the skycaps unload the luggage and had it checked for the couple. Radu made sure they were checked in and their tickets were in order before entering security. They passed through Romanian security without any trouble. They doubted it would be that easy once they reached America. They boarded the plane and went to their places in first class. Radu and Alina's seats were behind theirs to protect their privacy from prying ears.

The other staff had left yesterday to open the house for their arrival. They waited until the plane was airborne and the "fasten seat belt" light was off to recline their seats and catch a bit of a nap. Next thing they knew, Radu and Alina were waking them. They told them the plane had landed to refuel. Alex looked out the window he saw French police officers standing around the plane. He waved to a flight attendant.

"Ma'am, is something wrong?"

"No, sir," she responded.

"The plane is surrounded by French police officers. I have flown through this airport many times. I have never seen this."

"It is a routine security check. They may come through and ask for your passports, but they usually do not bother first class."

"Thank you."

"You're welcome, sir."

Alex turned to Stefania and said, "I don't like this. Something is up."

As Alex started to stand, officers walked into the first-class cabin and asked to see everyone's passports. Radu and Alina pulled out theirs as well as Alex and Stefania's passports. They handed them to the officers. The officers took them and looked them over. They compared the pictures to the four of them. One of the officers pulled out a notepad and wrote down a few things. The other pulled out his smartphone, pulled up a picture, held it up to Alex, turned to his partner, and whispered to him.

"So, Mr. cel Tinar, where are you traveling to?"

Radu piped up, "That is Lord cel Tinar. I request you pay him proper respect."

Alex waved him back. "It is all right, Radu. He doesn't know any better. He meant no disrespect. Did you, officer?" Alex looked deep into the officer's eyes.

"No, I did not, Lord cel Tinar. Please answer the question."

"Well, officer, we are headed to the United States on official business, the matter of which I am not at liberty to disclose. As you can tell by our passports, they are diplomatic credentials. Radu and Alina are our personal attachés and, as such, have the same protections as we do. I do not mind answering a few questions as long as they decrease our delay."

"Yes, I do see they are diplomatic credentials, and we do not want to delay you any more than necessary. Why are you flying on a commercial airline?"

"Why, to decrease costs to our country. It is much cheaper to send us commercial even in first class than by private charter. I feel you can understand that, with the condition the world economy is in."

"I can understand that as well. Is this your lovely wife?"

"Yes, it is. Lady Stefania cel Tinar, daughter of High Lord Stefan cel Mare."

"I see. Everything seems to be in order. We will let you be on your way once all the coach passengers are checked. We are very sorry for the delay."

The officer walked out of the first-class cabin. Alex could hear him stop just past the curtain. He knew he was listening. He held his finger to his lip and pointed to the curtain. He complained about the officer's insolence. He played the detained diplomat to the hilt. He finally heard the officers move away from the curtains. He turned to Stefania.

"They were looking for someone. I think it may have been Rick and Saria. He was afraid. I could see it in his eyes. I could smell it. If I hadn't stared into his eyes, I think he might have been a bit more aggressive. He knew it was a bad idea."

"My dear, you are full of surprises. I have never seen anyone control a situation like that."

"Stefania, you don't rule a large clan of samurai and not know how to manage a situation. I am so glad I grew this ponytail, beard, and moustache. It totally changes my appearance. If he had had more than an inkling of who I was, we would have had trouble. I also think he was so stunned by your beauty, he couldn't think of anything else."

"You know, darling, it could have been you who stunned him."

She smiled, as he felt very uncomfortable. They felt the engines hum to life and looked out the window to see all the officers gone. They could feel the gate crew pushing the plane away from the gate. Before they knew it, they were once again airborne and headed to the United States and their mission. Alex watched as they flew across the coast and over the ocean. Strangely, he felt a little queasy seeing all the water. He turned to Stefania.

"Why would a seaman like me feel queasy looking at the ocean from the air? I have never felt that way before."

"I think it is a vampire's natural aversion to large bodies of water."

"Why do vampires hate water?"

"Well, imagine drowning and not being able to have the benefit of dying. For some reason, vampires don't swim well. We are not sure if it is a higher body density or what. I hope that you won't have to give up sailing, though. Maybe we can overcome it. I didn't seem to have too much problem when we went sailing."

"Wow, I had no idea. I am so sorry for making you go."

"It's fine. I had a lot of fun," she said.

Alina moved next to Stefania as Radu took Alex to the bathroom. She reclined the seats and closed the partition surrounding them. She placed the sheets on the seats and made them into a bed. She helped Stefania to change into a sleeping gown, and then began to brush Stefania's hair. Stefania leaned back and enjoyed the feeling. Soon Alina had finished, and Stefania took the brush and started brushing Alina's hair.

"My mother used to do this when I was a child in Spain. She always insisted in doing these kinds of things for us instead of the servants. I always thought I would do it for my children. Then the man I thought I loved turned me into a monster. I will never be able to have children."

"I am sorry to hear that, milady. To have one of your greatest dreams dashed like that. What is it like to be bonded to another vampire?"

"Oh, it is wonderful. It is as if your best friend is constantly with you. It makes the pain of the thirst less. Though it has its disadvantages, especially when your mate has internal turmoil like Alex. I can feel that turmoil and the self-loathing of what he has become. But the good outweighs the bad."

Radu carried a small bag to the bathroom to help Alex freshen up. He helped him change his clothes and clean up. Radu handed him a set of pajamas to put on that had his new initials embroidered on them. Once he was dressed, Radu gave him a pair of slippers, then unlocked the door and let him exit the bathroom. Alex walked over to the suite. Alina opened the curtain enough for him to enter and lie down before closing it and returning to her seat.

Stefania was lying on the bed, dressed in a silk gown with gold embroidery. Her raven hair was carefully brushed and held back with gold combs. Her pale, olive-colored skin was a contrast to the white sheets she was snuggled into. She peeked over the edge of the sheet at Alex. He smiled at her, pulled down the sheet, and climbed under it. She had a smile from ear to ear.

"Alina brushed my hair over a hundred strokes. I haven't had that done since I was a child. It felt so good. We have another ten or twelve hours left in our flight, so I thought we should get a good eight hours or so of sleep."

"Great idea. Off to sleep we go," Alex said.

He reached over and kissed her. He clicked off the light as they lay down and snuggled together. Soon they were both asleep. Alex's sleep was fitful and full of nightmares. He could see Nickolea standing over both their dead bodies and the bodies of many more vampires. He had an army reaching out to the horizon behind him. Alex tossed and turned.

Suddenly his dreams changed to a peaceful scene of open fields and beautiful flowers. He calmed and tossed less. Stefania held her hand across his brow, whispering words of comfort and calm. Finally, his sleep became perfectly calm, and his body relaxed. Stefania lay back down beside him, her face white and her eyes wide with the knowledge of what he was dreaming. She kissed his neck and hit her buzzer for the flight attendant.

The flight attendant arrived seconds after Alina. Alina asked for a drink for Stefania. As the attendant walked away, Alina pushed her arm into the curtained area, gritted her teeth as Stefania bit deep, and drank. She removed her arm from the suite to accept the drink for Stefania. Her arm did not show a single mark. She handed Stefania the drink and two small white pills. Stefania thanked her and took them.

As the attendant walked away, Alina turned to the curtain and whispered, "Sleep well, mistress, my blood is yours."

Stefania went off to sleep. Alina walked over to the area she shared with Radu. She leaned into his shoulder and cried. He patted her head and consoled her. He whispered in her ear, "She was in pain. Otherwise, you would have felt nothing. You will get used to it, my daughter. Our family has served theirs for generations, and after what your great-great uncle did to her, we owe her a much greater debt. Because of our family, she almost lost her one true love and her own life. Tell her tomorrow it was painful, and she will make sure it is not the next time."

"Yes, Father, I will do that. You must now get some sleep."

"Thank you, Alina, for your concern, but I am not feeble yet. I will watch over the young lord, as is my duty. Once we are settled into our new home then I will sleep. Now rest, my child."

Alina drifted off to sleep. Radu watched the curtains and the area around them. He sat watching until the attendant came to him and let him know it was about an hour until they landed so they could make sure the lord and lady were ready to exit the plane. Radu woke Alina. Once she was awake and straightened, he stood to rouse their masters. As he stood, a man ran from the second-class cabin with a knife and headed straight for him.

Before anyone could move, the suite's curtain flew open, and Alex leapt out. His vampire speed and reflexes kicked in, and he got to the man before he could attack. His fist lashed out and struck the man full in the face. Blood and broken bone flew from the man's head as Alex crushed his face. The man's momentum stopped, he crumpled to the floor. An air marshal ran through the curtain in time to see the man fall to the floor.

He looked at Alex and bowed at the waist. He covered the man's head and moved him from the cabin to a small area in the front out of sight. Radu was visibly shaken, as was Alina. Stefania came out of the partitioned bed in time to see the body being dragged away. She looked at Alex and then to Radu and Alina. She pulled Alina into the partitioned area and changed the bed back to seats. She sat her down. She was still shaking.

"Lord Alex, he moved so fast and saved my father's life. That man was going to kill my father, but he came out of nowhere and saved him," she stammered out.

"Yes, Alina, you help and protect us, and we help and protect you. That is the way this arrangement works," Stefania answered.

"Your bite hurt me last night," she stammered out between sobs.

"I am very sorry. It will not again."

Stefania continued to console Alina while Alex pulled Radu into the bathroom area for some privacy. Alex checked the man for injuries. Radu was still in shock. Alex splashed his face with cold water. Radu snapped out of it.

"I am sorry, my lord. I failed you. You had to come to my rescue."

"No, you did not fail me. You were his target, not me. Why was he attacking you?"

"He was a Tepes, an impaler. They are a fringe group that kills vampires and any human who helps or assists them. They feel vampires are pure evil and so is anyone who helps them. Once we were dead, he would have gone for Stefania, then you. Again, my family owes yours a great debt. Stefan saved my great-grandfather from a Tepes, and now you have saved us. Your family is great and noble, which makes my great-uncle's betrayal even greater."

"What betrayal is that?"

"Lady Stefania must never know, my lord."

"Okay."

"Nickolea is my great-uncle. He used our family to get close to Stefania and convince her of his 'love.' Once he had done that, it was nothing to get her to change him and take him back to the US. Once they were there, he shot her, stabbed her in the back and pierced her heart and both lungs. If not for her rapid healing, she would have died. As it was, she appeared to, and he left her for dead. She recovered enough to return to the Colony, and her parents nursed her back to health.

"She returned once she was strong enough to stop him. We are not sure what happened, but she could not kill him. It is my family's greatest shame. That is why we will serve your family un-til we can avenge his wrong and repay all the kindnesses we have received from you."

"Stefania does not know?"

"She has no idea of our family heritage. My grandfather and father committed suicide after it happened. Stefania's housekeeper raised me. Stefan and Ecaterina offered to take me in themselves, but the housekeeper said it was inappropriate for a vampire couple to raise a human child, especially me."

"What a burden you carry," Alex said. "As a human, I carried the burden of every human death at the hands of rogue vampires. As the Lord of the Divine Shadow, I was charged with the protection of all humans from rogue vampires. As a human, I was vulnerable, so my identity was kept secret even from the Enclave that directed many of our actions. So I understand great burdens. Go now, get our travel kits. We have to get ready."

Radu took a deep breath and pulled himself together. He went to get their travel kits to prepare for their arrival at LAX. Alex looked out the door to see Alina doing the same thing to help Stefania get ready. Radu returned with everything they needed to prepare themselves. Soon they were finished and they moved to the partitioned area to dress in their finery for arrival. Once they were finished, Stefania and Alina emerged from the partitioned area. Stefania was radiant in her seafoam-green dress with gold embroidered trim.

Alex was amazed at how beautiful Stefania was. Even when she was at her worst, she was the most beautiful woman he had ever seen. She always looked poised and smelled wonderful. The fragrance he always smelled on her was the most beautiful smell he had ever experienced. He sat beside her in their seat, holding her hand and feeling her soft, silky skin.

His vampire senses were just as amazing as his vampire reflexes and strength. He could smell as much or as little as he wanted to. He could smell the nervous perspiration on the passenger in seat 43b in coach. He could hear the heart racing of the passenger in 22c as the plane started its descent. He still did not know how he'd known the man was coming for Radu. Suddenly in his sleep, he'd seen the man and knew he had to act fast to save Radu.

He was snapped back to his immediate time and place as he felt the plane start to jostle as it approached LAX from the ocean side. He felt every small updraft that was adjusted for by the computer that the pilot did not even feel in the yoke. He looked out the window to see the beautiful Technicolor blue of the ocean. Soon he saw the approaching runway. As they flew over it, he could see every pore of the concrete tarmac. He was not ready for the screeching of the tires as the brakes, then the jet brakes, kicked in. He reeled from sound. Stef rested her hand on his shoulder. He felt comfort in that gesture as he got his composure back.

Before he knew it, they were stopping at the gate, and Radu and Alina were collecting their belongings. They exited the plane as the door opened. The smell of jet fuel and sweat permeated his nose. They hurried down the jet way and walked out the door into the busy terminal. They passed through the secure area door to see a man holding a board that said "cel Tinar."

Radu recognized the man, and they approached. He handed the baggage claim tickets to a small group of skycaps who disappeared into the crowd. Soon they returned to the area with their baggage. They continued to the loading area, and Alex and Stef got into the backseat of the waiting limo. Soon all their belongings were loaded into the limo, and they were off. They were both on full alert since they were in enemy territory.

Alex pulled out his phone and texted Kinoshi, letting him know they were back in Los Angeles. Soon they reached the transfer point. Alex and Stef transferred to a sports car, and the luggage was transferred to a van. Alex got behind the wheel and pulled out of the parking lot. He drove all around the city as if they were tourists newly arrived into the Los Angeles area. After about four hours of driving from place to place, they headed to their new home in Bel Air. An hour later, they arrived and pulled into the garage.

They breathed a sigh of relief as Radu opened the door into the house. He signaled for them to come in. It was beautifully decorated in a Romanian style. They walked in, and Amaya greeted them and gave them the grand tour of their new home. Alex headed straight for the sword room. It was an exact replica of how he left it, except it now had a Romanian Calvary saber embossed with his initials on the guard. He walked back into the sitting room, and he saw Kinoshi sitting on the couch. He jumped up when Alex walked into the room.

"Alexandrel, the plan is progressing on schedule. With the clues we have left, the police should find the 'den' anytime. Then we will see how the target responds."

"Very good, Kinoshi. How are anti-rogue operations progressing?"

"Excellently. We have eliminated two more rogues in Europe and had three messy ones in the Russian Federation, but it was cleaned up pretty well."

"Messy? That is not our normal. What happened?"

"Three drunken Russians walked into the alley as we dispatched the rogues who were going to ambush them. However, the team leader was fast thinking—made them think they were hallucinating. We haven't heard anything else, so I think it is fixed. The local Enclave members have been notified according to protocol."

"Yeah, damn drunken Russians. Are you going to stay a while?"

"I can, if you'd like. I know you have had a long, hard flight."

"Of course I would, Kinoshi. You are always welcome here, my friend."

Radu walked over with a large glass filled with blood. "Sir, you will need this. It is donor, but it will have to do."

"I am good right now, Radu," Alex responded, pushing the blood away.

Radu looked very sternly at him. "Sir, you need to drink this. You have not had any in a couple of days. This is life now."

Stef looked at the concern in Alex's face. Alex took the glass and wrinkled his nose as he drank it. She smiled at him scrunched her lips, talking in baby talk.

"Take the nasty medicine, my sweet little man. It will help you grow into a big, strong vampire."

"Not funny, Stef, not funny at all," he grumbled.

He drank the entire glass and felt more energized, stronger. He knew that drinking the blood was unavoidable. However, that did not make it go down any easier. Radu handed him a second one, and Alex went over to sit on the couch. He sipped it while he spoke with Kinoshi about everything that was going on.

Kinoshi pulled out his tablet and pulled up a map of the LA basin. He had red marks where the most recent attacks had been, blue ones marking rogue kills. He had a few yellow ones marking innocents that the Shadow had killed to lead the police to the "den." Alex tapped each of the red and blue ones. The crime scene pictures of the red ones were turning progressively more gruesome. Nickolea was getting out of control. The video of the vampire interrogations with the blue dots made Stefania look away. Alex watched and listened intently. He listened to every word that was extracted from them. No one would give up Nickolea's location. Alex looked intently at the screen. Then he started to notice a pattern in the dots. He noticed an area in the middle that was almost devoid of any attacks. He tapped the area of the map to enlarge it. He hit a remote that lowered a projection screen and projector so Kinoshi could send the image to the projector.

"He has to be right here," Alex pointed to the approximate two square-mile area. "There are no obvious kills here. He is arrogant but not stupid. He isn't going to hunt on his doorstep. He knows that would lead the Shadow right to him. Have we scouted this area?"

"Yep. Only old warehouses and industrial buildings. We found nothing that would indicate a nest or operating base."

"What about a storehouse? He could have a storehouse of blood, maybe enough to feed an army." He snapped his head to Stef and Kinoshi. "How much blood does it take to make a vampire?"

They looked at each other. "Theoretically? Just a few drops. Why?" Stefania asked.

"Maybe all the blood is for him. To replenish after he drains large amounts of his own."

"To make an army," Stefania finished his statement. "He

would need privacy for that. If the Enclave were to get wind of it, there would be nowhere he could hide. If he found the right kind of people to make into vampires, he would have a perfectly loyal, near-unstoppable army."

"This is not good. However, we cannot bring it to the attention of the Enclave without absolute proof. Besides, what are they going to do, other than make him an outlaw, call in the Shadow to dispatch him and his minions, and potentially put you at risk?" Kinoshi asked. "No, we have to finish this."

"Have the Shadow search the area. Secrecy is our greatest ally so keep it quiet. Do you think he suspects the Shadow is behind the vampire deaths?"

"Alex, as you now know, the Shadow is acting as the hand of the Enclave. If he doesn't, then he is a lot more arrogant or stupid than we thought."

"Well, he is definitely not stupid," Stef chimed in.

"No. That he is not. Arrogant, manipulative, greedy, definitely, but he is definitely not stupid."

Stefania listened closely and was amazed at the person she'd once thought was a simple psychologist. She watched the "Puppet Master" at work. That is what the Enclave had called him. No one knew who he was, but the Divine Shadow had taken a very large change in their direction under his leadership. They were now effectively the enforcement branch of the Enclave. She wondered now exactly how much Alex had known all along. She now fully understood the questioning when she had admitted to him she was a vampire and the very cold look she received until she had given him acceptable answers. She would be very afraid to be in his crosshairs, even with her years of experience.

"Sir, your glass has not changed," Radu mentioned.

"Thanks, Radu," Alex stated as he picked up the glass and drank about half of it. "You know, it is starting to become palatable."

Satisfied, Radu walked back to the other room. Stef watched him.

"He sure is attentive to you, Alex. One of the most attentive valets I have ever seen. Father said their family was one of the best, and we were proud to have their services. I can see why. Alina is just as attentive. She knows when I need her before I do."

"Maybe that is their 'knack.' Everyone has one."

"Knack?"

Alex looked oddly at her and continued, "I thought you would know about the knack theory. The theory is that everyone has an innate special ability that goes back to prehistoric man. I know a guy who has a great sense of direction. He almost never gets lost. Myself, I can almost see an attack before it happens. Since becoming a vampire, it has become even more pronounced. Kinoshi can tell when people are lying. What is yours?"

"I am an empath. I can feel people's pain and can take it away. It is viscous: I can touch it, feel it. It doesn't matter whether it is physical or emotional pain, either. It all works the same."

"Isn't that hard on you?"

"Can be, but I don't do it for everyone, only people close to me. I'm nice, not a saint."

They all laughed.

"Alex, we should go on a hunt with the Shadow tonight. It will be great to see you in action with vampire reflexes."

"Oh no, you boys will have to pick another night. I have to teach Alex how to hunt for fresh blood if he is to survive." Stef stopped them before they took a step. "Drinking donor blood will only help you subsist for so long. Plus, he needs to know why the Gluts act like they do."

"What does that mean?" Alex looked at her, and she returned his look with an innocent one.

"The reason that the donor blood tastes so bad is the additives in it. Fresh blood has none of that, and it almost gives you a high."

"What about the victim?"

"Oh, since we only take a little, all they get is a feeling of euphoria, and some victims have even had an orgasm. As long as you prep them correctly." She looked apologetically at Alina. "If not, all they feel is excruciating pain."

"So how do you do this 'prep'?"

"Well, I have already told you how vampire saliva has healing properties. Well, it also acts as a numbing agent. You just run your tongue along the area you are going to bite for a few seconds beforehand, and it becomes instantly numb. You then bite, drink, and then run your tongue on it again for a few seconds, and poof, the bite marks disappear."

"So in other words, I have to be making out with a girl and lick around on her neck, then bite her?"

"Yep, works well."

He looked at her funny. "And you're okay with that, me making out with a strange girl at a club?"

"Well, let me clarify that. I am okay with it as long as you are on a hunt, on a hunt for blood, blood to help you survive. It is in no way sexual."

"Well, all righty, then. How do I get them to let me lick their neck?"

"You whisper to them."

"Whisper? How are they supposed to hear me whisper and do what I say?"

"Not that kind whisper, dummy. Have you ever heard of dog whisperers and horse whisperers? Well, vampires are human whisperers. By using that ability, we can convince regular humans to do what we want. It is not a compulsion. They can resist it. It just makes them feel it is the right thing to do. You can't make someone do something they feel is wrong, like kill someone or rob a bank. But you can get them to go in a dark corner, or somewhere alone, or with a friend."

"So, how do I do that?"

"Well, you kinda talk in a throaty tone, like this," Stefania changed her voice to a deeper, sultrier voice. Alex could feel the thoughts she had mentioned.

"So kind of like this: come to me, children of the night," he responded in his best Dracula voice with a similar tone.

"Ha, ha, very funny," she said sarcastically. "But you got the point."

"Did you ever use that on me?"

"Nope. Never needed to. You were way too easy. You slut,"

Stefania said.

He laughed. "Well, I guess we should be getting ready. It is getting into the evening. Maybe we can catch dinner out before we catch dinner."

"Nice one, my lord," Kinoshi said.

"I have to make light of it to make it palatable in my mind."

"Alex, the first time is always the hardest. Both to start and stop," Stefania warned.

"What does that mean?"

"Your first taste of fresh blood will set off a feeding reflex. You have to fight that to prevent draining your victim dry. Fresh blood also has an intoxicating effect. That is why I am going to be there. As your mate, I will have more of an effect on you than anyone else, and I will need every advantage I can to get you to stop." She turned to Kinoshi. "Kinoshi, I will need you as backup on this. If I can't get him to stop, you will have to make him stop."

"Yes, my lady," Kinoshi responded with a bow of respect.

She turned back to Alex. "My lord, let's get ready and go on a hunt."

They left the room. After a while, they returned, dressed for a night out. Kinoshi had also changed in the interim. They walked to the front. Their car was already pulled out and ready for them. Alex got behind the wheel, and they sped off. They continued for a few minutes before Stefania continued with Alex's lesson.

"Be careful to run your tongue all over the area you are going to bite. As I said before, your saliva has an anesthetic in it. If you don't, the bite can be very painful. You will have to lean your head back a little to allow your teeth to move into position. Like you did with me. Make it a subtle motion. I will kiss your neck as you get ready to bite, to make it look like your head motion is in response to me. Let the blood drain out—do not suck on it. It will come too fast. Once you have drunk a small amount, once again run your tongue over the area you bit in order to distribute the healing factors evenly. I should probably have you practice a couple of times on my neck before we have you do it to a real victim.

"When we stop at the club, we need to make out a bit in the parking lot. I want you to try the techniques on my neck. Does that sound good to you?"

"Sure, I love the thought of making out with you. This is weird, getting lessons on making out with strangers by my future wife."

Stefania looked at him a little strangely. "So you want to make this charade a little more permanent?"

"Everything about you—your smell, the feel of your skin, the softness of your kiss, the gentleness of your caress—makes me feel so at peace. Besides, who else should I spend the rest of my life with? I do remember the tears you shed while I lay dying in your lap as you asked my permission to raise me. I distantly remember all the care you gave me while I fought for my life. As far as I know, you did not leave my side. That tells me that you like me a little. Besides, didn't you say we were mated? How could I marry someone else?"

A tear came to her eye. "You don't know how happy that makes me."

She leaned over and kissed him. She snuggled to him as they drove the rest of the way in silence. As they arrived at the restaurant, Kinoshi pulled in behind them. They got out and waited for him. He stepped out with a beautiful woman. Alex and Stefania looked at him curiously. He smiled and shrugged. They went in.

The hostess stepped up to them. "Do you have a reservation?"

"No, we do not," Alex replied.

"How many in your party?"

"Four."

"This way," she said walking toward the dining area.

They followed. She weaved among the tables until she arrived at one in the back corner. The gentlemen seated the ladies and then themselves. The hostess distributed the menus and asked if they would like a wine list. They deferred, and she took their drink orders. She disappeared into the crowd.

"Kinoshi, who's your friend?"

Kinoshi cleared his throat at his error. "This is Su Li. She is my . . . friend. Su Li these are my dear friends, Alex and Stefania cel Tinar."

"It is very nice to meet you," Su Li said in a reserved tone.

"I am sorry for Kinoshi's rudeness. I am very glad to meet you," Stefania said, offering her hand.

Su Li shook it as the server walked up, delivered their drinks, and took their orders. She then collected the menus and headed back toward the server station.

"So, Su Li, what do you do?" Alex asked.

"I am an interior decorator specializing in feng shui design. We met when Kinoshi had me decorate his house."

"And what do you do?" she asked Alex.

"I am the head of an international law enforcement organization," he said jokingly.

"Co-head," Stefania interjected.

Kinoshi rolled his eyes and said, "Don't tease her." He turned to Su Li and said. "They are diplomats, aristocrats from ancient Romanian families. They just wish they were something cool."

"Hey, we are cool." Alex pouted.

Su Li looked at Kinoshi and smiled. The server arrived with their food. The easy banter continued while they ate their meal. When they were finished, Alex picked up the tab and left a sizable tip. Kinoshi teased Alex about his generosity as they walked to their cars and left for the club.

Soon Alex and Stefania arrived at the club. There was a large crowd at the entrance. He turned to Stefania and swept back her hair. He leaned over and stroked her neck with his tongue. He felt the hair stand up on his neck as he felt her sharp exhale. He then leaned his head back ever so gently. His fangs moved forward like a serpent, and he bit. He could feel her body tense as he swept the blood with his tongue. Her gentle movements told him she was having a very erotic experience. After a few seconds, she found her voice.

"That is enough," she said. "Any more could cause the victim distress. Remember, we are supposed to share. Besides, you should only drink a small amount at first. It decreases your risk of entering a blood frenzy."

"What is a 'blood frenzy'?" he asked as he swept her hair back in place.

She looked a little abashed at forgetting to mention it. "A blood frenzy is when you lose control of the thirst and you kill your victim by ripping open a major vessel to drink their blood more quickly. It is not a good thing. The more frequently you feed in small amounts, the more it will help you to learn to control it."

"So how was my technique?"

She took a deep breath. "Actually, quite good. You're a natural at an unnatural process."

"All right, I think I am ready."

"Let's go. Kinoshi will arrive soon, and we should have our first victim prepared when he gets here. He will help me to stop you if things go awry."

"Sure."

He got out and walked around to help her out of the car. They bypassed the line and walked up to the door, the bouncers recognized them and let them in. Stefania scanned the club for other vampires out hunting. Seeing none, she took a deep smell of the club, looking for the telltale scent of an alert vampire. Again, she detected nothing. She led Alex to a booth in the back of the club where the light was the dimmest. Their sensitive vision allowed them to see clearly in the near darkness of the club.

They moved to the dance floor looking for prey. Soon they spotted a pretty, young woman dancing with her friends and several men trying to dance with her. Beside her was a woman to whom no one was paying much attention. They moved toward her, and Alex turned to start dancing with her. She looked surprised at first, and then started dancing with him. He introduced himself as Alex. She said, "I'm Megan." As they moved around the dance floor, Stefania moved over to dance with them. Megan became even more surprised that they were both dancing with her instead of her friend. They slowly cut her from the group and got her over to a side close to their booth. Alex caught a strange smell and turned to see Kinoshi entering the club.

He quickly returned his attention to their prey. Stefania had already begun kissing her on the neck. Alex kissed the other side. He ran his tongue across her jugular and the muscle running beside it, and felt her body shudder in response. He instinctively knew she was ready. He whispered in her ear in a normal voice,

"Would you like to come with us to our table?"

She waveringly responded, "I don't think I should."

"You will not regret it," he said using the Voice in a whisper.

Her eyes grew wide for a fraction of a second, and she nodded and started to walk with them. They moved to the booth. Stefania sat inside and Alex on the outside. Alex turned to Megan and started to kiss her neck. He slowly progressed to a gentle rotating of his tongue. He felt her body tremble, and he leaned back his head, just enough to shift his fangs. He bit deeply to access the underlying vessels.

The blood flowed into his mouth, tasting sweet and intoxicating. He felt the desire to drink more and more, but continued only to take what flowed out. He intensely fought the desire to suck at the wound. The thirst struck him so hard, he could feel his entire body ache and hurt. His throat burned as the thirst struck him. The only thing that helped was the blood flowing into his mouth.

Stefania pulled his head away. He resisted with all his strength. She touched his cheek comfortingly, and he suddenly stopped fighting her, though the thirst still raged within him. She leaned over to drink some of the flowing blood and then sealed the wound. The girl was lying back in ecstasy, moaning. The bite wound was completely gone except for a couple of very small discolorations.

They continued to kiss her neck. She finally sat up straight again. She smiled at the couple and turned to kiss each one on the mouth. She started to return to her friends when she could walk straight again. Stefania walked her to the bathroom. Once they were there, and Stefania was sure they were alone, she leaned over to her ear.

"You had a very good time tonight, but you will not remember with whom. You will just remember that he was a lovely man and made you feel better than anyone has in a long time," she told her in the Voice.

Stefania walked out and left her staring into a mirror, absorbing what she had been told. Stefania walked over to Alex and kissed him deeply. She saw the tears in his eyes. She knew the thirst still held him. She moved to the dance floor alone and picked another victim. She quickly moved her to the booth and to Alex. She prepped her neck and bit her. She presented the blood to Alex. He quickly started to drink. After a couple of swallows, he felt the thirst start to subside. He licked the woman's neck and sealed the wounds. He then whispered in her ear.

"All you will remember about this is that you had a very good time. You had a wonderful time dancing and met a beautiful couple who made you feel better than you ever have," he told her in the Voice.

She stood up and walked back to the dance floor. After a few minutes, Kinoshi walked over and sat down with three drinks. He looked at Alex to determine his condition.

Stefania asked, "Where is Su Li?"

"I thought it best to take her home. Alex, is the thirst sated?"

"Yes, it was the most horrible feeling I have ever felt. Is it like that for everyone?"

"The thirst strikes everyone differently," Kinoshi replied.

"My body was wracked with pain. I thought I was going to die. Does it get better?"

"Only if you consume fresh blood. Stefania will help you to hunt on a regular schedule in order to keep it away. On my way over, our agents intercepted a couple of Nickolea's Gluts before they sprang an ambush. They are holding them, waiting on you to interrogate them. I have your uniform in the car. Stefania, can I borrow him for a bit?"

"I will come with you. I have a disguise with me in my bag."

"You carry a disguise in your bag?" the two men said in unison.

"I do hunt rogues occasionally. I don't just help at-risk teens and stalk prominent psychologists."

"Let's go."

They went out to Kinoshi's car and retrieved Alex's uniform. As he finished changing in a nearby alley, two men walked up to him. One brandished a large knife and the other one held a chain. The one with the knife spoke first.

"Hey, homes, look. This dude thinks he's a ninja," he said, looking at his friend. He turned back to Alex. "Give me all your money, or we're gonna kill you."

"I would think twice before I tried that if I were you."

"Oh, so you are a big, bad ninja man, huh. You gonna cut me with your sword, huh?"

"No, I think I will just beat the hell out of you with the scabbard."

"Oh, the scabbard, huh, homes. So then I can cut you and get your white outfit all bloody."

"Well, the only way you'll get blood on me is to wipe it on me when you fall unconscious."

"You're a dead man, asshole."

The man lunged at him with his knife. Alex sidestepped it easily and hit the back of his hand with the scabbard. The man's hand reflexively opened, dropping the knife. Alex spun around and hit him in the back of the head, knocking him unconscious. Alex then looked at the other guy. He could smell the fear on him. He could see the minute tremors in his hand. A millisecond later, the guy dropped his chain and ran. About that time, Stefania rounded the corner.

"What happened here?" she asked as he tucked his sword into his belt and secured it.

"Ah, nothing. A couple of guys wanted my money pretty badly. This one"—he pointed to the punk on the ground—"thought he wanted to cut me with his knife, so I showed him the error of his ways. I think he will see his error a little clearer once he wakes up."

Stefania shook her head and walked back around the corner. Alex secured the black scarf around his mouth and nose, leaving only his eyes showing. Stefania looked back and saw they had changed to a steel-gray color. He leaped up, grabbed the edge of the roof, somersaulted over the edge, and landed on the roof flat-footed.

Kinoshi was standing on the roof already and gave him mock applause. Stefania landed on the roof right beside him. He stepped forward, and she looked at his outfit. His white uniform was trimmed in gold, and he wore a black scarf over his mouth and nose. His belt was a black sash with gold trim. His sword was tucked into it in a black eelskin-wrapped wooden sheath. It was the sword he'd shown her the first time they'd spent the day together. She realized the significance of that now.

Kinoshi wore a black uniform with a red trim. He wore a similar scarf around his mouth and nose. His eyes were a golden color, like the eyes of a cobra. He also wore a black sash, but his had a silver trim. His sword also was in a black eelskin-wrapped scabbard tucked in his sash. She could see now that how they held themselves was identical. Both were coiled steel springs, ready to release.

Alex looked at Stefania for the first time since they were changed. She was dressed in a frilly white shirt and black leather pants. Her hair was covered and tied with a red bandana. She wore a white bandana covering her mouth and nose. Alex noticed her eyes were a deep green with a hint of gold. She was wearing swordsman's leather gloves and a rapier secured to her belt. He had never seen one like it. It had a decorative hilt and guard.

Kinoshi silently signaled them to follow. He leaped to the next building. They followed and crossed the gulf without difficulty. They continued jumping rooftop to rooftop until he walked through a door of one and silently slipped down a couple flights of stairs. They followed him. He led them down a dusty old hallway. They could tell this was an unused hallway of a deserted building. Finally, they entered a room toward the end of the hall. There were five other members of the Shadow standing around two vampires secured to chairs.

"Have they talked at all?" Alex asked in a deeply accented voice.

"No, lord, they have not, but we have not started yet," one of the Shadow replied.

Alex turned to one of the bound vampires. "Where is your sire?"

"We will not tell you. You are betraying your own kind," the vampire answered.

"No. We are killing vampires who have betrayed their entire race. Blatantly killing humans puts us all at risk. The Enclave has issued a death warrant for all followers of Nickolea Dalakis. If you help us stop him, they might be merciful. If not, I will carry out the pronouncement here, but not until after the hunger takes you."

"I will never betray my master. He will kill you like he did the lover of that weak bitch dame of his."

The anger welled up in Alex. Kinoshi started to move to stop the vampire's ranting. Alex held up his hand and pulled down his mask to show the prisoner his face. The prisoner recognized who he was. Alex protruded his fangs, bit the prisoner on the shoulder, and drank. The vampire screamed in agony. After a minute or two, he stopped and sat in front of the prisoner. The prisoner finally stopped screaming. Alex looked in his face and saw his lip quiver.

"Ahh yes, the hunger starts," he said in an almost singsong voice. "Yes, it starts as a desire. Then it changes, slowly turning into an agony. So what is your opinion of Nicky now? Is he still the mighty powerful lord you thought, now that you know how he has failed in such a simple task as killing a human, failed to turn me into a beast once my lover tried to change me to save my life?"

The prisoner stammered, "You are a vampire. How could that have happened? You were supposed to turn into a Reaper."

"Let's just say Nicky boy is a failure," Alex said, fangs still visible, in a voice just louder than a whisper into the vampire's ear. "It is not easy to kill a Lord of the Shadow. So where is he? If you tell me, maybe you get to live." Alex's voice was now a whisper into the vampire's ear.

Alex smelled the fear on him. He could also see the hunger starting to take effect. The prisoner's shakes were worse and more obvious. The clan members around him grimaced as they watched. When the prisoner failed to answer, Alex stood and walked over to him. He reached out his hand, and one of the Shadow handed him a straight razor. Alex took it and slit the prisoner's wrists.

"Are you sure you don't want to speak?" Alex said as he watched the vampire's wrist heal only to slit them open again. As they healed, he took the razor ran it across the vampire's neck with the dull side against the skin. The cold steel caused gooseflesh to rise on the vampire's neck. Alex flipped the razor over and slowly slit his victim's carotid artery and the blood spurted across his face. With the loss of blood, the hunger was starting to take hold. He could feel the anxiety, the fear, and the hunger in the vampire as it grew.

Stefania had been furious about what the prisoner had said, but that anger was starting to turn to pity. She saw the anger in Alex's eyes. She saw the total lack of pity in them. She wondered what was behind all this hate. She looked at Kinoshi, who was also becoming a bit queasy.

Alex turned to them and said, "You may want to step out for the rest of this. It will not be very pretty. Maybe I will get some information. Kinoshi, toss me that thermos of blood before you go."

Kinoshi tossed Alex a thermos of blood and saw Alex place it on a table right in front of the prisoners. Alex opened the cap where the prisoners could smell it. Then Kinoshi led Stefania out, followed by the remaining members of the clan. Alex was alone in the room with the prisoners. As they closed the door, they could hear the prisoner begin to scream the most horrible, blood-curdling scream. It lasted for a few minutes, and then abruptly stopped. After a few more minutes, Alex opened the door, covered in bright red blood. He took a towel from one of the Shadow and wiped the blood from his hands. They looked past him and saw the first prisoner slumped in the chair, headless. The other prisoner sat untied, drinking blood from the thermos. He was shaking so hard, the chair rattled.

"He is willing to talk. Take all the information he has, then put him with the other prisoners you have."

Kinoshi looked at Alex very oddly. "Lord, we have no other prisoners."

Alex sighed. "Then we need to put him somewhere to await trial with Nickolea, unless you can get him some sort of clemency from the Enclave. He is willing to talk. I would hate to just behead him here." The vampire's eyes grew behind him.

"If you are granting him mercy, I will take care of him. We will find somewhere to put him."

"Yes, I am granting mercy only if he truly helps. I hope the information he gives is real and accurate." He turned to Stefania. "Darling, we should be going. They can handle it from here."

He took Stefania's hand and led her from the room. She looked at him, shocked. She took the towel and wiped the blood from his face. He pulled off his hood and she wiped as much blood from him as possible. She felt none of the hate or loathing she had while he'd interrogated the first prisoner. Alex was the perfectly calm, loving man he'd been before entering that room. She could not understand why she could not feel him after the door closed but she could feel him every other time. Maybe he had somehow shut her out of his mind to protect her. She would have to think more about this. They left the building and made their way back to where their car was parked. Once they were in it, she turned to Alex.

"Alex, what happened back there? It was as if you turned into someone else. I know everyone has a side they keep hidden, but you seemed to enjoy torturing that Glut."

"He worked for the man who is trying to get our entire race killed for his own personal glory. I had to get the information and I knew conventional techniques would not work. I am sorry you had to see that," he said, tossing the hood into the back seat and turning on the ignition.

"I just had no idea you had that in you," she replied, getting in beside him.

"I have a very deep hatred of a certain vampire. Strange that I am one and the love of my life is one. I guess that is something

I will have to work through. Which I will, once I kill one particular vampire."

"Nickolea?"

"No, the one who killed my parents."

"Oh, that one," she said quietly.

"His face is burned into my memory. He killed them and left me alive to suffer."

"We will find him together once Nickolea is dealt with."

"Let's just get home so I can shower and wash off this stench."

They continued their drive toward home. She watched the lights pass by until the lights started coming less and less often. Soon she only saw them as they passed a bus stop. She knew they were close to home. Soon they were pulling into the garage. As the door closed behind them and Alex turned off the ignition, she reached up and kissed him. They got out and headed in the house, pulling off their clothes as they walked into the bathroom and the shower.

Chapter XIII

Alex awoke to the morning sun in his face. Stefania was still sleeping next to him. He got up and dressed in sweats and a T-shirt, put on his shoes, and walked to the living room to go on his morning run. As he passed through, he saw Kinoshi sitting on his sofa. He walked over and sat next to him. Kinoshi was looking at a map on his tablet.

"What do you have, brother?"

"Well, we got a lot of information from your friend last night. More than we expected."

"So what do we have?"

"Other than Nickolea is not here? Well, we did get as much of his plan as the man knew. However, that was not very much. He is building an army—not of vampires, though."

"What kind of army is he building?"

"Reapers."

"Reapers, oh my god."

"Yeah, that is what I said too. Apparently, we have made this area too hot for him. He moved out with his blood and RX-34 supply yesterday. Only problem is our friend doesn't know where he went. I have spread agents around the world to watch for him to pop up. I am afraid it may be too late when we find him."

"Kinoshi, what do you know about dames and sires?"

"Just the basics; probably not much more than you."

"I am going on a run. I need to clear my head."

"I'll inform Stefania when she awakens. She knows the most about dames and sires. Do you have an idea?"

"Yeah, I will discuss it with her when I get back. Feel free to raid the fridge if you like. We have all kinds of refreshments and not-quite-so-freshments in there. I'll be back soon."

"Unless you have increased your route, you will be back a lot sooner than you expect."

Alex stepped out the door and started his run. He explored his new neighborhood as he ran. His vampire muscles were so much more powerful, and his stamina was tremendous. Once he completed several miles, he ran back toward his house.

As he finally was approaching his home, he was starting to feel the effects of his exertion. He was a bit winded as he walked into his kitchen and reached in the fridge. He unconsciously grabbed a bottle of blood and downed it as he would have a sports drink. Kinoshi and Stefania watched him, and both had a bit of a smile on their faces. He looked at them oddly, and then looked in his hand. Once he realized what he had drank, he dropped the bottle on the floor, watched it shatter, and the residual blood scattered everywhere. The housekeeper walked out, gave him a look, and cleaned it up.

"Your body will take what it needs. You worked out hard enough. It had to replenish. So it grabbed a bottle of blood," Stefania said in a consoling tone. "You are a vampire now. You will be required to drink blood, no matter how much you don't want to. Your body will get it one way or another."

"My brain detected it and sent my hand to it instead of the sports drink beside it," he said in disbelief. "And I didn't even notice."

They saw a look of horror appear on his face. Stefania jumped up, ran to him, and pulled him to her. He whispered into her shoulder, "I didn't even know. How can I control it if I can't even tell?"

"Darling, it comes with time. I wished I had been able to explain more to you before." She paused. "But I could not wait. I had waited four hundred years for you, and I couldn't let you go so soon."

Kinoshi stood and left the room to provide them with privacy. He knew how private Alex was and did not want to intrude. Stefania continued to hold Alex tightly. She slowly walked him over to the sofa so he could sit and they could be together more comfortably. Alex sat at her unvoiced command. She continued to hold him tightly as he began to cry into her shoulder.

"I have prided myself on self-control most of my life. I can't control this. How can I keep from becoming what I despise most?"

Stefania pulled him away from her shoulder and stared him directly in the eyes. Her voice was comforting but stern. "You will get control of this. You will not become one of them." She said the last as if she had bitten into a green persimmon. "You will be fine. I am here to help you and to guide you. Now straighten yourself up and get Kinoshi back in here so we can discuss this idea of yours."

Alex stood and walked to the bathroom and splashed his face with cool water. After taking several deep breaths and composing himself, he felt he was once again under control. He dried his face and walked out to see that Kinoshi had returned. He moved over to the table and opened up his laptop. He lowered the projector and the screen to show them something from it.

"Okay, I take it Kinoshi has brought you up to speed?" Stefania nodded. "Tell me about the connection between dames and sires and their progeny."

"Well," Stefania started, "there is not much to tell. Dames and sires don't have a true telepathic connection with their progeny, but we can feel their emotions."

"Can you tell where they are?"

"I don't know. I have never tried. But I am afraid to expose myself that much to him. I am sure it would be both ways. He would know for sure I was alive."

"Well then that is a no-go. Where do you think he would go to ground?"

"I have been thinking about that. I am not sure. He never talked about anywhere or anything."

"He has to have somewhere to hide. Maybe somewhere you lived. Is there someone he idolized? Is there anywhere he felt safe?"

"I don't know . . . Wait—when we were in New Orleans, we

spent a lot of time with the coven there. He made a comment about it looking safe, or felt safe, or something. New Orleans has the third-largest colony of vampires behind Paris and Romania. It also has one of the largest groups of Tepes in the world. So we have to be careful. Oh, Alex, crash course: stakes to the heart will not kill you, but they hurt like hell. Just so you know, silver bullets and holy items don't affect us, but Tepes do not know that. We need to keep the illusion alive along with not tolerating sunlight."

"So we only come out at night and hiss and hide our faces at holy symbols. So I guess I leave my cross at home."

"Yes, please."

"What about garlic?"

"It is wonderful on bread and in pasta."

"Funny, funny."

"Okay, let's see—avoid contact with holy water. It is hard to simulate burning from its contact."

"Radu," he called to his valet. "We need tickets to New Orleans, first class."

"Yes, lord, right away."

He left for the office and the master computer. Alex walked over and sat down. Stefania sat beside him. He looked at the map on the screen and turned to Kinoshi.

"Kinoshi, I need you to stay here and finish cleaning this mess up. Don't kill them all. If he has gone, then they may become reasonable. We don't need to commit genocide here. That makes us no better than he is. Actually, it will make us worse. So calm things down, and let's get the community back together and talking."

"Yes, master, it will be as you say. Once that is completed, should I join you in New Orleans?"

"We will see what is happening at that point. Come with me."

Kinoshi followed him obediently. They walked into the sword room. Alex walked around, admiring each one. He grabbed a collapsible rapier from one stand. He felt its weight and flipped it around until he got the feel of it. He closed it and dropped it into his pocket. He continued to walk around to the costume dummy wearing his uniform. He removed it, folded it, and laid it on the table. He pulled the Kensai sword down from the wall and stacked it on the uniform. Kinoshi looked at him questioningly until he realized what was going on, and he began to back away.

"No, Alex, I am not worthy. I am not a Kensai. I am not worthy of wearing your uniform and carrying your sword." He continued to back away from Alex.

"Kinoshi Kimura, stop," he commanded.

Kinoshi stopped. Alex raised a hand, and a Shadow came forth and knelt before both of them. Alex indicated for Kinoshi to kneel. Kinoshi did as he was bade. Alex first placed the mask around Kinoshi's mouth and nose. He then placed the hood over his head, and then bade him to stand. Kinoshi stood and Alex spoke.

"By my command, as witnessed by the Shadow, I bestow the sash of Kensai to Kinoshi Kimura." Alex placed the sash around his waist, and Kinoshi tied it. "Also by my command, as witnessed by the Shadow, I pass on leadership of the clan to Kensai Kinoshi Kimura," Alex held the sword high in the air and laid it across Kinoshi's extended arms. Kinoshi took the sword and tucked it into his sash. "With these actions, as witnessed by the Shadow, the clan shall now follow the leadership of Kensai Kinoshi Kimura. He is the high lord and master of the clan."

With the final pronouncement, the Shadow stood and bowed to Kinoshi and silently disappeared. Within minutes, five more of the clan entered to pay homage to their new lord. Slowly, every few minutes, a different group came until the room was almost full. Kinoshi slid on the rest of the uniform, turned to the assembled clan members, and spoke his own pronouncement.

"Let the Shadow bear witness. My first command is that Kensai Alexandrel cel Tinar will be raised to the title of venerated master, and the Shadow will always follow his guidance." Everyone, even Kinoshi, bowed before their new venerated master. "May his wisdom forever guide the Shadow."

Kinoshi looked at Alex, nodded with tears in his eyes, and led his clan out the door of the home of their venerated master. Outside, they all disappeared and were gone. Stefania looked at Alex and saw tears in his eyes. She hugged him tightly and led him out of the sword room and to the couch. They sat down, and she turned off the projector and turned on the news. Finally Alex spoke.

"So ends the last part of Rick Smythe. All that is left is Lord Alexandrel cel Tinar."

Stefania wiped a tear from his eye. "Yes, welcome to the life of a vampire. Welcome to the joy and the sorrow." She kissed him. "So much for the sorrow. Now time for the joy," she said as she led him to the bedroom.

Chapter XIV

Alex awoke and turned over to find Stefania gone. He jumped up, jerked his pants on, and headed to the kitchen. She stood at the stove, cooking. She looked up at him.

"Good morning, sleepyhead. Hungry?" she asked him.

"Sure, what do we have?"

"Steak rare, eggs done, and a nice big glass of blood to make us a big, strong vampire."

"You are so funny," he said sarcastically. He looked around and noticed the area was empty. "Where is everyone?"

"Radu and Alina are packing for our trip. I gave the rest of the staff the day off. So I decided to cook breakfast for us and thought we could eat on the back patio."

"Nice. Let me put on a shirt and meet you there."

"Okay."

Alex went back into the bedroom and grabbed a frilled white shirt. He looked in the mirror as he buttoned it and opened his mouth and protruded his fangs. He realized it was the first time he had truly looked at them since they'd developed. They looked a bit serpentine and lay across the roof of his mouth until he protruded them, then they lay just behind his canines. Looking at those fangs in his mouth was surreal. He was now one of the things he distrusted most. He tilted his head in different directions to look at them at different angles.

As he continued to look at them, he felt Stefania enter the room. She walked up to him, slipped her arm over his shoulder, and reached across his half-bared chest. She whispered into his ear.

"Yes, they are real, and this is a nightmare you will not awaken from. I have had mine almost four hundred years and still try to wake up."

"I find this so hard to accept. My inner vampire controls my every action. It is such a strange feeling—a little like I am an observer, not actually in control of my body."

"Your 'inner vampire,' as you call it, is actually your survival instinct. Your reptilian brain is running things to protect you from your higher thought processes. Once your conscious mind accepts this reality, the reptilian brain will relinquish control to you. Otherwise, you might do something dumb, like try to not drink blood. By the way, without blood, you will die a horrible, painful death. So don't even think about that route."

"Wow, are there vampire scientists who figure all this stuff out?"

"Actually, yes. The colony has a large research center. Maybe one day you can read some of the papers in the library."

"I would love that. Maybe once this mission is complete."

"It's a date, then. Come on, your breakfast is getting cold."

They walked out to the patio. After they had finished their breakfast and cleared the dishes away, they went back toward the house. Radu was standing at the door as they walked toward it. He had a look of concern on his face.

"What is it, Radu?"

"Should we be using commercial airlines so much?"

"What do you mean?"

"Well, my lord and lady should have a private plane. You should disdain commercial flights and only use them as necessary. I took the liberty of ordering a customized private jet. The best company to fill out the interior was in Chicago. It will be ready in a day or two, so I rebooked you on a flight to Chicago. I found a manor house in New Orleans with its own airstrip. So I thought we could land at Louis Armstrong International to make an appearance and have the pilot fly out to the property while you and Lady Stefania take a limo."

"Radu, that is absolutely brilliant. How much is all that going to cost?"

"You? Nothing. The Enclave authorized it. They felt your movement around the country should be a little less conspicuous. You have a teleconference with High Lord Stefan in fifteen minutes. He has information for you. I have the conference set up in the media room. Alina and I will continue packing your clothes and other necessary items while you are at the conference."

"Thank you, Radu," Alex said and turned to Stefania. "Better get our game face on, darling."

She smiled, and they walked into the media room. True to form, Radu had everything ready. They sat at the table and hit the conference button. They could see Stefan sitting in a large conference room with several other members of the Enclave and Colony council.

"Good morning, Father," Stefania said to Stefan.

"Good morning, Stefania," he replied. "How are things there?"

"Progressing. Is the assemblage ready for our report?"

"I believe they are."

"Let me start, then. Ladies and gentlemen, we have narrowed down Nickolea's headquarters here in Los Angeles, but according to one of his men, he has departed for parts unknown. However, we believe he is in New Orleans. We are moving to pursue him there."

"Excellent," Stefan replied. "This is your operation, so you continue to conduct it as you like. The Enclave has decided you are to meet with the covens in both Chicago and New Orleans to let them know how displeased the Enclave is with Nickolea and his actions. In addition, they need to know any groups found to be helping him will find the Enclave displeased with them also. Make sure any groups in the areas you visit are also informed of our displeasure."

"Yes, sir," Stefania replied.

"When you pick up your plane, you will have diplomatic papers that indicate you are emissaries of the Enclave that you will present to any group you meet with. You are also to meet with them in full dress. You know what I mean, Stefania. So," Stefan said, changing the subject, "why do you think he is in New Orleans?"

"Something he said when we were together. Seemed appropriate he would go to ground there," she replied, nodding her head.

"Good. Sounds like you have things well in hand. This will take as long as it takes. Good luck, and take care."

"Yes, sir. Hopefully we won't need the luck, but we welcome it anyway."

Stefan smiled, and when all the other members of the group acknowledged that they had nothing to add, they closed the conference connection. As Alex and Stefania stood up and looked around, they saw their luggage was sitting in the hall behind them. Radu directed the loading of the luggage, and Alina grabbed Stefania and dragged her off to her dressing room.

Alex watched the efficiency at which Radu carried out his tasks. He understood where all the tales of the daytime servants attending to sleeping vampires had originated. The loyalty Radu and his family showed to Stef and her family was amazing. Once the luggage was loaded, he reminded Alex he had to get ready himself. Alex went into the bedroom and found a nice black suit. Every time he looked through his closet, he found new things and more of his old things gone.

There were things he hated about being an aristocrat—the entourage that followed him around, the fact that he was always in the public eye, the itchy beard he now wore—but he knew they were necessary. Even once they captured Nickolea, he knew they would not go away. This was his new life. It was a life to which he hoped he could become accustomed.

He showered and trimmed his beard and got dressed. Radu walked in, straightened his clothes, and retied his tie. Radu looked at his shoes and retied them, making sure the laces and loops were perfectly even, and the knot laid just perfectly. He handed Alex a black cape with a black lining and a small cane with a silver handle shaped like a small dragon. Radu then pulled a top hat from a cabinet and put it on Alex. He looked at it, adjusted it, and then took it off to replace it with another. After a close examination of this one, he nodded his head in acceptance.

"This one, sir. Remember, gentlemen do not wear hats indoors. Keep your back straight and walk tapping your cane on the ground in a way that it is obvious you do not need it, and with a bit of a strut, confident but not arrogant. Nose slightly tipped up. Remember, you disdain common people. But, they do not disgust you—they are just below you. Now let me see."

Alex walked with his nose slightly tipped up and set the cane on the ground, walked halfway past it, and lifted it to put in front of himself once again. Radu walked around him, looking at his gait, stride, and posture. Alex walked around the room for what seemed forever until Radu was happy with his technique.

They walked out, and Radu packed the hat and cane in the remaining cases and had them loaded. Alex saw Stefania in an ankle-length gray semiformal gown covered in lace. The only jewelry she wore was a solitaire diamond ring. He stepped forward to her and took her arm. They walked out to the waiting limo. Alex helped her in, and Radu helped him in. Alina sat next to her, and Radu sat in the front next to the driver. They pulled out, and a large black SUV pulled up behind them.

Alex looked behind them and shrugged his shoulders. Stefania giggled a little bit as she spoke.

"Alex, you should be used to the escorts by now. People of our 'stature' always have large security detachments. They have followed us everywhere. I am surprised you didn't have a group of them when you ran the other day."

"They were probably there; I just didn't notice them," he said with a smile.

She laughed. "You are probably right. So are you ready for this? Do you understand the significance of the black cloaks?"

"I just know they are important. They indicate that you are a representative of the Enclave and on their business is all I know."

"Well, a single Black Cloak means your coven is being warned about some trespass. Two or more means someone in your coven or even the entire coven is to receive punishment or censure. The real thing is, when two Black Cloaks show up, someone usually dies. That is the significance of the cloaks. If two Black Cloaks come and no one dies, that means disobedience will result in the ending of a coven."

"Does that mean what I think it does?

"Yes, it does. When a coven is ended, all members are killed and the leader taken before the Enclave. Usually he is killed too, and his line ended."

"So are we to enforce this, or will they be watched?"

"We are always watched."

The motorcade arrived at LAX. Paparazzi snapped photos as they entered the airport, hoping they were important people. They stood by security while Alina and Radu checked them in. Before long Alina and Radu arrived at security. They passed through without difficulty. Soon they were in their first-class cabin. Alex breathed a sigh of relief. They watched out the window as the plane took off and climbed to cruising altitude.

Once the plane reached altitude, the flight attendants began serving refreshments. Alex looked around and saw several men in identical black suits. He sighed. He closed his eyes and tried to rest. Stefania took his hand and squeezed it. They laid their chairs back and napped. Soon the plane started its descent. They sat their seats up and waited for the plane to land.

They watched as the plane circled and passed over Lake Michigan and approached the airport. The pilot performed a perfect landing and taxied to the terminal. They deplaned and walked out into the main terminal. With Radu and Alina behind them, they started walking down the concourse headed for the tram to take them to the transportation area. Alex noticed the black-suited men from the plane were following them at a comfortable distance. A man in a gray suit wearing an airport name badge approached them.

"Lord and Lady cel Tinar?" he asked.

"Yes?" Alex responded.

"I am Jim Filbar. I am to help with your security here and to escort you through the airport. I apologize for my tardiness and that I did not meet you at the gate."

"Apology accepted," Radu said with disdain. "Lead on."

Stefania looked at Alex after the man turned around with a touch of curiosity in her eyes. Alex moved his eyes toward Radu. Stefania nodded in understanding. They followed the man through the busy airport. People looked at the party and then either looked quickly away or lingered almost to a stare. Many men craned their heads to catch a look at Stefania. Women looked Alex up and down and smiled. They finally came to the tram that would take them to the main terminal. Security stood at the doors and kept other passengers from boarding as Alex and Stefania's party entered and the doors closed.

As the tram began to move, the man looked at them and smiled. He began to speak.

"Welcome to Chicago. Our coven awaits your pleasure. We have scheduled a meeting for you tonight if it pleases your lord and ladyship. We will have transportation for you if you like."

"Transportation has already been arranged," Radu interrupted.

The man looked at Radu with an irritated look but only nodded his head in understanding. "Okay, then. Should we expect you tonight?"

"Yes, the lord and lady will meet with your coven tonight," Radu answered.

Alex and Stefania remained silent and continued to allow Radu to speak for them. The other vampire understood the unspoken comments of their silence and closed his mouth nervously without speaking again. The tram slowed to a stop, and the party exited. They walked out into the large open terminal. In the middle of the walkway stood an older man dressed in traditional chauffeur clothing. He held a sign with "cel Tinar" on it. Radu led them toward the driver. Radu thanked the airport escort and dismissed him. The man departed silently with a quick glance and a slight bow toward Lord and Lady Cel Tinar.

They followed the driver to the waiting limousine. The lord and lady enjoyed refreshments in the limo while waiting on Radu and Alina to return. Radu directed a few of the security staff to secure their bags from baggage claim and the freight counter. The bags were stowed in the back of a waiting black SUV. The security staff sat in the SUV, and Radu and Alina settled into the limo. Once everyone was settled, the driver left the airport and drove to the Waldorf Astoria Hotel with the black SUV close behind. Upon arriving, they exited the car. Alex took Stefania's arm, and they walked in with a line of bellhops behind them, all under Radu's watchful eye. Alina walked to the desk and handed them a sheaf of papers and a credit card. The clerk picked up the phone talked into it for a moment, then hung it up. Within minutes, a man dressed in a tuxedo came out and introduced himself to Alex and Stefania.

Radu stepped up to him and responded. The manager sweated a bit and continued talking to Radu.

"Welcome to the Waldorf Astoria. We are very pleased you have chosen our hotel, and if you need anything just ask. If you will follow me, your suite is this way."

The manager led the party to an out of the way elevator. Once inside, he closed the doors and placed a key card into a small slot. He pushed the P1 button. The elevator moved quickly to its destination. He led them to the door and placed the card in it. The red light changed to green. He pushed the door open to reveal a very lavish living area. The glass counters and table had brass fixtures and legs. To the side was a large round sectional sofa with a seventy-inch TV in front of it. The manager handed Radu the key card, and Radu handed him ten $100 bills. Alex and Stefania walked over to the sofa and sat down. Radu thanked the manager, and the manager excused himself. Once Radu safely closed the door, Stefania spoke.

"Excellent job, Alex. You showed that he was below you and that he was only good enough to speak with your servant. No offense meant, Radu."

"None taken your ladyship."

"When we talk to the coven this evening, let me do all the speaking. We will make them feel if you have to speak, someone will die. I want to make them recognize Alexandrel cel Tinar as an enforcer of the Enclave. They will be more likely to follow our direction if they see you as one to eliminate resistance."

"Why me?" Alex asked.

"Your bearing. It makes you appear dangerous. It demands respect. You need to wear your Romanian military uniform, including the saber. It shows that you are a member of the elite of the Colony."

"Aren't all vampires members of the Romanian military?" Alex asked, confused.

"Well, we misled you a bit. They induct only the elite vampires of the Colony into the military and they rarely receive a commission, especially of your rank. That will show them you are a person of authority."

"So I am of the upper echelon of the Colony?"

"Well, of course you are. You are my lover and lord. I am one of the highest-ranking members of the Colony. You have a hunter's cord. Not every vampire hunts rogues. There are a choice few hunters out there. Outside of the Shadow, you are a member of a very elite group. There may be ten or fifteen hunters. I want them to see that hunter's cord too. You will be surprised about the weight it carries. Especially with a sire/dame mark. You have killed vampires and do it routinely. They will recognize that fact."

"Really, not everyone kills rogues?"

"So that is what you got out of all that?"

"Well, yeah."

"You represent the most extreme authority of the Enclave, the power to end an individual or coven. People recognize me as someone who makes Enclave policy. They will recognize you as someone sent to enforce that policy."

"So with us together, they understand the importance of said policy."

"Correct," she answered, exasperated. "Now we have to get ready. Radu, do your best."

"Yes, madam," he responded.

Radu led Alex into the other room. He sat him at a vanity and began applying makeup. Radu reduced his natural color to a milky, almost-white tint. He helped Alex dress in his dress uniform. He placed the hunter's braid on his left shoulder. He noticed the braid had ten small red stripes and two large ones. Once the uniform was complete, Radu helped him put on the black cloak. It was a simple black velvet cloak with a red satin lining. Alex looked at himself in the mirror. The cowl did not interfere with his vision at all, but all he could see was from his nose down. The rest was in shadow.

"Disquieting isn't it, sir," Radu said.

"A little. So this is traditional for emissaries of the Enclave?"

"Well, we are a bit on the theatrical side, but yes. Remember, sir, let Lady Stefania do all the talking. You want them to think you are only there to kill. Because of a vampire's relative immortality, the only thing they fear is a hunter. If they think they can kill you, they may try. Be ready for anything. We don't know how far Nickolea's reach is. He must contact and convert as many groups as he can if he wants to survive a purge, and especially if he wants to take over like we think."

"A purge?"

"Yes, sir. It is when the Enclave deems it necessary to kill every vampire in an area. They call in all the hunters to the area and authorize deadly force on any other vampire, no matter their affiliation. It is the easiest way to destroy the threat of a vampire revolt, which is what Nickolea is trying to instigate."

"Isn't that a bit extreme?"

"Well, to stop a revolt that could eliminate the species, no holds are barred. Better to kill a few innocents and save the race than to let it fester."

"Do you think Stefania is ready?"

"Alina should have her about ready."

They walked out of the dressing area to see Alina and Stefania sitting in the foyer waiting. Stefania was wearing a beautiful white formal dress. Her face was a lighter tint of her usual milky color.

Her lips were a deep red. She wore a deep black eyeliner emphasizing her pale-gray eyes. Around her neck, she wore a beautiful platinum filigree diamond-and-ruby necklace. Her black cloak appeared to float around her. She looked toward Alex and gave a start.

"My lord, you do appear . . ." She paused for a second. "Fearsome," she then finished. Radu, bring the saber, the hunter saber."

"Yes, my lady," Radu said as he went into the other room.

"So, my darling, your job is to stand there and intimidate them. I will do all the speaking. Watch them closely. If Nickolea has extended his reach this far, and the Enclave believes that either he has or could soon, they may try something."

"Got ya," he said, winking.

Radu led them to the underground garage he had scouted earlier. The car was parked in a secluded area off the service elevator. Alex looked at Stefania. Only her ruby-red lips showed beneath the cowl of the black cloak. Her normally pale olive skin was a pasty white. Her gold-inlaid steel rapier hung from her side. Alex knew it would take off a head as easily as his cavalry saber. Both were razor sharp, and the diamond-honed edge would cut through the hardest of bone.

The car drove through the darkening streets of Chicago to the meeting place. Radu and Alina would stay with the car unless they summoned them. The nicer buildings began to give way to older and less-maintained ones. Finally, they arrived in the old lakeside area. Most of the warehouses were old and in poor repair. They arrived at one with several nice cars out front.

"This must be the place," Alex stated with a whistle.

"Yep, must be. You know the plan."

"Yes, I do. I expect them to try for you first. They will think you are the weaker one."

"You are probably right. Remember, decapitation is the only way to kill a vampire."

"Yes, but not the only way to stop one."

"What does that mean?"

"Who is the hunter here? I have a few trade secrets."

They stepped out of the car, pulled the cowls over their heads, and adjusted their black cloaks. The steel mesh in them made them a little heavier than Alex liked, but it was a necessary precaution. He hoped there would not be any trouble but knew that it was probably a vain hope. They walked up to the door. Outside stood two younger men in black suits with shoulder holsters. They also had swords at their hips. They opened the doors without a word and allowed them in. The doors closed with a metallic rasp. Alex did not flinch at the sharp sound. He was beginning to get used to his vampire senses.

He could smell the anxiety in the room. It was a large open warehouse. He could see some catwalks around the sides of the built-in shelving. He could hear people carefully moving around the shelving. He noted where everything and everyone was. They walked forward to the group of vampires in front of them. The leader was standing a little in front of the group. They stopped in front of him.

"The Enclave has requested we deliver a statement. They are displeased with the actions of Nickolea Dalakis. Furthermore, they are displeased in all vampires who participate in any activities that support him or further his agenda," Stefania announced.

"Who does the Enclave think they are, telling us what we can do and who we can associate with?" the leader responded.

"The Enclave is made up of representatives of every major vampire coven in the world. They are charged with the safety of all vampires and will not allow any single vampire or group of vampires to put the entire species at risk."

"We will not bow down before the Enclave like dogs. We are the dominant life form on this planet, and we should take our place over the human sheep."

"We are brothers to humans—we were all human at one point. The Enclave represents all vampire kind."

The leader screamed as he leaped forward, drawing his sword. Alex stepped forward, drew his saber, beheaded the leader, stepped back, and sheathed his sword before the man's head struck the floor. The entire coven stood in shock. The other coven members stepped back upon seeing their former leader's sword still in its scabbard. Stefania continued speaking without pause.

"Again, as I was saying, any action or inaction that promotes Nickolea's agenda will incur the Enclave's displeasure."

Alex could hear others moving around. Suddenly he dodged toward Stefania as a vampire fired his pistol from behind them. He pushed her back and placed himself between her and the shooter. He reached behind his back, pulled out a throwing knife, and struck the attacker in the neck. Blood gushed from the vampire's throat. Alex threw four more knives into other vampires that leaped out to begin firing. His accurate throws struck each one in a vital area that stopped them in their tracks. They fell to the floor.

The group in front of them each drew a sword. Alex threw back his cloak and pulled two sabers. He cut into the group like a buzz saw. Stefania watched as his blades flashed, severing body parts as he passed through them. He carefully removed each one's sword arm and knocked them to the floor. The ones he identified as leaders, he quickly beheaded.

Within minutes, the action was over. Stefania scrambled to her feet, walked over, and removed the heads of the vampires he had hit with his knives. The remaining vampires scrambled to their knees. Their heads reached the floor. Stefania walked among them. Alex stayed by her side.

"How dare you? You attacked official emissaries of the Enclave. Who do you think you are? What arrogance you possess. You think you are so much better than we? Do you think you are somehow above reproach? The punishment for your crimes is death. My lord and I are empowered to execute you here on the spot, and you dare attack us. You have condemned your entire coven to death. We must now kill every vampire in this city and the surrounding area. Because of you, we have to kill our brothers and sisters. Why do you think they sent a hunter with me? He is an enforcer of the Enclave. Your actions have branded everyone a rogue." She turned to Alex. "Finish it."

Alex walked over and beheaded each in turn. As he beheaded the last one, he heard a noise in the upper catwalks. Using his enhanced vampire strength, he threw a knife toward the moving figure on the catwalk. The knife stuck in the wall in front of a young male vampire. He stopped dead in his tracks.

"P-Please don't kill me. Let me talk," he stammered.

"Come down, then, and quit hiding in the rafters!" Stefania yelled to him.

The young man scurried down and bowed before them. He appeared to be in his early twenties, but with a vampire, that could be misleading because of their timeless features. He was approximately six feet tall and had blond hair. His skin had not taken on the milky color of an elder vampire such as Stefania.

"Why were you hiding in the rafters and why shouldn't I kill you right here?"

"Milady, I came to speak to you and to request mercy for our group."

"Well, your leader and these—" She indicated the corpses with a sweeping gesture. "They made your group's opinion plain."

"No, milady, these are not members of my group. Once Nickolea visited and enlisted our coven, several of us left the coven and formed a separate group. We knew it was only a matter of time before the Enclave sent someone to chastise the coven. When I heard they were sending a messenger, we felt it was our chance to tell our side. When I arrived, they had already started attacking you. I hid in the upper catwalks because I did not want you to kill me before I could speak."

"So Nickolea was here and enlisted your coven?"

"Yes, milady."

"Where did he go from here? Where was your leader supposed to contact him?"

"He was making several stops, but I think he was headed to New Orleans."

"How many in your group?" Alex asked.

"Approximately six. There are a few vampires in the area who do not belong to either our group or to the other coven."

"Hmm, the solitary vampires are a problem. We do not know where they stand. They will probably be purged," Stefania said.

"What about us?" the young man asked.

"Hmmm. Your coven will have to speak to Enclave representatives. Tell them what you know and what actions you took. Also, tell them your fate was deferred to their mercy by Lord and Lady cel Tinar. You have one week. We will check in and make sure you have done so. If you have not, we will return to finish the issue. Do you understand?"

"Yes, Lady cel Tinar, I understand completely. With your leave, I will go immediately to make arrangements and collect my members."

"Go before I change my mind. No, wait. Gather all the keys and identification from your fallen brethren."

The young vampire took off as fast as he could to execute his orders. After collecting everything he held the items up to Stefania while kneeling with his head tucked. She accepted his offering and placed them on a table nearby.

"Now go."

The young vampire raced out the door. Alex stacked the bodies in the middle of the warehouse. He lit a match and threw it on top of them. They burst into flame. The fire burned white hot for a couple of seconds, and the bodies were gone. Alex watched as the blood on the floor rapidly decayed into nothing. He retrieved all his throwing knives and eliminated all trace of their presence. Stefania pulled out her cell and made a call. Soon several men arrived. She threw them the keys, and they removed the cars from the area. As soon as they were content that they'd eradicated all traces, they left the building. Radu met them as they walked out.

"Was your meeting productive?"

"Not very, Radu, not very productive at all," Alex said.

The trip back to the hotel was very solemn. Once they arrived and went back to the suite, Alex went to the bathroom to clean the swords and oil them. Stefania walked in while he was working and hugged him from behind, resting her head on his back.

"Stef, that was a useless loss of life. Nickolea will pay for this. How many more vampires will have to die before we stop him? When I was killing rogues, it was for the improvement of life for everyone. This was just a slaughter."

"Yes, my darling, I feel the same. Now we have to call the Colony and relay the information to them, and they will order a purge. Who knows how many vampires will needlessly die? The horrible thing about it is Nickolea does not care. All these brothers and sisters are just tools for his agenda. All this blood is on my hands. I should have killed him when I had the chance. The Enclave spared you and me to teach me a lesson. They wanted me to feel responsible for all these deaths. Well, they were right."

Alex laid down the swords, turned to Stefania, and pulled her head against his chest. "Stef, Nickolea is responsible for these deaths."

"And I am responsible for him. Therefore, I am responsible for these deaths. This is an important lesson you will have to learn. Vampires are not born. Other vampires create them. Therefore, their creator will always be ultimately responsible for their actions. If they do not take the lessons, if they do not understand the importance of secrecy, then you destroy them. I failed to destroy him."

"So if I failed to understand the lessons and the need for secrecy, you would have killed me?"

"I would have had to, yes, even though it would have broken my heart and destroyed me. I would have not made that mistake a second time."

"Well, no more playing around. We head straight to New Orleans, track him down, and put his head on a spit."

"You mean bring him to the Enclave for trial."

"Yeah, that."

She smiled at him. "Yeah, that. I know how much you hate him for what he has done to me. But he has to stand trial."

"Okay, this is your call, but I would rather take his head back, disconnected from his body."

"You realize it is now more than an individual acting alone. It is turning into a rebellion. With all the trouble he is stirring up, we have to prove the Enclave is more than a legislative body. We have to prove it is a powerful organization. We have to prove that it can enforce what it rules."

"I understand the last vampire-human war was a horrible experience. I certainly don't want another to start."

"So tomorrow we continue to New Orleans and put an end to this."

"Agreed."

Chapter XV

They walked out and explained the change in plans to Radu and Alina. They changed the arrival plans to be secret and set up a meeting with the New Orleans leadership. Alex and Stefania went in the bedroom to be alone as Radu finished the arrangements and began packing their luggage. As soon as everything was complete, Radu knocked on their door. Alex opened it.

"Lord, everything is ready. The car will be here soon."

"Thank you, Radu. We will be out momentarily."

"Very good, sir."

Alex closed the door and turned back to Stefania, her pale-olive skin only slightly contrasted against the white sheets. Her lithe body beckoned to him. He walked toward her. He bared his fangs and hissed as he approached her. She bared her fangs and hissed back at him. He leaped toward her, and she flipped him across the room.

As he flew over her, he grabbed her hand and pulled her with him. She twisted in the air and landed on top of him. He tried to flip her over, and she flipped him onto his stomach. He pushed himself to a standing position. She landed in a handstand, wrapped her legs around him, and pulled herself into a sitting position on his shoulders. She reached down and bit down deep into his neck. He dropped to his knees, and she let him go.

"Remember; use your agility, not your strength. You will never be able to overpower a Glut. If they grab you, you will have had it. So your best bet is to not get caught."

"Okay, but why would I ever get into a grappling match with

a Glut anyway? I will use my sword and take his head."

"Well, what if you don't have time to draw, or they disarm you? Remember, these guys can be really strong. It is better to be prepared. We go again."

He walked over to the door. He moved a bit faster toward her this time. She flipped into a handstand, and he ducked his head into her abdomen and flipped her over his head. He dropped to his knees as she reached for his neck. She missed and landed hard on her back. He spun around and bit deep into her neck. He then moved to her lips and kissed her.

"Much better, and to the victor goes the spoils," she said as she spun into his lap.

She pulled off her top and rubbed her bare breasts against his chest. He kissed her and stood up. As he stood, she wrapped her legs around his waist. She started kissing his neck. He loosened her from his waist and wriggled from her grip.

"We need to go. We have to finish this. I want nothing more than to have a romp in the bed with you, but we have to end this threat. This rebellion of his will just cause more useless deaths."

"Really? You will turn this down"—she pointed toward herself from head to toe—"to hunt down the bad guy. Wow, I didn't realize what sacrifices you would make."

"It is not a sacrifice. If we don't stop this, I might lose everything. So it is quite self-serving. Another war is not in anyone's best interest, especially ours."

Alex walked to the door as Stef put her top back on. When he opened it, he could see the luggage was gone. As they walked out, Radu stood and led them to the waiting car. They rode to the airport, and the car delivered them to the general aviation terminal. They walked out onto the tarmac. A Learjet sat in front of them with the pilot in the doorway. As they climbed to the top of the stairs, the pilot greeted them.

"Welcome, your lord and ladyship. The plane is ready when you are."

"Please take off once everyone is aboard."

"Yes, sir."

The pilot turned in toward the cockpit to start the engines and get clearance from the tower. Alex led everyone in and helped Stefania to her seat and sat next to her. Once everyone was seated, Radu picked up the phone to the pilot and told him everyone was ready. Within several minutes, the plane started moving. Once they were at their cruising altitude, Radu and Alina walked into the galley and brought back refreshments. Alex and Stef accepted them inattentively as they stared into each other's eyes.

"So what is our next step, Stef?" Alex asked.

"Well, we meet with the New Orleans coven. If we find the same welcome there, we will know where we stand. I hope they won't be as dumb as the last group. They will probably listen to us, make some empty promises, and try to get us out of there. After we meet with them, we start looking for Nickolea."

"We won't make the same mistake as we did in LA. We will be stealthy, not heavy-handed. That is why it is just us and not the entire Shadow," Alex replied.

"Ooh, intrigue. I like that. Looks like your investigative skills will come in handy."

"Yeah, we should start by asking them without directly asking where Nickolea is. I am sure he has loyal agents who will tell him if anything is mentioned outright, so we have to let any party interested tell us what they know without risking their lives."

"So we let them know where we are staying, which will be a meeting place. It will have to be somewhere easily defended. He has already shown he is not afraid to attack anyone out in the open. We also need to let them know about the Chicago purge. They need to know we mean business."

"We will have to make contact with local authorities. Can the Colony make the proper arrangements?"

"They should be able to. However, that could alert the local coven of how deep we are probing. I don't want him to take off again."

"Well, with just us doing the probing, he may just try to take us out. If we are lucky, he might try to take care of it himself.

Especially if we stop his first attempt. Our mere presence in New Orleans means the Chicago attempt failed. So he may feel it is necessary to eliminate us himself anyway."

"Okay, we have to make it plain that we were the Chicago emissaries. That way he knows they failed. Maybe we can stir him up a bit too. Say it was a pitiful attempt on our lives."

"Oh, that would stir him good. With his ego, it would absolutely kill him," Alex said, smiling.

The rest of the trip was uneventful. Alex and Stefania planned the meeting with the New Orleans coven as they looked through the plane's supplies. They found another two black cloaks. They had a titanium weave inside the lining, yet made no sound other than a simple quiet *swish*. The Colony had also included the proclamations and credentials they had been promised.

Soon the plane was on approach to the private airfield of the estate they had leased for their stay. They watched as the plane passed over Lake Pontchartrain, then over dark-green fields until the airfield was in sight. Soon they were on the ground, and Radu was opening the door. As they stepped out of the plane, a group of servants walked from the house. As soon as they reached the field, an older man from the group spoke.

"I am Phillip MacDonald, the butler here. This is Sara, the housekeeper. We maintain the grounds and facilities and provide all the needed supervision of the staff, so your personal attendants do not need to worry about those particular tasks and can attend to you. We have been informed of your special dietary needs, and that will be taken care of."

"Thank you, Phillip," Alex stated. "We welcome your assistance. I take it your staff was specially chosen?"

"Yes, sir, this estate has housed many . . . interesting . . . individuals," he said with a deliberate pause.

"Ahh, good to know. So how is the hunting in the area?"

"For you, there is a nice area on the outskirts of town. Our gamekeeper will be glad to show you the best spots."

"Excellent. We will need his assistance later this evening."

"Very good, sir. If you would kindly follow me, we will show you around the manor."

Phillip led them to a building with an SUV inside. They got in, and Phillip got in beside the driver. As they drove out of the building and around the estate, Phillip pointed out anything he considered important or interesting. Yet, as they continued to drive around, Alex began to feel more and more uncomfortable. Soon they returned to the manor house. They drove into an underground garage and parked, and as Alex and Stefania exited the vehicle, his uneasiness continued to intensify.

As they walked toward the stairs leading into the house, three men leaped out with stakes and another two with pistols. Alex leapt forward, pulled out his collapsible rapier, and clicked the blade in place. The two Tepes with pistols both fired at him. The forty-five-caliber slugs knocked him off his feet. One of the men with a wooden stake dove on him and tried to stab him in the chest.

Alex rolled from under him and heard the crunch of the stake breaking on the concrete floor of the garage. He rolled back and took the man's head with a quick flick of the saber. Stefania reacted quickly, drawing her own collapsible saber and clicked the blade in place. She flicked the sword and slapped one of the gunmen on the wrist, making him drop his pistol. She turned, bared her fangs, and bit the man's neck. She drank enough to refresh herself and pushed him toward Alex.

Alex caught the man and drank from the bleeding wound. He felt the hunger come and go. He forced himself to release the man and seal the wound. He pushed him to the floor as he headed for the next gunman. The gunman fired at Alex again. This time, he missed, and Alex grabbed him and snapped his neck. The remaining Tepes agents turned to run. Alex grabbed a nearby garden rake and threw it at the men's feet, tripping them. He picked up one of them and bared his fangs.

"Tell your masters to not bother us again, or we will drink your blood as we did your brother. We are not here to prey on humans but to police our own. Now take that other one with you and go. Do not return."

Alex set the agent down and turned his back to him. The man stood shaking for a moment and then turned, gathered his men, and left. Alex stood silently as the Tepes left. He began to shake. Stefania could see how upset he was. She walked over to him, and he buried his face in her shoulder.

"I have killed few men in my life who were not vampires. I do not like it. I grabbed that man and drank his blood by reflex. I had to force myself to stop. What if I can't next time?"

"You needed the blood, so your reflexes took over, and killing never gets easy."

Alex cried into her shoulder. She held him close and caressed the back of his head. Gradually she could feel him relax as the anxiety drained away. Slowly he pulled away from her. He walked over and looked at the dead bodies. Phillip jumped out of the SUV and ran, terrified, up the stairs as Radu came down. He ran over and looked at the bodies of the Tepes agents.

"Milord and lady, are you all right?"

"Yes, Radu. Apparently these guys think guns are effective against vampires."

"Actually, Alex," Stefania started, "I think they were using them to make you easier to stake. It did knock you to the floor."

"True. Well, hopefully they will think twice before coming back here."

"Maybe, or they'll just bring more agents."

"Nice."

"I'll take care of the bodies, sir."

"Thank you, Radu."

***

The Tepes lieutenant looked over the table at the remaining agents.

"So two demons killed two of your men and bit another. The male picked you up, bared his fangs, and told you he wasn't here to feed on us but to police their own?"

"Yes, sir."

"And you left?"

"Yes, sir. I have never seen one move so fast. Sam shot him, and he fell to the floor. Gil dove on him with a stake. He rolled out from under him and cut off his head as he landed. It was like he knew what was coming next. He even moved like he knew we were there."

"Hmmm, it seems there are two major factions among the demons. If they fight each other, maybe it will work to our advantage. So this super vampire is new to the area?"

"Yeah, they both are. Our agent in the house said they just arrived today from Chicago."

"Hmmm, our chapter in Chicago reported that the vampire attacks have all but ceased in the last few days. They have not even seen a vampire since their 'meeting.' Apparently, the meeting was with these two. Something big is happening, and we need to keep an eye on it. With luck, this war between demon factions will thin their numbers enough that we can wipe them out for good."

"You know, sir, we could help one side and then wipe them out after we have defeated the other. It wouldn't be immoral since they are creatures of evil."

"Not a bad idea. Let me think on this. I will come up with a plan. Yeah, I like that idea a lot."

Chapter XVI

Nickolea sat in his chair. Siobhan, a tall, curvaceous, stunningly beautiful blonde-haired woman, stood before him, giving her report. After she had finished, he stood and walked to her. He slapped her, and she flew across the room. She crawled back to him and groveled at his feet.

"Siobhan, I wanted information about the death of those two Enclave agents, and you bring me this?" Nickolea growled.

"But lord, I watched from the skylight like you ordered. The hunter drew his sword, removed Scott's head, and sheathed his sword before the head hit the floor. He moved faster than any other vampire I have ever seen. The female agent didn't even react. She continued as if nothing even happened. She did not even flinch when Scott jumped toward them. They had the entire situation under control. When the rest of the group attacked, he moved through them like a buzz saw, cutting off only the arms that held a weapon. He was lightning fast and laser accurate. There was a traitor on the catwalks, and he put a knife right in front of him from over fifty yards away. He cleared the man's nose by millimeters."

"Well, maybe your information is valuable after all. You may kiss my hand."

She crawled up the leg she was clinging to and kissed his hand. He lifted her to a standing position and kissed her. He ran his hand along her hip and across her buttock. She moaned quietly at his touch.

"Now go and bring me Sigmund. I have to prepare a welcome for these agents."

He stood there for a few minutes while she went into the

other room. She returned with a tall, blond, well-groomed man with piercing blue eyes. His beard was braided from his chin, and he wore a nice black suit. He walked confidently over to Nickolea. Once he was within a few feet of him, he bowed at the waist.

"Yes, my jarl, how may I serve you?"

"We have two visitors coming."

"Yes, lord, the emissaries of the Enclave are due here tomorrow."

"I want you to kill them."

"I understand and obey, my jarl. But, won't that bring down the wrath of the Enclave?"

"I don't care what those old men do. They are pitiful excuses for vampires who cower in hiding when we should be in charge. We are the alpha predators. Once we have killed their dogs, they will be too afraid to do anything."

"I understand your disdain for them, but what if they aren't too afraid and launch an attack? I realize that we will kill them, but how many of us will die?"

"Are you afraid of them? We will have hundreds flock to our banner when we show them how weak they are. We will have the strongest of our kind, the Gluts. All they will have are the weaklings, Thins. We will finally cull them from our numbers."

"We are weaklings, are we?" came a voice from the corner.

"Ah, Kenta Shinto, glad you could make it," Nickolea said to the dark figure approaching from the door.

"So we Thins are weak, are we?"

"Well, you are a Thin by necessity. Ninja must be quick and nimble."

"Well, you know I am only with you to get even with the Shadow for their treachery. Especially that human leader of theirs."

"Okay, Shinto, we'll get him. What do you think of the agents we have coming?"

"Well, I think the hunter is a Shadow. He is possibly a Kensai. Only problem is, I have killed all their Kensai except one."

"How is that a problem?"

"He is a human, and that hunter is definitely a vampire."

"So couldn't he have become one?"

"He would have to have ended over a thousand years of tradition."

"Why is that?"

"The remaining Kensai is the master of the clan, the Lord of the Shadow. For the last thousand years, only a human can rule the clan. However, they could have already replaced one of the Kensai I killed, too. But I doubt that."

"Why do you doubt that?"

"The only member good enough to make a Kensai is Kinoshi, and he is still in Los Angeles wiping out your coven there. They are currently being purged," Shinto said in a flat tone. "He is carrying out the will of the Enclave. Everyone thinks you fled in fear. I know better, but others do not."

Nickolea's face turned bright red. "Purged? Those reprobates dare purge my coven?"

"Even more, Kinoshi sent a group of their clan to purge Chicago too. I am just letting you know so you can get this situation under control."

"Shinto, I need you to go to Paris to put phase 2 into action. You are the only one I can trust with this."

The ninja bowed. "Yes, Nickolea, I do as you ask. It serves my purposes as well."

With a puff of smoke, the ninja disappeared. An uneasiness deep in Nickolea's gut started to settle with the man's departure. He noticed the other vampires in the room also became a little less tense. Nickolea could not understand why Shinto made him feel that way. Perhaps it was the fact that he had no control over him. Shinto felt absolutely no fear. Well, his usefulness was about to end. He turned to Sigmund.

"Like I said before, end them."

"Yes, my jarl," Sigmund replied and left the room.

Nickolea sat and leaned back into his chair. Siobhan ran over and sat at his feet with her legs behind her. He reached down and scratched her head. She looked at him with longing eyes. When he did not seem to respond, she looked back down, dejected. He continued to scratch her head reflexively, and she lay at his feet.

Chapter XVII

Alex walked over to the mirror and adjusted his cloak. His dress uniform from the Romanian military matched in color and texture. He bared his fangs and looked at himself in the mirror. He had been a vampire for months now, and he was having difficulty getting used to it. He cautiously touched the serpentine fangs, sharp as hypodermic needles. They tapered from needle-sharp tips to the size of the tip of a new crayon at the base. They were designed to pierce the skin and underlying blood vessels and then expand the hole without tearing to allow a controllable blood flow. A vampire was designed to leave its prey alive. *Leave it to a human mentality and hunger for excess,* he thought, *to turn it into a murderous thing.*

Stefania walked up behind Alex. She ran her arms around him.

"Keep playing with them and you'll go blind," she snickered. "They are incredible pieces of art, aren't they? Perfectly designed for what they do. Believe it or not, after four hundred years, I still look at mine in awe. Yours are so beautifully formed. I have not seen many like them. Mine are, yours are. Strangely, though, Nickolea's are not. Maybe I should have taken that as a hint he should not be a vampire."

"Why do you say that?"

"His fangs are rough, not smooth. They tear instead of gliding in. Like I said, they are imperfect. Father told me that but I didn't listen. I should have slain him when I saw them, but I thought I loved him and he loved me, so I felt a few imperfections were acceptable—even against Father's advice."

"Now I am really confused. The formation of the teeth are a determining factor of if someone should be a vampire? So you kill anyone without perfect teeth?"

"No, silly, just with teeth that are not smooth. Rough teeth make holes that do not heal correctly; they are a genetic throwback to a more primitive ancestor. That particular mutation puts the species at risk, so we usually destroy them. Well, the extreme cases like Nickolea. Even his mentality is a throwback to that same ancestor. That is why he has to be stopped, no matter what."

Alex turned around and kissed her. He wiped away the tears that formed at the corners of her eyes. She looked up at him and smiled a gentle, loving smile. He smiled back and turned back toward the mirror to adjust his uniform. He turned back and noticed what she was wearing. Stefania had a black seventeenth-century Spanish doublet over a billowy white shirt. She wore tight leather pants with black riding boots with a flat sole. She wore her saber on her side. The black cloak of the Enclave rode comfortably on her shoulders. The hood draped across her back, blending in with the doublet.

"Expecting trouble?" he asked.

"Always. I noticed you are wearing a katana instead of the saber. I take that to mean you are expecting trouble also."

"Feels better in my hand. It also cuts cleaner—if I need to cut."

"Do you really think they will surrender him peacefully?"

"No, he has them very deeply under his control. If you see him, point him out to me. I don't even know what he looks like."

"Will do, babe. If you are ready, let's go."

Alex nodded his head and pulled the hood up on his cloak. His face disappeared except for his lips and below. The creamy white of his skin accentuated the pale pink of his lips. Stefania noted how his color had lightened. She was concerned he was not drinking enough blood. He needed as much energy tonight as he could muster. She signaled Radu. Radu turned and walked over to the refrigerator and pulled out a bottle with dark-red blood and returned to Stefania. He handed it to her and stood in front of Alex, blocking his way.

"Alex, hold on a second," Stefania said.

"Yes, Stefania?" he asked as he turned around and saw the bottle of blood in her hand. "What is that?"

"A bottle of fresh blood."

"And what is it for?" he asked with a raised eyebrow.

"You. You need to drink it before we get there. You are too pale. It tells me you are not drinking enough. I want you fully in control of your head there. If you are hit with the hunger while we are fighting or trying to negotiate, it could be bad. Now drink it all."

She shoved the bottle in his hand. He tried to resist, but she was stronger and more determined than he was. He reluctantly opened it and drank the bottle dry. It was a touch sweet with salty undertones. It was like no other blood she had ever given him. He turned it back and drained the remaining drops. He felt his body fill with energy. He even felt a slight bit giddy.

"What was that?" he asked.

"Fresh donor blood, without the preservatives," she replied.

"What else? I have tasted fresh blood. This is different."

"It was from a pregnant donor. It provides more nutrients."

"What? Blood from a pregnant woman?"

"It is all right, Alex. It was a willing donor, and there was no risk to the mother or the baby."

"How can you be sure of that?"

"Hmmm, I don't know . . . over three hundred years of experience?"

Alex backed off a bit. "Okay, okay, sorry I got upset. It just caught me off guard, is all."

"It is probably the blood. You felt the euphoria, right? That is the feeling I have been telling you about. That is why Gluts are gluts."

"Wow. Yes, I did. Interesting feeling. I might have to research a bit more." Alex smiled.

"Let's go now that you are ready."

They walked down the stairs to the garage and entered their car. Again, Radu sat in the front with the driver, and Alina sat in the back with Alex and Stefania. The driver moved easily through traffic. They were in the car for what seemed an eternity. Alex began to feel nervous. He could tell something was wrong but could not locate it. Stefania watched him as he began to squirm visibly.

"Alex, what is wrong?" she asked.

"I am not sure," he replied. "Something is wrong, and I can't pinpoint what it is. It is like a general feeling."

"Like not all is right with the universe?" she asked playfully.

"Kind of. It's like it is all around us yet nowhere."

"We'll be careful."

"It is going to take more than that."

He pulled out his phone and started dialing. He held the phone to his ear and waited impatiently for the other person to answer. Soon she could tell someone had answered, and he said a single word. "Initiate." He then hung up the phone and threw it out the window.

Before Stefania could speak, they pulled up to the meeting place. Alex stepped out of the car with his hood fully in place. He placed the katana in his belt. He cracked his knuckles and waited for Stefania to join him. She walked over to him. Her hood was in place, and they started to walk toward the door. Two vampires in black suits stopped them at the door.

"This is a private party. I need to see your invitation."

Alex pulled out the katana and removed the arm blocking his way. He sheathed it and turned to the vampire.

"Never bar my way again," Alex said matter-of-factly.

They walked in the door. The other guard touched his mic.

"They're coming in."

The door closed behind them, and they could see the warehouse was filled with vampires. In the back was a raised catwalk with a stair leading up on each side. On it stood Sigmund, with a black-suited vampire on each side. The vampires on the floor divided as they approached the catwalk. Alex and Stefania took note where each member of the crowd was. Soon they approached the catwalk, and Sigmund addressed them.

"Welcome to our small gathering, esteemed representatives of the Enclave."

Alex did not raise his head. "Step down. You will not stand above us."

"But this is my rightful place," Sigmund responded.

"You will step down here, or you will not be able to. This disrespect will not be tolerated."

"If you think you can make me, hunter, do so," Sigmund said with contempt.

Alex leaped onto the catwalk, drawing his sword, and cut Sigmund's beard even with his chin. He then grabbed his braided ponytail and flipped him off the catwalk and onto the floor. He turned and chopped the heads from the two guards standing next to Sigmund and flipped back to the floor. The crowd stood perfectly still in shock.

"So you are below me now," Alex said with his boot across the back of Sigmund's neck. He turned to the remainder of the crowd and raised his voice loud enough for them all to hear.

"Lack of respect and disobedience to the Enclave will not be accepted. Anyone giving assistance or hospitality to Nickolea Dalakis will face the displeasure of the Enclave."

The crowd shuffled in place. They were visibly nervous. Alex looked around. Another vampire stepped out on the catwalk. Stefania let out a nervous gasp. Alex recognized him; this vampire's face was burned into his memory. He realized Nickolea Dalakis stood before him, and he was the one who'd killed his parents and left him an orphan. Alex's mouth formed into a snarl. He prepared to leap when Stefania placed her hand on his arm, stopping him.

"Hello, Nickolea," she said.

"Saria, or should I say Stefania, who is your pet?"

"Nickolea, you will surrender immediately, to be brought before the justice of the Enclave. If you do not, this will not go well for you."

"Saria, you never were very good at threats. You have no authority in your voice. You are too weak. That is why you have that thing with you. You cannot kill anyone yourself."

"Nickolea, you have always confused mercy with weakness. I

only give you the opportunity to help yourself. If you surrender, the Enclave may have mercy on you. If it were up to me, I would have already taken your head. But that is not the Enclave's desire."

"You are sorely outnumbered. With a word, my faithful will rip you apart."

Alex grabbed the immobilized Sigmund by his hair and flung him over his shoulder into the crowd.

"You mean like that one?"

"Why don't you kill her and join me? We can be gods over men, as is our right."

"You don't know me, do you, Nicky?" Alex threw back his hood. Nickolea stared into his eyes. He saw the flame of hate.

"No, should I?"

"I have killed many of your minions around the world."

"And?"

"I did it while I was still a human. So you see, you are not so much greater than the ones you want to rule and feed upon as you desire." Alex turned to the entire crowd. "Not a single one of you was born a vampire. You were all created from humans. If humans are so weak and beneath you, then what are you if not just as weak?" He turned back to Nickolea. "You are so weak; you could not even kill me. You sent your best with a poisoned blade and still could not kill me."

Nickolea looked at him closely. "You are that human that Saria cared so much for." He stepped back. "You should be dead. You should have turned into a Reaper and Saria would have had to kill you herself."

"I overcame that little surprise you left for me. You are not quite so superior, are you, if you cannot beat me. You could not kill a mere human, could you? I am also that little boy you left for dead after murdering his parents in cold blood."

With that statement, Alex leaped up into the air, landed directly in front of Nickolea, and struck him on the shoulders, driving him to his knees. He then fastened a set of multicolored manacles onto his wrists. Nickolea jerked against them, and he felt two needles slip into his wrists.

"Those needles will drain the blood from your radial arteries. You of all people should know what will happen next."

Alex turned around and saw Sigmund standing in front of the crowd, snarling and holding a sword. He charged forward.

"Save the jarl, kill the intruders," he screamed with a heavy Nordic accent.

The crowd surged forward. They had drawn their swords and advanced toward Stefania. Alex leaped down in front of Stefania, pulling Nickolea with him, and dropped him between them. He looked back at Stefania.

"Get him out of here," Alex said.

"I will not leave you. He'll keep," she said as she pulled her sword into a guard position with the crowd approaching them.

As the crowd broke over them, Alex punched Sigmund, snapping his neck. He moved with clean precision as he removed one head after another. He watched as Stefania did the same. He dodged and caught a blade across the ribs as he flipped back around to take the head of the sword's owner. He slowly moved so that he was back to back with Stefania with Nickolea between them. He rapidly removed head after head. He had to kick the bodies away.

The crowd was starting to thin, but they seemed endless. As they were starting to be overcome, the windows shattered, and ten white uniformed figures entered the room. They started to attack the crowd from the back. Soon the tide began to turn, and the crowd started to splinter as the members started to break and run for their lives. Finally, the battle was over. Alex walked over to the leader of the white uniformed figures.

"Thank you Taiga," he said.

"Yes, Venerable Master," he replied in a thick Japanese accent. "Lord Kinoshi would have been here himself, but he was stuck in Los Angeles cleaning up."

"I understand. I am very glad he sent you."

Alex walked over to Stefania. Her cloak and clothes were

sliced in multiple locations. She had deep wounds in multiple stages of healing. She reached up and kissed him. He leaned to help her up and felt the cut across his side. It had closed, but it remained very tender. He looked down at his clothes and saw many cuts and slices through them. Stefania walked over to him and wiped blood from his brow before it could drop into his eyes.

"Well, my darling, all we have left is to bring him to the Enclave for their judgment," Stefania said.

"He can't pay enough for what he has done."

Chapter XVIII

The Tepes lord commander looked at the report his lieutenant had handed him. He carefully read every word, frowning as he moved to the end of the report. He laid it on the desk, stood up, and walked over to the window in his office, staring out at Lake Pontchartrain. He remained silent for several moments, just staring outside. Then he finally spoke.

"So this group that came here from Chicago had help. A large group of ninja, samurai, or something. And those twelve demons killed approximately fifty to one hundred other demons?"

"Yes, Lord Commander, that is accurate."

"Who are these creatures?"

"Well, the ten that joined the fight late are from a large organization in Japan. The only name for them we can get is the Shadow. A Caucasian led them until recently, when he disappeared. The Order of the Tepes members in Japan has been watching them for some time now. It seems they are a kind of vampire police force."

"A vampire police force? So they hunt vampire criminals? They should kill themselves, then. They are all murdering demons. So what can anyone tell us about this super vampire?"

"Nothing, sir. He is new on the scene. The Order in Los Angeles seems to think he is somehow related to this Shadow. After he appeared there, the numbers of the Shadow increased exponentially. They have reduced the numbers of demons in LA by over three-quarters. They have decreased the numbers in Chicago by half. They just started showing up here in the last few days."

"This is concerning. We may not be able to fight this new force of demons as easily as the ones before. This makes them more dangerous. We need to capture one. So we can interrogate him."

"Capture one, sir?"

"Yes, capture one. We need to know what is happening. Also, bring in the creature you already captured. We need to find out what all this is about. I can't have a bunch of unknown factors running around, causing me problems," the lord commander said, holding out his hand, exposing a large gold ring with a ruby set into it.

"Yes, Lord Commander."

The man kneeled, kissed the ring, stood again, and left the room. The lord commander walked back over to the window and stared out over the lake once again. Soon there was a knock on the door. Without turning around, the lord commander spoke.

"Enter."

Two burly men brought in a pale-skinned man and dropped him in front of the lord commander's desk. He fought against his bonds and hissed at the guards. The lord commander turned away from the window and approached the vampire. The vampire bared his fangs, and jumped for him. The lord commander quickly turned sideways, and the vampire missed his neck. The vampire landed in a heap and one of the guards put his foot on the vampire's neck. The vampire lay still on the floor.

"Release it," he ordered.

The guard took his foot from the back of the vampire's neck. The guards pulled the vampire up to his feet by his bonds. The vampire screamed in pain. He stood looking at the lord commander, trying to look into his eye. The lord commander stared him in the eye. After a second, the vampire looked away from him.

"So devil, who is the super vampire?" the lord commander finally asked.

The vampire looked at him and spit on him.

"Answer the lord commander," one of the guards said.

The vampire spat on him too.

"You foul devil," the guard punched him as hard as he could in the abdomen. The vampire doubled over. He spat out a little blood on the floor.

The lord commander signaled the guard to stop. He pulled out a bag of donor blood and held it in front of his captive. The vampire started to salivate uncontrollably. The pain was approaching intolerable. He had not fed in days. He lunged for the bag. The lord commander held it just out of his reach. The captive continued to scramble for the bag.

"Tell me what I want to know, and it is yours," he told the captive.

"I'll tell you anything," he hissed. "Just give me the bag. I can't take the pain anymore. The hunger is consuming me." The captive reached for the bag again with his mouth, and the lord commander pulled it away.

"Who is the super vampire?"

"We don't know. He is an agent of the Enclave. He just appeared one day," he said, stretching for the bag.

The lord commander pulled it away again. "What is the Enclave?"

"It is the collection of all the leaders of the major vampire covens. They make decisions that relate to the entire vampire species," the captive replied.

"Hmm, interesting. Where is this Enclave held and when?"

"I don't know. Only people invited know when and where. But I think they are held in the same place every time."

"Okay, you can have this," the lord commander said, tossing him the bag of blood.

The captive vampire grabbed it from the ground in his mouth, pierced the plastic with his fangs, and sucked it dry. The Tepes watched him as he consumed the blood. They saw his withered body regain some of its mass. His arms and legs fleshed out, and his skin seemed less wrinkled. As he fought his bonds, they seemed to strain more against his muscles.

The lord commander watched and took mental notes of what was happening. All this would go into his report, including all the information on this Enclave. The lord captain would be very interested in this new information. He signaled for the guards to take the prisoner away. He needed to keep this one alive to give him more information. Once he had one of the Shadow, he could get enough information to make vampires an endangered species, a much-endangered species indeed.

Cɦᴀᴘᴛᴇʀ XIX

Alex dragged Nickolea's unconscious body up the stairs into the jet and threw him into a seat. He buckled him in and covered him completely with a blanket, then closed the curtain and signaled Stefania that she could come inside. She cautiously looked into the plane. When she could not see the unconscious Nickolea, she walked in and sat in her chair. Alex sat in his. Soon the plane was moving down the runway, and the plane was airborne.

Once the plane was at cruising altitude, Alex and Stefania snuggled on the couch. After a few minutes, Radu and Alina brought a glass of blood to each of them. As he sipped at his, Alex realized he was finally getting used to the taste of blood. It was actually beginning to get pleasurable. He saw Stefania continuing to glance back toward the compartment where he'd secured Nickolea.

"Darling, he is secured and unconscious," Alex reassured her.

"I know, but this day has been so long in coming. The fact that he is on the same plane as we are makes me as nervous as a long-tailed cat in a room full of rocking chairs."

Alex looked at her, perplexed. "I haven't heard that saying since my grandmother died."

"Well, I am about four hundred years old now, you know."

"True. So once we are out from under the Enclave's thumb, what do you want to do?"

"Hmm, I haven't thought about it. You are really good at this hunting down fugitives stuff."

"Well, I have been hunting Nickolea a long time."

"So he is the one who killed your parents?"

"Yeah, that is why I joined the gang as a teen. I wanted to learn how to kill. I wanted to be comfortable with it. I just didn't have a taste for killing humans. Now killing vampires, that was a horse of another color. Once I met Kinoshi, I found out about the world of rogue vampires. I decided that would give me experience in killing vampires. Since the one I was looking for was a rogue, it would give me a chance to hunt him too."

"So why were you so reserved with me once you found out I was a vampire? You did not think I was a rogue, did you?" She looked at him in horror.

"I didn't know. You didn't act like any I had met. I had to be sure. I had already had one love affair with a vampire that went wrong."

"The coworker in New York—Britney, right?"

"Yeah, she was sent to seduce me so she could kill me. I thought she was human, so after a while I told her what I really did."

"So she set about to end you."

"Yep. I wonder if it was by Nickolea's order."

"Maybe. It could even have been by the order of Shinto."

"Perhaps, but we will probably never know. I am sure she is long gone from here."

Again she looked toward the back of the plane. "One thing still bothers me. He was too easy to capture. I don't understand that. Why didn't he fight back?"

"He was just outclassed. I was faster and smarter. I didn't give him time to react."

"Yes, but Nickolea didn't go to the bathroom without a back-up plan. We never found the blood or RX-34 storage either."

"He just got overconfident and made a mistake. As for the RX-34, maybe all he had was the vial he had given to Shinto to kill me. Maybe we were misled about the whole Reaper army thing."

"Possibly. I hope we aren't just missing something, though. He was too easy to capture."

Stefania looked at Alex's glass. "My lord, your glass is empty. Should I have Radu refill it?" she said playfully.

He looked down at the glass. "Yes, my lady, please do."

She touched a button on the side of the couch. Radu appeared. "Yes, my lady. What can I do for you?"

"Please get Lord cel Tinar another glass. He apparently likes this vintage."

Radu looked at the glass and Alex. Alex nodded his head and smiled. Radu smiled back, headed to the front of the plane, and brought out a crystal decanter. He refilled both Alex and Stefania's glasses. He then disappeared into the front of the plane. Stefania smiled at Alex and snuggled into his chest as they continued to sip their drinks in silence.

They woke to the captain announcing their descent toward the Colony's airport. It would still be another hour or so until they landed. Stefania led Alex to their private suite. She undressed and stepped into the shower. Alex undressed and followed her. She had already lathered a natural sponge and handed it to Alex. He stood behind her and ran the sponge across her bare breasts.

She tilted her head back into his chest. He kissed her neck as he continued to wash her. He continued down her tight abdomen. He scrubbed in small circular motions. She turned around and kissed him. She took the sponge and ran it across his bare chest. She chose her motions carefully. She ran the sponge down his tight abdomen and across his washboard abs.

He reached forward and kissed her. She tilted her head back and bared her neck. He bared his fangs and bit deep into her neck. He tasted her sweet blood, and he could feel the spasms of passion flowing through her. He licked her neck and shifted his head. She leaned forward and bit deep into his neck. He could feel the pleasure run through his entire body. She licked his neck. The sensation of her rough tongue was a pleasure of its own.

They finished their shower and headed out into their individual dressing rooms. Radu and Alina awaited them. Radu helped Alex into his dress uniform he had prepared. Alex looked at him questioningly, but Radu did not speak until Alex was fully dressed and ready to meet anyone.

"Lord, I pulled out the dress uniform because we received a message from the Colony. The Enclave has assembled, and you are to head there immediately with the prisoner."

"What? I thought the enclave wasn't for another several days."

"Apparently, as soon as word reached the Colony of Nickolea's capture, they started the wheels in motion."

"I will wear my saber, then. This is Enclave business and, by default, Colony business."

"Yes, my lord."

Radu headed to return the katana and retrieve the saber. Alex walked out into the main area and saw Stefania dressed in regal attire, wearing her Spanish coronet. Radu walked in and belted the saber on Alex's waist as Stefania looked on. Alex looked at her, and she nodded in approval. He sat in his seat next to her and fastened his seat belt. He could feel the plane's steep descent.

"The saber was an excellent choice, Alex," Stefania said.

"I thought it appropriate," he replied. "Since we are on Enclave business."

Stefania smiled. They looked out the window and saw the ground rushing up. As it seemed to get uncomfortably close, the pilot pulled up, and the plane was on the ground a few minutes later. Radu and Alina placed the black cloaks of agents of the Enclave around their necks. Radu walked over and opened the door of the plane. Outside was a twenty-man security team. Alex dragged Nickolea to the door, and the security team closed around the bottom of the stairs. Alex brought him to the bottom, and they put him into the back of a van with several members of the security team. Alex and Stefania got into a waiting SUV with Radu and Alina. The motorcade drove over to the assembly hall where the Enclave waited.

The large assembly hall rose before them. There were large groups of security officers spread out around the route. Thousands of vampires from all over the world had come to see the proceedings of Nickolea Dalakis. Alex and Stefania watched the crowds, looking for anything out of the ordinary. They expected a rescue attempt. They knew how Nickolea's followers revered him. The trip was uneventful as the motorcade stopped in front of the assembly hall.

Alex and Stefania stepped out of the SUV as the security team brought Nickolea up to them. The entire entourage walked into the building. It was a short trip to where the Enclave waited. As soon as their entourage entered and the courtier announced them, a team of the Shadow walked up to them led by Kinoshi. They relieved the security team and led Nickolea behind Alex and Stefania. Soon they were in the middle of the hall. Alex stepped forward to the microphone.

"Honorable members of the Enclave," he started. "As agents of the Enclave, we were entrusted with the task of hunting and capturing the fugitive known as Nickolea Dalakis. We stand before you after completing this task. We consign to you the criminal known as Nickolea Dalakis."

He stepped back. A security team dressed in the black cloaks of the Enclave stepped forward and took Nickolea from them. They dragged him away through a door in the back of the room. An older man Alex did not recognize walked forward to the microphone.

"As the speaker of the Enclave, we accept the prisoner. We also exonerate you from all charges brought before you on this and previous matters. Your responsibilities to the Enclave are completed. Alexandrel cel Tinar and Stefania cel Tinar, please be seated. The Enclave has other business to attend. But you will be recalled."

They were escorted to a booth off to the side, where they were asked to wait. They looked at each other and over to the Colony representatives. Stefan sat in the booth. The blank look on his face revealed nothing. He looked over at Kinoshi, who also had a blank expression. Alex and Stefania looked around them. The booth was similar to the booths of all the representatives but was slightly different. They both started to pull back their hoods but the security officers near them stopped them. As soon as they were settled, the speaker started again.

"Honorable members of the Enclave, with the severe nature of recent events and the quantity of these events, the motion has been made for a Council of Covens to be formed. This Council of Covens will consist of ten representatives elected by the Enclave. These representatives will represent the Enclave in situations such as this to prevent the inconvenience of calling a full enclave. This council will hear grievances and cases that do not require the full enclave. This council will have a group of agents that will carry out punishments and capture fugitives.

"Who will second this motion?"

"I will," Stefan stated.

"The motion has been made and seconded. All in favor signify with the green paddle."

A wave of green flowed across the Enclave. The recorder counted the paddles.

"All against, signify with a red paddle."

A flow of red passed across the Enclave. It was significantly smaller than the green. The recorder counted the paddles.

A voice came from the back. "How can we be guaranteed the council will act in the best interest of the Enclave?"

"It will be chosen by the Enclave. Every member sits at the pleasure of the Enclave. Should the members of the populace think the Council is not acting in their best interest, they can replace the members. In addition, the agents will be agents of the Enclave, not of the Council. They will maintain the interest of the Enclave.

"Will Alexandrel and Stefania cel Tinar please return to the platform?"

Alex and Stefania stood and walked back to the center of the room where the microphone was. As soon as they arrived, the speaker continued.

"Lord and Lady cel Tinar, you have shown great dedication to task and great resourcefulness by capturing a fugitive who has eluded many others. You have been chosen by the Enclave by unanimous vote to lead the corps of agents to the Enclave. Will you accept this honor?"

Alex and Stefania stood in shock for a several seconds. Alex was first to find his voice.

"This is a great and unexpected honor the Enclave offers." He looked at Stefania, and she nodded. "We accept."

"Then you may return to the box of the corps," the speaker stated.

There was applause throughout the assembly hall. Stefan and Kinoshi both had large grins on their faces. As Alex and Stefania arrived back at their box, two agents stood and walked over to them. They bowed to them and seated them. Within minutes, Radu and Alina walked to the box to stand behind them.

The speaker continued, "The Enclave has voted to form the Council of the Covens. The elections will begin after other business has been completed. The proceeding of Nickolea Dalakis will begin tomorrow morning. The meeting of the Enclave will now come to a close."

Everyone filed out of the assembly hall. Stefan and Kinoshi walked over to the couple. A couple of the black-cloaked agents remained in the box, waiting patiently. Both Stefan and Kinoshi were smiling broadly. They hugged both of them. Stefan kissed Stefania on the cheek.

"So, daughter, how does it feel to be one of the most powerful people in the world right now?"

"Surreal, definitely surreal. I take it you two had something to do with this?"

They both looked innocent.

"Who, us? Why would you think that?" Kinoshi asked.

"Well, perhaps it was the smiles you both had," Alex answered.

"Well, it is definitely well deserved. You two have hunted and captured probably the most notorious fugitive in all of vampire history," Stefan stated.

"That is evidence enough of your ability and tenacity. Well we will meet you at Stefan's house. These gentlemen have waited long enough," Kinoshi said, indicating the other agents.

"We'll see you there," Stefania said.

Stefan and Kinoshi left the booth and headed for the door. They signaled to Radu and Alina to follow. The two walked out with them. The assembly hall was now completely deserted except for the four agents in the booth. Two agents walked up to Alex and Stefania. They bowed at the waist.

"Lord and Lady cel Tinar, please follow us. We will show you to your new office," the first agent stated.

They indicated for Alex and Stefania to follow. They led them out of the hall and down a hallway leading deeper into the building. After several turns, they walked up to a large black walnut door with two agents standing at attention. The large, heavy door opened easily with the pull of the second agent. They walked into a large room ornately decorated with wooden carvings. Two large ebony desks sat toward the back of the room. Two other doors led into the room.

Alex and Stefania walked up to the ornate desks. They ran their hands across the perfectly smooth wood. All the carvings were detailed and well shaded. The chairs were made of ebony, and the seats and backs upholstered with fine black leather. The cushions felt so comfortable, it was like sitting on nothing.

"This is your office," the first agent started. "The door to your left leads to the chambers of the new Council. The door to the right leads to the agents' wardroom. An agent will always staff the door we came in and the one from the Council chambers. No one will be allowed in without an appointment. No one."

"Excellent. Have all the agents assigned here arrived?" Stefania asked.

"Well, Lady cel Tinar, all the active agents are assigned to this office. If you would like, we can call everyone in. However, I recommend sending word for them to report back after their assignments are complete. Most of their assignments are coming to a close anyway. Yours was the only open-ended one left. We have several agents here in the facility, and several more are on their way. We currently have twenty active agents."

"Thank you for the report. We will let everyone's assignments expire, and then we need to see everyone here in this office. By the way, feel free to call us Stefania and Alex."

"Thank you, but I prefer to call you by your titles. That is, until you choose code names, which you really should do before the meeting."

"We will take it under advisement," Alex responded. "We need to head home. Thank you for your time."

"It is our pleasure. We have waited a long time for this organization to get some real structure. It has been too haphazard for too long, and it is too important to remain that way. We are also very pleased to have the famous cel Tinars to make up the leadership."

The two agents bowed and headed toward the wardroom. Alex and Stefania headed back out the way they had come. The agents watching the door saluted as they exited. The building was eerily quiet. They could hear the click-clack of their heels as they walked. Soon they reached the door outside. A carriage waited on the drive. Radu sat next to the driver and stepped down as they walked closer. Radu helped Alina from the carriage and assisted Stefania in. Alex assisted Alina in the seat next to Stefania, then accepted Radu's assistance into the carriage himself. Radu climbed back to the seat next to the driver. The driver popped the reins to get the carriage moving.

The carriage slowly moved through the streets of the Colony. Stefania looked out the window to see the stars that had thrilled her so much as a young woman. They had changed but not enough that she cared. He smiled to see such glee in Stefania's eyes. Soon the coach arrived at Stefan and Ecaterina's home. Radu helped Alex and Stefania out, then Alina. He sent the coach along as he rang the doorbell.

Stefan opened the door and welcomed the entourage in. Alex shook Stefan's hand. Ecaterina came up and hugged them both. Soon Esmeralda walked in. She ran up to Stefania and hugged her. She grabbed Alex too. Soon she released them both and looked up at them.

"Can I go to America with you now that the bad man is

gone?" she pleaded.

"If it is okay with Mother and Father, you can go back with us," she said, looking at Ecaterina.

"Stefania, I know you will take good care of her. So you have our blessing," Ecaterina responded.

"Cool," Esmeralda said.

"We are not leaving for a little while, so don't pack your bags yet."

"Ahhh," Esmeralda said with a cute pout.

Stefania turned to Stefan. "Father, we are tired. We are going home and will see you in the morning."

"As you wish, my darling girl."

They said the rest of their good-byes and walked out the door. They walked down the street with Radu and Alina behind them. The stars seemed brighter than usual to Alex. Soon they were at their front door. Radu produced a key and unlocked it. He then opened the door and escorted them in. Alex and Stefania walked to their bedchamber, fell onto the bed, and fell asleep.

Alex awoke after a few minutes to Radu trying to remove his boots. He stood and undressed and put on pajamas and prepared to go back to sleep when Stefania leaped straight up. She walked into the dressing room where Alina helped her into her sleeping gown. Alex and Stefania both went back to bed and fell sound asleep in each other's arms.

The rising sun woke Alex. He looked around. Stefania was still asleep beside him. Their clothes were hanging from valet trees, waiting for them. Steaming cups of coffee sat on warmers on the serving shelf. Alex smiled. He sat up on the side of the bed. As he stood, Stefania rolled toward his edge of the bed. She opened her eyes. She saw the steaming coffee. She quickly sprang out of bed and grabbed one of the cups.

"My coffee," she said as she held it protectively.

"Wow, I knew you loved coffee, but that much?" he said, smiling as he picked his up and sipped. "Chocolate raspberry truffle, hmmm."

Stefania smiled at Alex and looked over at their clothes. She frowned at the formal attire Radu and Alina had set out for them.

Alex smiled a little bit of a smile. He caught a touch of a fragrance. He took a deep breath and smelled. A large smile came across his face.

"Our staff is here. I smell eggs over medium, lightly toasted whole wheat bread, and steak cooked rare. With a glass of fresh-squeezed blood."

Stefania began laughing so hard she almost spilled her coffee. Almost.

"Fresh-squeezed blood." She chortled. "That is probably the funniest image I have ever had. I saw a cartoon man being twisted and blood running into two glasses by a cartoon vampire with huge fangs."

Alex started laughing. They both had a good laugh before heading into the kitchen. The small table was set with two plates. Everything was as Alex had mentioned, including the two glasses of fresh blood. Alex picked up his glass, smelled it, swished the glass, and took a small sip and swished it in his mouth. Stefania started laughing again. The staff looked at them as if they were insane.

Alex looked up at Radu and said, "That is a fine vintage. Has quite a nice body to it."

Radu rolled his eyes as Stefania cracked up again. Alina had to cover her mouth so her father could not see her giggling.

"Lord cel Tinar, it is very good to see you laughing, though the jokes are a little on the tasteless side."

"Radu, I am sorry. I guess it is the sense of relief that the mission is over. The danger is over. Nickolea's reign of terror is over."

"Yes, it is a time for rejoicing. But also a time of sorrow," Radu replied with a tear in his eye.

"Why is that?"

"Nickolea Dalakis is my great-great-uncle," Alina said.

Radu cut a look at her but then responded, "Yes, he is the shame of our family. We are remorseful about how he treated Lady cel Tinar. That is why my family swore we would serve your family from now till eternity."

"How can that be? Radu, you are a von Landon," Stefania said.

"It is the name of the family that raised me after my father and grandfather committed suicide when Nickolea betrayed you, Lady cel Tinar. Lord Stefan and Lady Ecaterina were going to raise me. The housekeeper said it was not proper for the lord and lady to be burdened with a human child, especially an infant. I am glad my mother died in childbirth and did not have to face that shame.

"Lady cel Tinar." Radu bowed before her on one knee. "I beg your forgiveness for the actions of my great-uncle."

"Radu, stand up this instant," Stefania snapped. "You have no responsibility for what that beast did to me."

Radu quickly stood. "But Lady, his actions have shamed our entire line."

"I grant you and your descendants pardon from any actions of your ancestors against me and mine," Stefania pronounced.

Radu smiled. "Lady cel Tinar, thank you, you have no idea how long I have carried that shame."

"Well, Radu, carry it no longer. I also release you from your vow to serve our family into perpetuity."

"That, Lady, I will not let you do. We owe you that much. Besides, I like taking care of your family. How would Lord Alexandrel get dressed in the mornings without me?"

"And Lady Stefania without me?" chimed in Alina.

"Your continued service is requested. However, we do not expect you to attend the proceedings. Nickolea will be executed, and I don't expect you to stand through that."

"Nickolea gets what he deserves. I will not shed a tear for his deceitful hide. I only shed a tear for the suffering you have had at his hand and the risk of your and Lord Alexandrel's life because of him. We will stand with you."

"Well, we'd better finish breakfast and get ready. It wouldn't look good if we were late. Oh, and Alina, we will go shopping later. You need some new clothes. We can take my little sister too."

"That would please me, Lady Stefania."

They finished their breakfast. Radu and Alex headed to one

dressing room, Alina and Stefania to the other. Once Alex had showered and dressed, Radu held up his new black cloak. Alex looked at it and hoisted it to his shoulders. Next, Radu pulled out his new hunter's tassel. It was a full loop with a ten-inch tail hanging down his chest. It was filled with small stripes. It now bore three thick stripes. Alex looked at it as Radu put it on him.

Soon they stepped out of the dressing room. Radu placed Alex's circlet on his head. Soon Stefania stepped out of her dressing room. She wore a traditional seventeenth-century formal Spanish gown. The greens and blues were woven together in different patterns. She wore her royal coronet, as always. Alina settled the new black cloak on her ladyship's shoulders and connected the clasp. They walked outside and entered the carriage that was waiting for them. It carried them to the door of the assembly hall. Kinoshi and Stefan were waiting outside for them.

"Are you two ready for this?" Stefan asked.

"Ready for what?" Alex asked.

"You will be required to stand as accusers of Nickolea, Stefania as his dame and you as his brother. This is the worst kind of accusatory process. You must stand before him the entire time. You think you can do this, Stefania?"

"Yes, Father, I can," she said with an absoluteness Alex had never seen from her.

"Excellent. Let's go in, then. It is amazing that you two have your own booth. As agents of the Enclave, you are also officers of the tribunal. You are also the executioners."

"Well, I am sure one of our men can handle that. I will assign one of them," Alex stated before Stefania could say anything.

Stefania shook her head. "No, this is something I need to do."

Alex looked at her, surprised. "Are you sure?" he asked.

"Absolutely," she stated resolutely. "I must see this to the end."

They walked into the hall. The halls were already crowded as they made their way into the entry chamber. It was a cavernous room with banners strung throughout its rafters. Two agents stood at the entrance to the hall, each holding a glaive. They saluted as Alex and Stefania approached. They returned the salute and walked in. An entourage of agents stood just inside the door. They walked with Alex and Stefania as they headed for their booth. Once they arrived, Alex turned to the group.

"So are we responsible for escorting it out?"

"The Shadow has requested that honor, sir," one of the men answered. "I didn't think you would mind, under the circumstances."

Alex nodded. "Excellent idea. Kinoshi can handle that."

"Actually, Lord Kinoshi was not the one who requested. It was Lord Taiga, Lady Amaya and a group of the Shadow from Los Angeles. Ten of them, as a matter of fact."

Alex looked at Stefania and nodded. She nodded back.

As the hall began to fill, they all pulled up their hoods. The hoods shrouded their faces in darkness except for their mouths, and each of those were expressionless. Soon the hall filled. At exactly nine, the speaker of the Enclave walked out to the microphone. As he tapped it, the room became as quiet as a tomb.

"Good morning, honorable members of the Enclave and members of the public at large. We are here today to hear the accusations against Nickolea Dalakis, charges brought by his dame, Crown Princess Rosaria of Spain, House Habsburg, now known as Stefania cel Tinar, and his brother, Daimyo Richard Smythe, Venerable Master of the Shadow, now known as Alexandrel cel Tinar. Sylvester von Habsburg of the greater Austrian coven prosecutes the case. The defendant has chosen to represent himself. Will the accusers please approach the podium?"

Alex and Stefania walked from the booth and headed for the podium. The assemblage watched them with interest. Once they arrived at the podium, the speaker called for the prisoner.

"Bring forth the prisoner, Nickolea Dalakis."

A large door in the back of the building opened, and a group of members of the Shadow in full uniform led Nickolea to the podium. None of them wore the black and red of a Kensai. Nickolea stood, defiant, in front of the assemblage. Several of the public attendees averted their eyes so he did not see their eyes. Once he was in position, the prosecutor walked out and stood before him. He first turned to Stefania and Alexandrel.

"What are the charges?"

Stefania spoke first. "Nickolea failed to accept the teachings as I presented them. He felt himself above the Law. In failing to accept the teachings as dictated by the Law, he has committed treason against the vampire race."

"As my brother, he attempted to murder, then to discredit and emotionally torture his dame. He sent others to try to kill our dame and me instead of taking that task unto himself. Therefore he has committed treason against our line," Alex stated.

"By inciting others to commit treason and then be executed for that treason, he is responsible for the unnecessary deaths of hundreds of vampires. He is also responsible for the wanton deaths of hundreds of humans. These murders were committed in the open, with blatant disregard for the secrecy that has protected our race for millennia. For this, the Law is plain: he must die. Any vampires created by him will submit to me, his dame. If they refuse, they will also be destroyed."

The prosecutor turned to Nickolea. "How do you plead?"

Nickolea stood straighter as he snarled, "I plead indifference."

The prosecutor looked at him strangely, as he continued.

"I plead indifference because the results of this proceeding will mean nothing. This enclave is made of weaklings unwilling to take control of the future and release the limiting traditions of the past. We are the superior race. We are the alpha predators of the Earth. We should not move in shadows and hide from our inferiors. We should harvest them like the sheep they are."

"As their superiors, we should be shepherds of the sheep, not the wolves. You are a wolf, and as such, you must be destroyed in the interest of the species. Does anyone stand for the accused?"

The room was dead silent, then in the back of the hall scuffling could be heard. Someone was trying to step forward and was being restrained by people around him. Someone whispered in his ear and he stopped fighting against them.

The speaker walked up to the podium.

"Since no one stands for this cur and he is damned by his own words, the Enclave decrees he is to be executed immediately."

"You may kill a single wolf, but you cannot kill the whole pack. By killing me, you only make me more powerful!" Nickolea taunted as Stefania walked up to him. She drew her sword and with one swift blow, she removed his head. Stefania dropped the sword. It fell to the ground with a loud clang. She picked up Nickolea's head and held it facing the crowd. There were several gasps in the room as the eyes blinked for the last time.

"It is over," she proclaimed to the enclave.

She dropped the head. She and Alex walked out the door and headed for their office. As soon as they reached it with Radu and Alina, they closed the doors, and they heard the agents shift to a guard stance outside. They threw off their cloaks, and Stefania shoved her face into Alex's shoulder and sobbed uncontrollably in relief.

At the same time in Paris, Kenta Shinto stood in an old warehouse on a raised catwalk. He looked over the hundreds of humans receiving two transfusions: one of Nickolea's blood and the other of RX-34. He watched them start to transform.

"Rise, my children. Rise," he said, dramatically raising his hands, palms up, above his head. He smiled as the first Reaper finished its transformation.

Acknowledgments

Writing a novel can be frustrating and time consuming. I would like to thank my daughters, Lizzy, Rachel, and Becca, and my son, Thunder, for their brutal honesty. I would like also to thank my wife, Sherry, for all her support and encouragement during the writing process.

I would also like to thank my cover designer and artist Aidana WillowRaven. Her interpretation of my ideas helped bring the images of the book to life. Also, my editor, Lynda Dietz, who's keen eye and sharp pen helped to keep my writing streamlined and on target.

ABOUT THE AUTHOR

J.T. Buckley is a Science Fiction and Fantasy enthusiast. He has written science fiction and fantasy for over twenty years. His main two series, Terra Rising and Blood and Steel, have sold copies all over the world. He is an avid traveler and currently lives in Colorado with his family.

CPSIA information can be obtained at www.ICGtesting.com
Printed in the USA
LVOW11s0423051114

411839LV00001B/2/P